I0683779

COUNTRY FOLK

Country Folk

Cadan Henry

BURDEN BOOKS
Indianapolis

Copyright © 2010 by Cadan Henry
All Rights Reserved

www.cadanhenry.com

Published in the United States by
Burden Books, Indianapolis

FIRST SOFTCOVER EDITION 2010 NOVEMBER

This writing is a work of fiction and any similarity to situations, locations
or someone living or dead is coincidence.

Burden ISBN 978-0-578-06185-6

BURDEN BOOKS
PO Box 501938, Indianapolis, IN 46250

PRINTED IN THE UNITED STATES OF AMERICA

For E.E.C

COUNTRY FOLK

1

Sandy liked to walk along the river when she was feeling this way or that way or to try and understand what exactly the day had shown. She was never so at home as when she was by the water. She knew she couldn't be the only one who felt that way but seemed to be the only one who acted on it. Cold days, warm days. Getting surprised by the rain happened on occasion. She didn't really care. There was always shelter nearby. A towering tree, arms out to catch the water. How do you feel old tree? She would ask. Then laugh maybe out loud. A tree couldn't answer, she knew. But it did. It did answer. That was the reason she always found herself in the woods by the river to begin with. Because like so many things that actually could talk she found the silence and confidence of the outdoors as good as any speech she had ever heard. The natural world was a new way which liked to intersect and swarm her own.

It was usually after school before anyone got home that she was able to make her escape. Finally away from the clamp of formal education she was able to do what taught her the most. There was no destination in mind or stretch of river she planned on walking. Whatever got her attention was where she paused. Sometimes nothing got her attention till a long way down. The evening bugs started to make their noise and if she was still pointed away from the house by then she knew she was a long way down. But the journey reminded her of a kitchen faucet. It just depended on how long it was till she was filled up. Going back too early meant missing the new tone that fell down and any new animals that came around. Sometimes one deer or a group would reveal themselves from seemingly nowhere. But this thrill

9

only ended in a sort of sadness because she really wished she could run off with them instead of going back. The language of deer couldn't be that far from her own she imagined. Maybe if she just concentrated a little harder they might understand. The deer told her that their fur wasn't really brown but gray in the fading light to blend with shadows. Men couldn't be trusted so the deer agreed long ago to change from brown. She had somehow realized this before being told but appreciated being reminded. The color gray. The color between two worlds. Dark and light. The deer were far from captured by this middle ground but owned it. They dismissed the light as something entirely rewarding. And dwelt near the dark for comfort while they foraged. Nothing had stolen more from them than being seen in the open light so they stepped back after talking to the one in charge and made this arrangement.

Dark was well on its way now but Sandy Toolering sat unconcerned on a log held in a stack of debris sticking out in the slow moving current. She sat comfortable with her legs drawn up and arms wrapped around as she looked out. The mind of nine year old girl should be sweeter she reckoned. Not so tedious and run down. Or constantly imagining running off with deer. What is it about the way I was born that makes *me* so gray? she wondered. I can't prevent myself from wanting to hide in a place in between, too. But she was stronger than that and had a confidence too, that not so many saw but that kept her spirits up most days and made her feel alive and protected. She felt she really hadn't been born yet and was just waiting until she was called away for what might be her real job. But that confidence inside would remind her of why she was here and that right now was going to be her patch of days.

The river turned brown to black. Permanent night closing. The river got the name Blue River but her father liked to call it Smoke River because it was always rising. Sandy usually

10

timed her return walk with the finishing light. It made her mother crazy with worry. Sandy never quit doing it this way and for some reason was never really severely punished about it. Some sort of contract had enacted itself between her and her mother while her daddy was usually too distracted to notice. She rushed back in the half dark, saplings and low branches swiping her cheeks and forehead. Sometimes a tip aligned itself perfectly with one of her nostrils and went reaching for her sinus cavity which was a terribly strange feeling. Or she would trip over an exposed root, cursing because she knew it was there. The perils of almost running on the path at dark. Especially with no moon and eyes squinted to protect precious sight.

The leaves on the trees had grown big this wet mid-spring in the south end of the state. It was much warmer than usual for the time of year too, and the woods came alive as if they had fallen out of bed.

The glow from the back door guided her the last few hundred feet, silhouetting branches for easier travel. She leaned on the woodpile momentarily, thudding her feet into a log before going in. The pneumatic spring closed the door while she sat down to untie her laces.

"Sandy's home!" came her mother's voice.

"Is that you, Sandy?"

"Yes, its me." She scurried up then went into the kitchen in her socks, loving how warm her feet felt after an adventure.

"What are we havin?"

"You're going to eat it anyway, right?" said her mother.

Sandy just groaned. Her mother nodded knowingly.

"Sandy, its still dark too early for you to be out this late."

"No its not."

"Sandy, I mean it. There are too many things that could happen."

"No there's not."

11

"Sandy, I won't argue."

Sandy went into the dining room where her father was already seated at the table.

"Your uncle Durry can take you explorin," her mother called.

"Hell, Durry don't wanna see you that much, girl," said her father. "He ain't always gonna come over jist cause you wan im too. As lonely and wifeless as he is, he don't always wanna be with some kid." He was half smiling, knowing he was getting away with a lot.

Sandy ignored him and sat down at the table, unfolded her napkin and put it in her lap.

"I think he likes to come over," Sandy said finally.

"Of course he does," said her mother walking into the room. She gave her husband a shaming glance.

"Just a substitute," he said. "Truth is, I don't know what my brother likes. Seems like all he's ever done is work anyway. Only cares about work. Work, work, work." He was laughing now.

Sandy was also laughing at the way her father said it. Sounding like a duck or something.

"Durry does what he wants," her father started again. I know he likes comin over to see us but one day he's gonna have to get a family of his own."

Sandy's mother was returning to the kitchen. Sandy could only see the back of her head but wondered what the expression on her face might have been at this point. Her father served himself some green beans, still smiling but expecting to be trounced any moment for his bold reasoning.

Sandy's mother returned placing the platter of broiled pork chops down in front of her husband. "Perry, that makes no sense," she said simultaneously. Perry only stabbed a chop and dropped it to his plate. The bone knocked the dish.

"Is anybody gonna pray?" his wife asked.

"Oh, just eat," returned Perry.

12

Sandy only looked around the dining room and thought how much she liked her house. It wasn't a mansion. But it was there by the river and woods which fit whatever mood she might be struck by.

"Why can't you just act like a normal person? Durry's family and that's it. He comes around and is welcome like anybody else. He's not asking you for money or anything or drinkin all your liquor."

"He doesn't drink at all, remember," he reminded his wife.

Sandy remained a spectator while enjoying a particularly moist pork chop.

"Eat some beans," said her mother quickly. Sandy spooned a couple beans onto her plate.

"So far your brother doesn't drink and works for a living," Sandy's mother reported before picking up her pork chop and taking away a rigorous bite. Sandy was impressed by her mother's indelicacy.

"Look at you! That pork chop might as well have been my head!" Perry said.

Gwen was only a little embarrassed.

After a moment: "Don't be jealous of Durry. You've had just as much luck as him. But you have to start with him every time. You two aren't boys anymore and have to get along. You're just stuck, Perry."

"I ain't stuck! Can't believe you'd imagine anything *like* that! He just makes me uncomfortable, you know. I don't understand im. We don't always get along and that's probly why."

"You have to try."

"I don't have to do anything. When he gets a normal life or somethin... Gits his own life, I'll understand im better. Until then..."

"He *was* married."

"And he didn't pay attention to what she was doin and he lost her."

"It's over now."

"Yeah, so he should get on with it."

"He has women."

"Where'd you hear that from, the bulletin board at the grocery?"

"You know he does, just nothing permanent yet."

"I *don't* care. Hand me them beans, Sandy."

"Sandy, what'd you do at school today?" asked her mother.

"I can't remember. Nothin good."

"I read today that young boys are getting dumber."

The whole table laughed.

"Gwen, where do you get these things?" said Perry. He hauled in another pork chop.

"Sandy, do the boys seem slower?" she pressed.

"I don't know, mom."

"Well, I believe it's a sad fact that those boys are losing their minds to all that violence and sexual content."

"Good Lord, what the hell are you sayin?" Perry could hardly believe his ears as he tried to eat his dinner.

"Sandy are the boys aggressive? Going after you or anything?"

Sandy just looked at her plate. Not because boys were going after her but because she was too embarrassed.

"Oh my God. Will you just eat, please? This is all hurting my stomach."

Gwen looked at her food and ate. Sandy never thought her mom was that weird. She did watch a lot of news shows. Maybe that's what happened, she thought.

"Boys just swing on the monkey bars same as they always have," Perry mumbled.

Gwen let it pass.

"What's the matter down there?" said Perry after a time.

"So if Uncle Durry gets his own family he won't want to see us anymore?"

"Sandy, I'm sure he'll always want to see us. Of course, he will. Don't listen to your father. Your uncle will always have time for us."

"Don't tell my daughter not to listen to me."

"Well, not when you tell her things like that."

"She should listen to me no matter what I say."

"And she does, but she has to learn about you and your brother."

"There is nothing to learn about me and my brother. He does what he wants to. I don't owe him a damn thing. He comes over here and you both go crazy and she goes off with him somewhere then you go off somewhere too." He took a big drink from his beer can.

"Well, honestly, with him here to watch Sandy, I can finally get a few things done. So that's what I do."

"You can't do any of those things with me around?"

"Not really. Your always here and won't get out of the house long enough for me to get caught up."

"You just said you have to go *out* to do things."

"What I mean is I need time to git caught up."

"You're caught up. I don't know what you're talkin about."

"I'm just saying, when he's here it seems like I can git caught up without everybody bothering me."

"Who the hell is bothering you!"

"Oh, God, just forget it." Gwen smiled at Sandy.

"I can't believe that everybody's bothering you."

"Not all the time, you know. But sometimes I need to do some things for myself."

"I don't even want to know what that means!"

"Let's just stop, okay? Did you like dinner?"

"Damn good pork chops, momma," he said.

"Damn good, mom," seconded Sandy.

15

"Sandy…"

"What?"

"Don't talk that way, it scares me."

"*He* said it."

"Your father is a grown up."

"Yeah, I'm a grown up, little girl." His teeth came though his smile. Mostly, Sandy imagined, to irritate her mother.

Sandy swallowed another bite. "Well, it was *good*."

"Thank you," said her mother.

"Do you see what you teach her, Perry?"

"Never heard that talk before, have you?" Her father winked at her.

"Nope," Sandy replied.

"The hell you haven't!"

"Perry, my God!"

Perry ignored his wife while he looked at the girl. He was going to make her regret crossing him.

"I've heard it before," Sandy finally admitted.

"Doesn't matter. I don't want to hear it. Perry, are you crazy? Come in here, Sandy."

Sandy picked up her plate and went into the kitchen. Perry remained at the table briefly then stepped outside and lit a cigarette on the front porch. A bit of a retreat from being ganged up on.

Sandy helped her mother clean up in the kitchen, wiping pots and glasses, not saying much. Not because of any tension but because of some release from it. Either can leave you without a desire to talk much.

"Sandy put those dish towels in the laundry room then go upstairs and git started on your homework."

"Okay." She did as she was told then was on her way through the living room to the stairs. She heard the television in the back room where Perry was. She liked to finish her homework quickly and join him there before bed. Perry let her watch the same shows he was watching without a care.

16

Said it was good for the girl to see the way it really was. Sandy could usually get away with it for about thirty minutes before her mother hunted her down and sent her off to bed. Sometimes a mother is just too tired to enforce policy no matter what her children are doing. Sandy also knew this, turning it to her advantage whenever she could.

She finished her homework in about an hour and took a shower and put on her pajamas. She stared at herself in the mirror curiously while brushing her teeth. Then even more while she brushed the knots from her tangled brown hair.

Her bedroom was cozy but unusually austere for a young girl. She pulled down her bedding then stared out the window into the black. Nothing outside was revealed. Only her reflection in the pane of glass. Their house was too far off the main road to receive any illumination from a street lamp. Sometimes she caught a set of headlights flashing through the trees far off. When the windows were open in summer she could sometimes even hear the *whirrr* of car tires on the blacktop.

Sandy could hear her mother was upstairs now. Knowing she'd be preoccupied for the next few minutes, Sandy silently descended the stairs to visit her dad. She liked to sit on the floor right in front of the set usually but if she got cold she curled up next to him like a winsome cat.

In all his days Perry would never admit it but it was during those times that he felt closest to his daughter. The warmth of his best cat and sipping a beer in the dark with the TV on.

17

2

Perry met his boss at about 7am to replace a broken water heater in a farmhouse basement out on 550E. When he pulled up there were still wisps of fog starting where the field began some distance behind the house. He was working as a helper with Butz Plumbing these days. The profession was new to him but a welcome income since what happened with his last job. There was still some speculation by certain friends and other gossips in the Engadine area about what happened exactly or who was surely to blame but in the absence of a better coat hook the guilt was on Perry. The most popular version of the story was that Perry was having an inventory sale out the back door of High View Electric. The company taking its name from the fact that it sat on a bluff above the road and looking out toward a shallow valley. And because the place was on such high ground and in plain view of traffic going in both directions any passerby could easily observe whatever outside activity there may be. No one knows who alerted the owner of High View but Perry was questioned by his boss about some apparent stock inconsistencies that now stood out quite blatantly. Perry said he had no idea what was going on and that anybody could check his truck and his house if they weren't satisfied. He said the account lists had always varied a lot since he'd been there and that he tried to fix some of it but it took too much time away from his basic duties as warehouse co-manager. He also told his boss that if he spent more time at the business that he'd know all this same as he did. With nothing to prove that Perry *didn't* do it and the comment that was made he was asked to leave. Upon telling his wife what happened, Perry found that she understood completely and believed

18

him all the way. Of this he was relieved and truly surprised because he'd made what he thought were smaller mistakes in the past that had been received much more poorly. But this time his wife surprised him along with his brother.

Perry and Allen Butz together hauled the ruined water heater out of the basement. They then told their customer they would have to come back that afternoon with the right make and model and finish the installation. Perry followed Allen to the shop in town where he stopped inside for a moment then went after the new unit over at one of the suppliers. It was not that Perry had wanted to become a plumber but with his new reputation and very few opportunities in the area he had to try it. Frankly, Perry had no idea what he wanted to be. He had never given it much thought. Only that it should be fun and pay a lot. Since he'd never found that he just took whatever he could get from whoever would hire him. He was forty-one now but felt better than he ever had. He had gotten most of the stupidity of youth out of his system and felt good generally most of the time. But there had been some stupidity. That's one reason he married Gwen. She was older than he was and he needed that. Before her he had always gone for the rather pretty, easy types. He realized at one point that there had been an endless line of them hung out like cheap bait if you weren't paying attention or cared where you ended up. His first wife was a perfect example of some easy bait. He was young but he soon discovered that she had no intention of working or contributing in any way other than helping him stay drunk most of the time. When they were both drinking he often found he was the one getting beat up. Though he didn't ever not swing back. She came down on him one time with a chair when he wasn't looking and believed she had killed him by accident. When he came to she was leaning over him speaking softly and he raked her off with so much force she lost her breath. When they finally split it was almost like they had never

19

known each other at all except on some otherworldly plane. And after her he liked to visit that plane as much as possible only by himself.

Allen called and told Perry to meet him at the jobsite again. They wrestled the new water heater inside and Perry was left to finish the balance of the job. It wasn't that hard and it was good to be put on the spot Allen said. Perry smiled simply and set about getting it done. The farmhouse still had the old knob and tube wiring from a long time ago. If Perry had to plug in one of his tools the lights would hesitate or pulse. He felt like he wanted to offer the old man some advice about re-wiring but decided he was too new at the job to go and try to inform people. The farmer said Perry could take a roll of chicken wire with him if he wanted so he could build a rabbit cage for his daughter. The man didn't spend much time in the basement but talked at length in the kitchen. He said he and his wife imported gifts and novelty items in the winter and traveled around to home shows to sell them.

Gwen dropped her daughter off at school on the way to the Smoothstone Nursery. She worked there four days a week for ten hours each day and some Saturdays but only if necessary. She was originally hired to answer phones and handle billing but like any job where you demonstrate ability she was soon working with customers and doing a lot of the buying. She was even past the point of having to get Bret Smoothstone's approval before writing a check over fifty dollars. It helped a lot because chasing down the owner or waiting while he was on the phone shot her patience quicker than a difficult customer. She found herself outdoors more and more helping people select assorted flora for their landscaping. She discovered a creative aspect within that increased in fortitude daily. Though technically, handling the books was still her responsibility she found time in the after-

20

noons to wrap up collecting from their commercial clients. She was also just starting to become involved with servicing these larger accounts, too. The couples buyers were fun and had a lot of questions and usually took direction well; the professionals knew exactly what they wanted and worked her on price. It all balanced pretty well but the real fun was helping completely lost homeowners select beautiful living things to surround their dwellings. That was truly satisfying. If the perception of the job became too complex she was even allowed to refer them to one of their professional clients for help. There were many smaller landscapers she knew of that were mostly Hispanic owned. But the larger and older operations weren't minority owned. In a small town just over the Ohio River from Kentucky change didn't go over too well. The large firms were convinced the Mexicans were taking away all the business and minority owners had no doubt that *whitey* would stick together so offered blistering low prices. But it became a duel that kept everyone from being too complacent. Eventually quality firms with affordable pricing lead the market and that is who Gwen rewarded.

"You finish with those people out front?" Jill asked. She worked the register and did a lot of the clean up and watering.

"Yeah, all done. Have to order some things though. What's in stock is never enough, you know?" Gwen said.

"I heard her out there and thought she was going to gather seeds in the woods and grow things herself!"

"Yeah, a whole lotta patience."

"How much they goin to buy?"

"About eleven-hundred dollars."

"I think the husband liked you."

Gwen laughed. "Why?"

"He kept lookin at your butt when you bent over!" Jill burst out laughing.

21

"My butt?"

"Oh, I think so."

Gwen kept looking through a catalog.

"Hey, how's Perry doin? Behavin himself at his new job?"

"Yeah, he is." Gwen was busy looking up an order.

"Can you believe that? Was he really stealing all that stuff or what?"

"He says he wasn't and I believe him." Gwen *loved* hearing this from nearly everyone she knew. If they didn't ask specifically they came at it from the side.

"I think the owner was just pissed. Had to blame somebody. I would." She nodded, assuming a look of authority.

Gwen wanted the subject to go away.

"Well, Ron says he hasn't seen anything he might recognize on eBay." Jill laughed again.

Gwen sneered.

"I'm just kidding!"

"I know."

"It's just nice to see sometimes things happen to other people!" Now Jill really laughed.

Gwen wanted to smack her. Not because of the heavily used topic but because she was trying to work. "Oh, they do," she said finally.

A customer came up to the register handing over a credit card. Gwen escaped outside to tag the sold items. She wasn't officially anyone's boss but she upheld so many duties. Sometimes she and the other employees were confused just how much authority she had. She found it beneficial to act as if she had none.

Eduardo was on the other side of the lot off loading a delivery with the fork truck. Gwen approached and watched the men working. She got a good feeling from so much constructive activity. Eduardo waved to her and always gave a respectful smile. Say all you want about those people, she

22

thought. But they work hard and are always kind. You never had to decide if you liked them or not. It was automatic and usually so was trust, she mused. The company hadn't had a problem with theft since Carl Knighter used to run mulch to his friends after hours a few years ago. One of his customers inadvertently turned him in by calling and specifically requesting Carl to make another delivery. He gave back two hundred dollars and quit on the spot.

"Gwen, move that," Eduardo pointed.

Gwen nodded and rolled away a small tree in the way of the fork.

"Thanks!" he shouted.

Gwen looked at the driver's manifest and began the count. Bret came out and stood next to her.

"Goin good?" he asked.

"Yeah, we got Macintosh's order in."

"Good. I'll go in and call im. We could use the money." He winked and walked away.

Spring shipments meant a lot of tulip, magnolia and dogwoods. Clients loved the amazing flowers, though most were short lived. Gwen's particular favorite was pear blossom. Not a lot of odor but so much for the eyes. I've got to get Bret to give me a break on a couple trees, she thought. Perry will bitch but he'll plant em. Maybe along the drive.

Gwen started thinking about picking up Sandy. Sandy complained she had a headache that morning but by spending a little time with her daughter in the car the untimely headaches usually went away. She remembered now that Sandy said she'd be taking the bus home. It was just the time she wanted Gwen was sure.

"Hey, what about these guys," asked Jill.

"Who? What?"

"Larry at Marine Life called about his order."

"I did tell him probly today, didn't I," Gwen said.

23

"He said no problem but let im know when. He needs it soon."

"I know. I'll call im. And I gotta call Modern."

Jill got busy ringing up someone else.

"Charlie's comin in after a while," said Jill eventually. "Says she's off a half day."

Gwen thought about when she met Perry in Louisville. It must have been years ago. She wondered how far they had come. She didn't see one bit of distance to measure if they had advanced at all. She only felt heavy for a moment at the realization of the time that had passed. Sort of a blank satisfaction rolled through her. The stone knowledge of never being able to go back and desperately trying to uncover anything good or worthy that lie ahead. *Whatever.* They moved because land was cheaper and her sister was there. Neither Gwen nor Perry could really stand the city. Large towns only made them feel lonely. They had both agreed on that. When they were single and only cared about work it made more sense but with a baby on the way nothing soothed her like the idea of rural life. Perry got in less trouble too. He was less alien to himself and didn't act so high strung. The drinking curbed and anguish retreated.

"Charlie's comin in? She say what time?"

"No. Only she'll be here in a while."

"Okay." Charlie, really Carlene, was Gwen's daughter from her first marriage. The first union so long ago it could hardly be remembered. Gwen thought about it sometimes, mostly for her daughter's benefit. The man was never heard from again after the divorce. Neither one had sought out the other since. Gwen would wonder how this affected Charlie. Charlie was pretty young during all of it and Gwen always hoped she wouldn't bring it up. Gwen always hated that part of her life and shut it out.

24

Gwen went to the *extra* office she used when she wasn't in front and made her calls. She worked on orders, looked at the schedule. She saw she was working Saturday. She wasn't surprised. It was the season again and business was rapidly picking up. Which reminded her of several other things she needed to do. Anyway, the weather was supposed to be nice and Perry would probably have to work too. Maybe I could get Durry to stop at the house and check on Sandy, she thought. She sat down at the desk and looked at the clock. She wanted to pick Sandy up today but couldn't. Gwen did a few more things before going up front again.

Jill and one of the other girls were talking by the register. "When Charlie comes I can watch everything," Jill said.

"That's okay."

"Really, do what you need to and I can watch everything."

"Maybe. I might, thanks." Gwen had a sense of duty that guided her. She depended on it and sometimes others resented it.

Charlie came in about three o'clock and she talked with Jill while Gwen handled a couple more customers. Gwen was glad the money was coming in. It would put Bret in a better mood but make him want even more. The bills mounted during the winter. Sales were good thru December with seasonal stuff but soon evaporated till April. Bret needed money now to buy as much stock as he could. He was used to it, though. Heck he'd been doing it fourteen years.

"Charlie, you look so nice. You didn't gain a thing over the winter," Jill said.

"Still the same me?"

"Oh, yeah, darlin, you look so nice."

"Well, thanks."

"Your husband feelin alright?"

"We're alright, you know."

25

"Good." Even under the benign scrutiny of someone like Jill, Charlie seldom became excited. This tendency did not agree with her anxious eyes. Charlie was not as sturdy looking as her mother and had a more rigid body and darker hair, usually held back in some way. She smiled at Jill and went over to Gwen.

"Almost done. How did you get off today, I wonder?"

"I took a half day. I had to go to the doctor."

"No problems?"

"Just a physical." Gwen had a thought that her daughter was always going to the doctor for some reason. It was an expensive way to get attention even with insurance. "Do you still want to go to the store?"

"Yeah, one more minute. And we have to git Sandy. I don't want her on one of her adventures tonight. I don't feel lucky this afternoon."

Charlie just looked at her.

"You know, she's always on some mystical adventure somewhere. And if I wait too long she won't eat or eat something bad."

Charlie's gaze appeared a little more distant. "Okay, well, is it okay if I just stand here?"

"Of course, I'm sorry. You're not in the way at all. One more second... Okay, let's go."

Charlie came up with what might have been a smile.

They waved to Jill on the way out and Charlie followed Gwen in her car over to the house.

Sandy was outside with Perry throwing a Frisbee in front of the porch. Perry had a beer in his hand along with a cigarette. Gwen saw that the Frisbee was the one made to look like a smashed rubber chicken. Sandy will like it, Perry told her at the store. Gwen shook her head and reminded herself that she did love him. Turns out, Sandy did think it was an amazing gift. Gwen couldn't look at him for the rest of that morning.

"What are you doin home?"

"Hi Charlie," Perry said, ignoring Gwen's question. He awkwardly flung the Frisbee to Sandy. "Well, I'm home."

"Did your job finish?"

"Gotta go back in the morning. They had to kick us out."

"Oh."

"Hi Charlie," said Sandy. She gave Charlie a great smile that made her feel more relaxed.

Perry looked the women over. "Why do I think there's no dinner tonight?"

"We'll bring you back somethin," Gwen said.

"What time?"

"Not too long."

"Yeah, Yeah. Right after I couldn't wait any longer and had to eat half a pie or somethin."

"Nooo...." Gwen tried to reassure him. Even with working, she didn't mind setting the table and making most of the meals. It was because she wanted to spend time with her family. She also wanted Perry and Sandy to eat right. She knew both of them would eat anything as long as it tasted good. Sandy ate a pound of sliced baloney one time with a Coke when Gwen was late. She just peeled off the plastic rind and squirted mustard on each slice, rolling them up into tubes. Perry said he just told her to eat some baloney if she was hungry. He said he didn't think she would eat the whole thing like appetizers.

"Well, I'll try to hold on," Perry said. He awkwardly threw the Frisbee to Sandy again now with a laugh.

"You'll be fine," Gwen said. "Sandy, do you wanna come with us to the store? Just about an hour, sweetheart."

"Guess I gotta go to the store," Sandy told her dad.

27

Perry picked up the smashed chicken Frisbee spilling a little beer. Gwen wondered why he had to smoke *and* drink *and* play catch at the same time.

"Don't take too long," he said.

"We won't. I know you're hungry."

"Okay."

The women and Sandy got into Gwen's car. Perry eyed them with a funny face.

"I was *playing* Frisbee," Sandy said.

"Maybe it'll be light enough you can play when we get back," Gwen said.

"I hope so," replied Sandy. She looked out the window and thought about how squishy the Frisbee had felt.

"Where do you wanna go?" asked Charlie.

"Wherever, just for some basics," Gwen said.

"The Wagon Wheel," yelled Sandy.

"We have to get groceries first, honey."

"She likes the Wagon Wheel?" asked Charlie.

"They have those burgers she likes."

"The French fries, mom."

"I know, you like the fries."

"I *love* the French fries!"

The chain store parking lot was pretty full. It always was. Frustrated after trying to find a good spot Gwen nearly pinned some old man against his Malibu.

"Almost got im," said Charlie. Gwen offered a small wave to the guy.

"Perry says you need to make sure they're dead," Gwen said. Sandy leaned up now.

"What?"

"Yeah, Charlie. If you hit someone you need to make sure they're dead so they can't sue you."

"Perry…" mumbled Charlie.

"Is that what dad thinks, mom?"

28

"He was only jokin me, hun." Gwen did sort of believe it though, and therefore, so did Sandy.

"C'mon everybody," urged Gwen.

Sandy watched the old man drive away but could not imagine him dead.

Gwen took out a small list from her purse reciting a couple things to herself.

Sandy yanked a cart loose from the row but Gwen commandeered it. "Mom!"

"Sandy, go find a bagga carrots and one nice white onion."

Sandy looked at her mother for a moment then went into action. She couldn't tell the difference between carrots so she pulled out a bag that was easiest for her to reach. The onions were different, though. She didn't like the ones pointy on the ends but larger and rounder. She figured pointy ends meant they were bitter. Rounder meant better eating and sweeter. The skin also needed to be as white as possible. This helped determine the sweetness. She wanted to take a bite out of one while she was looking to be sure but didn't think Gwen would like it. She finally selected a very white medium-sized round specimen. The choice actually made her feel proud.

Sandy returned and gently placed the vegetables in the cart. Gwen didn't really check to see if they were okay. Charlie walked along with her arms folded.

"Toilet paper, Sandy. Get a large pack of something on sale. Something we usually get."

"One of the boys at school says his mom cleans his bottom in the kitchen sink."

"I don't think so, Sandy," said Gwen. Charlie shook her head. "You know Durry's coming on Saturday, I think. I have to work so you two can keep an eye on each other."

"What about Dad?"

"He never knows what his schedule will be."

29

"Okay." Sandy went off on another errand.

"She's so independent," observed Charlie.

"I think it's the way she was born."

"Ross says he wouldn't mind having kids."

"Just be sure."

"I know."

Sandy looked at all the toilet paper but then realized she had a few minutes on her own. She went farther down the aisle noticing the man on a roll of paper towels and thought he was ideal. She went past the feminine hygiene products quickly because she wanted to put off having to think about that for as long as possible. Then she thought about Popsicles but decided it would be better to eat those in June. She returned to the toilet paper section and hefted a package.

The three walked together at the back of the store. Gwen picked up some more essentials. Ground beef, orange juice, milk. Sandy shook a container of yogurt.

"I'll get you some of that if you want."

"Really?"

"Yeah."

"Is it good?"

"Its really good," responded Gwen.

Sandy put the container in the cart and shrugged. She noticed the package of chicken parts that were also there. "How do they get these in perfect pieces?"

"They have to cut up the chicken," Gwen said.

"Must get boring," said Sandy.

"Probly does."

"What about chocolate, mom?"

"What do you think, M&M's?"

"Yeah, peanut maybe."

"See if you can find em."

"C'mon, Charlie, help me find em." Charlie hesitated then unfolded her arms and walked behind Sandy.

Sandy began to scrutinize the entire candy section.

30

"We better go," said Charlie.

After some more indecision the original idea prevailed.

They all regrouped at the checkout line where Sandy started to stare at the magazines. She couldn't decide if she liked any of the people on the covers who seemed to be looking back at her. None of them made her feel any better.

"I'll cook when I come home from work on Saturday," Gwen said.

Charlie thumbed a magazine.

"What're we havin?" asked Sandy.

"Don't know yet, maybe grill out."

Sandy thought she'd like to tear open the bag of M&M's. "Uncle Durry will like that."

"I hope everybody will."

"We have to hurry or Dad's gonna be mad."

"I know."

"We have to git to the Wagon Wheel or he's gonna kill us."

"Kill me, maybe."

"You don't want that, mom."

Charlie actually smiled.

"Then let's go eat," said Gwen.

When everyone was sleeping Friday evening the wind came. It knocked loose every dead branch throughout the property. There had been no rain, only severe wind that made the house creak and bent the trees. It hadn't kept Sandy and her parents awake but they remembered how it sounded as they went to bed.

Sandy was outside by eight Saturday morning examining her empty rabbit cage. She thought she'd like to get another rabbit. It was something to look forward to on a Saturday morning or after school. Something to be kind to and feed. Something furry! Her mind exclaimed. But the last pink eye went out bad. Something had eaten its feet all the way off.

31

Perry said it had to be the raccoons. Durry said it had to be coyotes. It was horrible anyway. Sandy had come out to find the rabbit on its back exposing the four shredded stubs. She didn't scream but got terribly angry then cried when her mother finally came out to see. Sandy said she would never get another rabbit. It was too sad what happened. But now after all the wind and the desperate way the trees had shed some of their heavy branches she thought it would be good to get another. Her dad said he could redesign the floor of the cage to be solid somehow instead of wire like before so legs won't poke through.

When Sandy returned inside her father was at the breakfast table just looking out into nowhere with a coffee cup in his right hand. "What's it like out there?"

"You doan wan me to tell you."

"Sandy, dammit..."

"Branches everywhere. Little ones. Big ones. It looks like it rained branches, dad. There's a lot. I didn't even go up to the street."

"I knew it. Start pickin up summa the little ones, okay? Put em in the burner pile and I'll take care of em later. Doan worry about the big ones, I'll git those. And don't *you* burn any of em! I don't want you doin that. Just try to get summa the smaller ones."

"Do I have to do it today?"

"Sandy, just pick up some of em. While you're outside, you know? Make a game out of it. See how many you can count."

"I'm gonna go back out and see." She slugged back half a glass of orange juice.

"Good."

"Ahhhhh...." Sandy placed the empty glass on the counter by the sink.

"Durry comin over or what?"

"Mom said so."

"Well, I have to work for a while today so you and him can help out aroun here. I mean, jist try to get the smaller ones."

"Ok, dad."

Perry looked at her with a straight face. Sandy walked past him to go back outside.

The property behind the house wasn't that deep before it became wooded but in front of the house the yard went all the way to the road, maybe two-hundred yards. Sandy darted around like a boss pearl diver. She threw little dead branches into the brick burner then went to collect more. What she found out by the street brought her to a fast stop. Wow, she thought. A whole tree fell down! She went closer and saw that the trunk had been snapped roughly leaving a stump maybe three feet high and the rest completely separate. She walked beside the fallen tree to the end where it was jutting into the road. Wow! her mind said again. This is amazing! Sandy ran back to the house. She had to search for her father who was now upstairs.

"Dad, its amazing!"

"I know, what happened?"

"A whole tree fell over! You know that one back from the mailbox?"

"Yeah."

"It completely fell over. Its broken over. Only the stump left. Amazing!"

"Shit."

"I loved that tree," said Gwen.

"Its gone now, mom."

"Are you sure. I mean, is it completely destroyed?"

"Completely, mom. I don't think it can grow back."

"Perry, you better take a look."

"I will."

"Its in the road a little bit, dad."

"Shit."

33

"Perry, go take a look."

Perry made a noise in his throat.

"You need to come and see, dad."

"Yeah, I'll meetcha out there. Jista minute."

Sandy went downstairs and sat on the porch. When her father came out they went to look at the tree.

"Dammit. Just a mess."

"Not a little one, dad!"

"Nope, not a little one."

"What're you gonna do?"

"I've gotta git out here with a chain saw. Shit."

"Its not that far in the road, dad."

"Not too far." Perry stood and looked. He placed his foot on the log and pushed. The tree didn't move. Not a hope of rolling it back himself.

"Durry's comin, dad. He can help."

"Come on."

They both walked back behind the house to the garage and storage area. Perry looked for a chain he could attach to his tractor to pull the tree. Sandy watched him drag out the rusty links and put the chain in a compartment behind the tractor seat. He then told her to stand back while he started the engine. The tractor was mostly used for mowing but with three foot wheels was big enough to pull and haul.

"What're you gonna do, dad!"

"Pull that tree away from the road!" They were both yelling over the motor. Sandy ran behind Perry to the road again. He dismounted the tractor and looped the thick chain around a spot on the fallen tree. Then he connected the other end to the tow ball of the tractor. "Stand back!" Sandy stepped way back.

Perry pulled the tree clear of the road and more. He drug it along steadily, getting rid of any slack in the chain before hitting the gas. The tires ripped apart some of the grass when

34

he did. "Shit!" The impact of the fall had also created some deep gouges in the earth.

"You got it, dad!"

Sandy inspected some of the damaged ground with her feet.

"I'll have to work on it later."

"You gotta go?"

"Durry's comin. Your mother said he oughta be here bout ten." Perry undid the chain and placed it back in the tractor.

"You gonna cut it up?"

"Yep. Have to cut it up."

This time Sandy walked back to the house trailing her father on the tractor. Gwen saw her out the window from the bedroom. She called to Sandy when she heard the front door open.

"What!"

"Just come here, please."

"What?"

"Well, tell me, what did you see?"

"Big tree, mom. You'll see it when you pull out. Big tree. Really big."

"What did dad say? Was it the tree you thought before?"

"Yeah, same one. Dad said he thought it was an oak. Just got too old and snapped he said."

"Oh, God... Well, what's he going to do?"

"Cut it up he said."

"Unbelievable."

"Yep."

"Okay, Durry's coming in a little bit and we have to go to work. Your dad said he might only have to be gone for a couple hours but I'm gone till four. You guys can come and see me if you want."

"I don't think so," Sandy said.

Gwen was a little hurt. "Why not?"

"I doan wanna see a buncha fake trees, mom."

35

"They're not fake. They're jist not planted. You have to buy em and plant em."

"Okay, well, why doan we just see you when you come home?"

"Fine! Don't have to see your mother if you don't want to!" Gwen straightened her bra under her sweater. Sandy appeared impatient.

"I'm gonna go eat, mom."

"I'll be down in a minute."

Sandy retreated to the kitchen and filled a bowl with some cereal. Her father came in and said he had to go. "Tell your mother I had to leave. Maybe I'll be back in a couple hours. It depends on if they're ready for us or not." Perry messed his daughter's hair.

"Don't!"

"Gotta go!" Sandy heard him drive away in the truck over her own crunchy bites. She also heard the floor creaking above where her mother still was. She thought about what color rabbit she wanted. She thought more on the fallen tree.

"Nice day out today, Sandy," said Gwen as she entered the room. She had taken a minute to inspect the front yard from the window in the living room.

Sandy didn't reply.

"Didn't think it was going to be so nice today after all that wind last night. And no rain. That's so strange."

"Wind blew all night, mom. There's sticks and branches all over the yard. Dad said I had to pick em up."

"Shouldn't take you too long."

"Durry will help me and then we'll be done faster."

"Don't you charm your uncle into helping you, Sandy. Your father told you to do it. You can finish it quickly and then you can go do what you want."

"It's a lotta stuff on the grass, mom."

"Your father left?"

"Yeah, he said to say he was leavin."

36

"Well, thank goodness it's a nice day. Where did your father tell you to put the sticks?"

"Some of em are branches, mom."

"Where did he tell you to put everything?"

"In the burner."

"But don't burn anything, right?"

"He already told me."

"I'm serious, Sandy. I don't wan any fires aroun here. That wind'll do somethin terrible I'm afraid. So jist leave that to your father."

"Yes, mom, he already told me."

"Well, Sandy, you have a thick head and we have to tell you many times usually before you listen. But its only that way with dangerous things, with other things you're pretty good. But dangerous things seem to draw you in. Its almost like you can't resist."

"I just like to have fun, mom."

"I'm not angry with you, I just worry about you. I doan wan anything to happen to you. I couldn't bear it if anything happened to you." Gwen wasn't prepared for what she was feeling.

"You worry all the time, mom. Nothing will ever happen to me because I'm careful. You don't have to worry."

"I do worry."

"Why?"

"Because you're not a boy! You'll think that you can do something but you can't. I'm afraid you'll just get ripped apart."

"I won't get hurt, mom, because I like the way it feels."

"What?"

"I don't know. Alone and wondering what will happen next. It's a great feeling. Its like I hear everything talking at the same time."

"Just sometimes please obey, okay?"

"I do listen, mom. I do."

37

"Okay." Gwen turned to the sink and put in some dirty dishes. It was good to splash and make noise after being reminded how deeply she cared for her little girl. It made her throat tight how much.

Sandy moved the spoon around her empty bowl.

Gwen stepped to the refrigerator and removed two hard-boiled eggs. She peeled one, rinsed it, and held it out for Sandy. Sandy smiled and took it.

"I didn't know we had these," she said.

Gwen nodded and ate hers standing at the sink. She sprinkled on a little salt. Sandy dipped hers in the salt she had poured into the empty bowl.

"Durry comin or whutta you think?" Sandy asked.

"He'll be here soon. Sometimes he's late."

Sandy popped the last piece of egg into her mouth and stood up. Gwen came over and got the bowl.

"I have to go now sweetheart, why doan you wait on the porch?"

"Yeah, I'll wait on the porch, maybe pick up some more sticks."

"Get that done, you know?"

"Yep." Sandy went out the front door and sat down in a brown wicker chair on the front porch. Part of a bush obscured her view. She crossed and uncrossed her arms. She decided to pick up sticks. She filled the big brick burner till it had twigs poking out high in a big twig bunch.

Gwen came out and started her car, an old sky blue Camry. She waved to Sandy in the yard then stopped. "See you tonight. You won't be by yourself long."

"Bye."

Gwen waved again and drove slowly down the drive. Sandy looked up a couple times watching her go. She noticed her mother was at the end of the drive for an awfully long time. Then she saw Durry's truck and the two were talking.

Sandy began to run around the yard picking up sticks as fast as she could. She hadn't even started in back but there wasn't too much back there. But she still had to work her way all the way to the street. She ran around picking up sticks with one hand, trying to hold as many as she could with the other. "I can't even carry that many!" she cursed. She'd throw one lot into the burner then scamper up the yard picking up more. She missed a lot of the little ones hiding in the grass but was just concentrating on the bigger ones then anyway.

Durry's truck rolled up right in front of her on the drive. "Dad got you workin?"

"Yeah, you comin to help?"

"I'd tell you put em in the truck but I think the ground's still too soft out there."

"There's some big ones."

Durry turned off the engine and came out of the truck.

Sandy was beaming but suddenly felt very calm and very excited at the same time. "Help me with this one," she said.

By himself Durry hefted the branch. He walked it over to the already full burner and set it down beside. "Summa these are gonna have to be cut up."

"Dad's gonna cut everything up he said."

"When's he comin back?"

"He doesn't know, maybe a couple hours."

"Whuh d'ya wanna do?"

"Go up the river."

"Up the river?"

"A long way."

"Okay, lets finish these big ones first."

"So… we're goin?"

"Of course we're goin."

They stacked the big branches next to the burner and picked up most of the smaller ones, stuffing them into the burner with their feet sometimes or one of the bigger sticks.

39

Durry leaned up against his truck when he was finished and looked at Sandy. "Let's go," she said.

They started along the trail behind the garage and down the slope entering the first area of trees beside the river. Sandy found a kid-sized stick she used to poke or whack things with or move a low hanging branch out of the way. Durry stayed right behind her even though it was more fresh-air and exercise than he was used to. It was a challenge keeping up with her but every time he went on those kind of excursions he'd realize he wasn't as out of shape as he thought.

Most of the early part of the trail was so familiar to Sandy that she usually went quickly by. The adventure lie in whatever was undiscovered still some distance ahead. When there was an opportunity like that day she intended to fully exploit it. And there was no one better to go with than Durry. He shared her own sense of wonder at the unknown and also had the energy. No one else ever cared to go with her and some days it was just crucial to have some company. Uncle Durry never refused even at times when he clearly would rather be doing something else.

The river was full and the edges round like always during spring. Moving slowly with a lot of swirls. They stopped to look at a family of turtles sunning themselves on a protruding rock. The big one was the first in the water when they came too close. The little ones soon flopped off the rock to join.

It was always difficult to measure distance when hiking but after what Durry thought was about a mile and a half they decided to sit down on some large rocks by a shallow. Sandy had only been to the spot twice before so she knew they were pretty far down. She felt pleased with their progress and took the rest as a reward for something earned. She still didn't think they were far enough, though.

"My dad keeps askin when you're getting married."

"I was gonna marry you but you're so small."

He thought Sandy might blush but she didn't.

"I think he worries my mom talks about you too much."

"What does that mean?"

"Maybe my mom will like you better."

"My brother worries a lot."

"That's what my mom says."

"I like your mom. She's always treated me well. We just get along that's all. I think its great how we all get along."

"Me too," Sandy said.

"Another woman is a possibility."

"Do you ever think you're too old?"

"Yeah."

"Thirty-six isn't too old."

Durry was impressed and disappointed she always remembered how old he was. It wasn't something he cared to concentrate on. He also felt embarrassed about being vain. In so few areas was he self-conscious except his age.

"You're right."

"Everyone's married aren't they?"

"Yep. Or crazy. Or drunk."

"I might go crazy," she announced.

"Do you feel confused?"

"Nope. I'm just not like anyone else."

"Everyone thinks the bold are crazy."

"So I might not lose it?"

"There's a good chance you won't."

"I'm glad because I imagine its pretty dark."

"What do you mean?"

"If your brain is so jumbled you must always be in the dark."

"I think that's probly right."

Sandy loved it when Durry supported her. "Do you know anyone like that?"

"You just have to swing a dead cat."

"And you'll hit one?"

41

"Yeah."

They smiled at each other.

"What kind of woman do you like?"

"Not sure."

"Like this," she said. She pursed her lips and pushed out her chest.

"You got it."

Sandy took off her shoes and went wading. The muck sucked her feet down till she was gooey all the way to her calves. Durry said he always thought it was a disgusting feeling. Sandy only smiled. She felt the unknown objects buried in the mud jabbing her legs but went out even farther. She said she wanted to catch a snake. Durry said he'd watch.

"Maybe a water moccasin," she said.

"After he bites you I'll use you as a raft and float home."

Sandy hissed.

"Don't think they live in the mud."

"Yeah, but they slither along the bottom in the shallow part."

Durry leaned back to catch some sun.

"Do you feel like you're on vacation?" she asked.

"I kinda do." Durry's eyes stayed shut.

She screamed then laughed.

"You think its funny but I wouldn't be lookin for any water moccasins."

"There's none out here, do you think I'm crazy?"

"Just a girl who can fool her uncle."

"What did you think was gonna happen?"

Durry heard the big splash next to him.

"I think I see that water moccasin."

"You wouldn't want anything to happen to your little niece?"

"Nothing really terrible."

"But somethin small?"

"You go far enough out and you'll sink down deep in the mud but I don't know if that's gonna be small."

"I *am* starting to sink."

"You're just gonna to be somethin else for stuff to get caught on goin down river."

"What!"

"Wait till it rains."

Sandy made her way back over. She rinsed her legs in an area where the bottom was mostly gravel. She waited for her feet to dry then put her shoes and socks back on.

"Let's go," she said.

"Do you want to?"

"Yeah, let's go up a little more."

"A little more." Durry felt outdone but it would pass.

They found an area so lit up with flowering trees it was decided they had gone far enough. Sandy admitted she had never been to that spot and couldn't believe how beautiful it was.

"I feel like fishing," she said. Just sitting here around all this waiting for a fish."

"I'd like that too."

"Why don't we do it sometime?"

"It really is nice"

Sandy waded out again but the bottom was mostly gravel. Durry looked at the trees and couldn't believe it. He had never seen that many pink and white blossoms outside of Gwen's nursery.

"Ohhhhh...."

He turned to see Sandy had fallen in a sink hole. She was wet to her armpits.

"Sink hole."

She gave an awkward laugh. She was straining to get to more shallow water. Durry watched her slosh back to the bank.

"Soakin wet now."

43

Sandy pulled off her shirt and began wringing it out. Durry felt little surprise. Perry said once she wouldn't wear clothes at all if it were up to her. Durry was now starting to smile, shake his head.

"You just might go crazy."

"I'm just wet."

"What about shoes?"

"I'll put em on." She was as confident as ever. She went over to the edge again placing the shoes and socks nearby. She rinsed the grime from her feet then leaned against a tree to put on the socks.

"I could just keep goin but we probly oughta begin the other direction," said Durry.

"Okay." Sandy was putting the shoes on over her damp feet. "Great here, isn't it? We need to come back."

"Nobody'll believe it."

Sandy stood up and wadded her shirt in her hand.

"No shirt?"

"Don't need it."

Durry would lead the way this time, keeping some of the branches from swatting her exposed skin. He even laughed to himself as he walked. He laughed because he thought how different everybody was. Just because they're family doesn't mean you can predict a thing. Here was absolute proof. And from a nine year old. He was afraid she'd hear him laugh and inquire. The sound of walking in the woods was enough cover, though. The legs of her damp jeans making that scraping noise, too. Women, he thought. Once they decide something you can only sit back and watch the action. He always held that knowledge in high regard.

"Those branches aren't whackin you?"

"A little."

"Some hillbilly's gonna see us an think somethin different."

"I don't care."

44

"Maybe some kinda poison ivy or somethin."
"I'll be fine."
"Ok."

Durry used to be like that too. Not caring what anybody thought, even reckless. God knows the things he did. He used to think it would take ten lifetimes of clean living to erase so much bad. But everything changes. To survive he felt he had to make friends with many of the things he despised, authority, institutions. He would adjust his play. There was always that part of him, though, that was beyond any capture. The unbreakable part. The part that no matter how much darkness confronted him could never be minimized or obliterated. Obviously, he treasured time spent with other independent types, those hard to wrangle.

"See, no hillbillies," said Sandy.

Durry just laughed. They were coming up behind the house.

"Here come the pioneers." Sarcastic, Perry was in front of the garage putting fuel in the tractor.

"When did you git home, dad?"

"Bout and hour ago."

"What time is it?" asked Sandy.

"Maybe three or four," Perry replied.

Sandy was pleased at how long she and Durry were gone. It was a good, long adventure she reckoned. She looked over at Durry in acknowledgement of this.

"What'd you do to that shirt?" Perry asked.

"It's all wet."

"Well, go inside and git another one then come back out here an help in front."

"I have another shirt," she said.

"I know, now go git it."

Sandy put the shirt around her neck and went inside.

"How long has she been lookin like that?"

45

"Topless all the way back."

"She's always doin that."

A pause.

"Workin on that tree?"

"Yeah, got off early today so I'm gonna do it while I'm in the mood."

Perry started the tractor and went around front. Durry just stood in the drive looking after him. He always felt alone around Perry. It was often hard for him to accept that they were brothers. He knew Perry probably felt that way even more. But they had reached a certain place where they could at least be around each other, which was pretty new. Before they had only wanted to kill each other. At least he was sure Perry had wanted that. Their parents split up and disappeared one hundred years ago. So the brothers first tortured themselves then each other. Durry didn't have any family of his own and adored Gwen and Sandy. They pretty much adored him back. He was still pretty handsome if nothing else. And having those two in his life really helped with the great sense of inadequacy that ate him to the center. Perry was even beginning to understand. He usually didn't act like it because he thought it would make him seem weak but he was as tolerant as he was able. Most often everything managed to balance.

"Are you staying?" Sandy was coming out the back door.

"Yeah, let's see if your dad can use us."

"You don't have work today?"

"It's Saturday."

"Yeah, but you always work."

"Someone else is doin it today."

Sandy smiled and they walked together toward the road.

"Go git that fire started!" yelled Perry. He was cutting apart the great tree trunk with a chain saw. His plan was to section it then take the main pieces to the side of the garage where the woodpile was and turn them into firewood. The smaller limbs would mostly be scrap and have to be burned. He wasn't sure at first how he was going to get the large sections behind the house then he found a large bolt with a diamond-shaped eye. It was going to be hell on the fine gravel in the drive but he also thought he had a way around that.

"What do you want us to do!" yelled Durry.

"Just collect all these branches and trim and get em in the fire!" Perry went back to cutting.

Sandy was stuffing all the branches she could find into the burner. She just wanted a big fire. Durry was in his truck looking for something.

"What are you doing!"

"Findin a lighter." He found what he was looking for then took a couple steps toward Sandy and tossed her the lighter. "Be right back."

Sandy nodded and immediately began flicking the lighter at a green leaf.

Sandy was still squatting down in her new shirt trying to get a fire going. Durry heard her cursing as he came up. She juggled the lighter between both hands. "It really gets hot!"

"You're just holdin it with the flame lit, aren't you?"

"Yeah." She said it like that was exactly what she was supposed to be doing.

"Step back now," said Durry.

Sandy watched him pour the gasoline over the collected debris. She thought she understood now. Durry lit a rolled piece of paper with the lighter then threw the paper into the burner. Whoosh!! Sandy felt the breeze from the ignition go past her. Amazing, she thought. "Why couldn't I do it!"

"Are you kidding!"

"No."

Durry smiled. "You can't burn it when its so green."

"You gave me the lighter!"

"So now you know."

47

"I can do it the other way!"

"No."

"My parents would sell me."

"May-be."

"Dad says people would pay a lot of money for a tender white girl!" Sandy burst out laughing.

"God, Sandy."

They watched the smoke and heat render the ash up high.

When Gwen got home she had to park behind Perry's pick-up which was parked behind Durry's pick-up which had been blocking the drive about two-thirds of the way up. Gwen didn't say anything but Perry had quickly made everyone aware.

She watched the two men working apart the wood. She felt a sense of loss regarding the tree. It always bothered her when anything natural met its end. Funny though, the same sentiment wasn't reserved for people. Weren't people natural? The answer was a quick *no*.

Morris Bardaxle stepped across the road after collecting his mail. He watched with his hands on his hips as Perry carved the balance of the thick trunk. He picked a moment when the saw was quiet: "You ready for me to sharpen those mower blades, Perry!"

"Nope, did it myself this year!"

Gwen watched as Morris' shoulders fell. She knew he'd been sharpening their mower blades each spring for years. There was never a charge, just as a favor. It was sort of an expectation. She wondered why Perry did it himself all of a sudden. Morris came over and talked with Gwen about the demise of the tree.

Talking over the noise got too tiring. Morris and Gwen realized that at about the same time. Morris waved with the hand that was holding the mail and started back across the road to the foot of his drive about a hundred feet away.

48

Gwen went over to Sandy who was staring at the fire in the burner. "How was your day?"

"Great, mom. Durry helped me pick up the sticks then we went along the river for almost four hours!"

"You have fun?"

"Of course! I loved it!"

"Thank Durry. That's a lot of time for him."

"He likes it too, mom."

"He enjoys his time with you."

Sandy looked at her mother.

"You're doin a good job out here. I'll see you later."

"Where're you goin?"

"Inside to relax then start dinner."

"Is Durry stayin?"

"Oh, yeah."

Sandy went back to staring at the fire.

Durry helped Perry bring the large sections of log around the house. They sat them up on end like tables and were tempted to start splitting them but Perry said he'd do it another time. "Let it dry out a little," he said.

Then they worked with Sandy cleaning up the scattered leaves and twigs. The fire was roaring again. Sandy thought it was much more exciting with her father and uncle helping. It was reassuring how little apprehension they had doing dangerous things. Right then Sandy recognized something in herself that could make her very happy or surround her in peril. Not danger once in a while like riding a bicycle with no hands but danger like a companion that wouldn't ever let her go. An unwanted influence that was always there. Similar to a person you would certainly look away from after seeing them up ahead. From this she wanted to look away but had a feeling that it was a great deal of her future she wanted to avoid. The idea made her weak. She decided then to become more mindful of the course she would choose.

Nothing to be overly concerned with at the time but not to be ignored either. My mind can get so run down, she thought.

The green leaves made the fire crackle loudly as all three stood and watched. The work was done. The orange leapt high amid thick gray smoke. Perry and Durry went to put the tractor and other tools away. Sandy monitored the fire until they returned.

"I'm goin to get a beer," said Perry.

Durry and Sandy remained to let the fire burn down. Sandy swept in the unburned sections of branch that had been left on the brick.

"There's a lot to think about," Sandy said.

"There always is." He didn't know if she was referring to the job they had just done or something else.

"It won't stop bein hard I can see."

"Most believe itsa mix."

"I think the bad is so just heavy when it happens."

"I don't know. Jeez. You have to work at stayin positive sometimes. Strange stuff can collect. You have a lotta people looking out for you so you doan need to feel alone."

Sandy smiled a little. "I have you and my mom and my dad. I had a rabbit but he got eaten. Maybe I'll get another rabbit. There's one that lives behind the woodpile. I've tried to catch him but he's way too fast."

Durry was relieved she was talking about something else. Even if it was her dead pet. "Maybe you can git another rabbit. We'll fix the cage and you woan have to go through that again."

"I been thinkin about it."

"Thinkin about a lotta things today I guess."

"Usually."

Perry was outside on the porch having his beer. Durry sat down in a chair nearby.

"What're we gonna do now?" said Sandy.

"What're you talkin about?" asked Perry.

50

"That was fun, so now what do we do?"

Both men laughed.

"Come here you little unshirted nudie!" said Perry.

"Why?"

"You do that when you're older and you're gonna be sirprised!"

Sandy didn't say anything. He would never understand she already knew that. And that's why she did it, because she still had the ability. Certain behavior that wouldn't be acceptable later was a gift. She sometimes greedily enacted it. That's how she understood herself.

The front door opened and Gwen came out with a beer in her hand. She looked over the expanse of the yard. Her eyes rested on the burner still producing large smoke. "The work crew looks tired."

"Just takin it easy mam," said Perry.

"You guys did a great job. I'm still sorry to lose the tree, though. But I guess it wasn't one of my favorites."

"We'll split it this summer and have wood for most of the winter," said Perry.

Sandy leaned against one of the porch supports, quiet.

"Everybody hungry?" asked Gwen.

"What are we havin?" said Perry.

"Barbeque chicken, so you better start the grill."

Sandy was only hungry for more adventure. She didn't care if she ever ate again. Food wasn't the pacifier she was thinking of. She wondered if Durry was of the same mind. He looked content, though, sitting with his legs crossed.

Perry got up to start the grill. It was just outside the back door between the house and the garage. He always used charcoal and thought gas was for pussies. Gwen sat down in his chair.

"Its nice you had the whole day," she said to Durry.

"I like it sometimes."

"Got any extra sticks of furniture for me over there?"

51

Durry looked at her.

"You had some nice stuff when I was over there."

"That was all work for other people."

"Really beautiful, like that bookcase."

"Bookcase?"

"Remember you had that old bookcase I liked."

"Maybe. Don't have it now though. We get it in and get it out. Not too fast but quick so we can get paid. The guys are good. But I know not to push em too much. Then they get pissed and the work suffers. We refinish lotsa stuff."

"Is that what you do, paint furniture?" asked Sandy.

"Sort of. The guys I have working for me prefer to call it restoration. You know, takin somethin that's been run down and makin it nice again."

"I like that."

Durry smiled at her.

"Does anybody ever want to sell something or just drop something off and never come back and pick it up?" asked Gwen.

"You mean what do I do with stuff they don't come back for?"

"Yeah, whutta you do with it?" Gwen had a mischievous expression.

"We don't have much of that, really. I can only think of twice. One time I know the couple was going through a divorce. And the other time we got into an argument bout the quality of the work. Anyway, they said they weren't going to pay. It was like an old dumbwaiter or something. I still have it somewhere."

"Okay."

"If somethin lands in my lap I'll letcha know."

"Appreciate it."

Sandy watched both of them but couldn't keep track of their expressions. She knew her mom wanted something for free but Durry couldn't help her. She thought he wanted to

52

but couldn't. Neither of them seemed very disappointed because they were both smiling strangely at the end.

Perry came around the side of the house. "Do you have the meat ready or what?"

Sandy started laughing.

"He's so loud," said Gwen grinning.

Perry laughed a little too. "What?"

"In a minute. The meat's inside but I still have to make the salad and finish this beer," said Gwen.

Perry saluted then went back behind the house.

"He'll have a couple back there, too," Gwen pointed out.

"Do you breathe paint fumes all day, Uncle Durry?"

He laughed. "We have some pretty good ventilation in the shop, sweetheart. But yeah, it can be pretty strong in there sometimes. When its cold outside the guys tend to wanna work without any fresh air comin in. The atmosphere can get pretty flammable."

"You mean there might be a fire?"

"Nah, there won't be a fire."

"But there could be a fire..."

"We're pretty careful. Nothing's happened yet."

"Paint catches fire?"

"Not really. But we have a lot of solvents around. We're careful, though."

"Oh."

"Sandy, go get Durry something to drink."

"Like what?"

"Ask him."

Sandy faced Durry and widened her eyes.

"A Coke, darlin, thanks."

"There better not be a fire," she said before opening the door.

Durry laughed and shook his head.

"And when I go inside you bet I'll have *another* beer!" said Gwen.

53

Gwen went inside to finish dinner with Sandy to help. Durry sat on the porch a little longer. He watched the birds jumping from tree to tree, the squirrels digging up nuts and the cars slide by in the distance. Though he had a nice house, it didn't exactly feel like a home. No one there to keep him company. No one there to make any of it matter. He believed in a Buddhist saying he had once read: 'If you're a talented musician but no one can hear you play are you making music at all?' Something like that. He couldn't stop thinking about the audience. He knew how important it was. He remembered how he had enjoyed it before. Taking care of something or someone else to live better yourself was no secret.

Durry finished his Coke then went inside. Just the sound of their voices changed everything. He leaned on the table and watched them with great appreciation. He stepped over to the back door and looked out. Perry took a sip of beer then splashed some on the meat cooking. He was singing something. It was humorous to watch him out of character. He didn't know anyone was looking. He spat out the words forcefully. He was still a rock n roller. They both were really. Durry liked all kinds of music but rock was listened to most. Perry was only rock. He referred to anything else as pussy music. Perry did sneak in a country song, though, not like he would ever tell anybody. He suspected he was a hick but also thought no one else knew. He sang and soaked the chicken with essentially backwash.

At dinner Perry was as happy as anyone had ever seen him. He passed plates cheerfully, said please and thank you. Gwen realized then how far they had come. Especially the men and that shitfuck life they came from. Left like weird-o puppets to dangle in that foothill wilderness for any relative there to take a turn at raising. She was told that their father's brother's wife had the most constructive influence. Tried to offer some kind of childhood. But the brother was a terrible

54

drinker. All those back in that woods were. Half of them made it themselves. Nothing like ripe liquor. All of them trapped by age twenty. At least they had no idea what else was out there. That was the unfair part. Never giving them a chance. But Gwen heard that woman did the best she could. Both boys got away. Across the river could still be seen as more than enough distance.

"Do you two ever think about the mountains?" asked Gwen.

"More like hills roun here," said Perry.

"I mean a long time ago."

"Those mountains..." said Durry. He made a jolted smile.

"The Appalachians..." whispered Perry, holding the "s".

"Every day," said Durry.

"I don't much," said Perry.

"Never?" asked Gwen.

"Well, I gotta go there this summer, so I guess I have to think about em again."

"This summer, why?"

"Great uncle says he's dyin, wants to give away the stuff from our grandfather and parents we never took."

"What stuff?" Gwen asked.

"Well, there's some guns and tools. I doan know. Been in storage for years. Probly a few surprises," said Perry.

"I didn't know anything," said Gwen.

"Sorry."

Gwen's eyes widened as she stared at her husband. He knew he had the advantage and smiled too much as he ate.

"What about you?"

"I knew, just wasn't sure what I was going to do," said Durry.

"What if you don't go?"

"Says he's gonna throw it out or give it away. Too much to worry about," said Perry. Durry nodded.

55

"You're parents are aroun *somewhere*. What is it, stuff they left or something?"

"I guess, I don't know. Haven't been there in a while." Perry was mildly irritated with so many questions.

"When duh you wanna go?"

"Maybe July. Have to see," said Perry.

"I'm comin too."

"You think so?"

"Yep." Gwen was amazed Perry didn't argue.

"I wanna go too, mom," Sandy said. She had been listening intently.

"You're gonna carry everything," said Perry.

Durry continued to eat without saying anything. He long ago dismissed thinking about returning to his birthplace. The memories were just in a perfect spot. Dammit.

"So you never got any of that?" Gwen asked.

"Well, of course not. We were gone. But now we'll go back an see," said Perry.

Durry looked up with some makeshift smile.

After eating they were able to talk. Gwen pressed the men for even more details, almost shocked she didn't know before. Sandy was excited to go somewhere new. She and Durry played blackjack on the table for a while. She missed when he would tickle her breathless or hold her up on his shoulders when he was over. She knew there was an unspoken rule against it now. Perry stayed at the table with them, finishing off a couple beers. For some reason he had felt tickled all evening. The hostess Gwen did some cleaning up, never being far from her family for long.

3

Durry's shop was right in town. There was an entrance that faced the street and also a bay door around back. Most everyone who knew the place came and went from the back. When the bay door wasn't open there was also a standard door beside it. Durry's role was as owner and overseer. His staff fluctuated from two employees sometimes all the way up to three. The third man, Mike, always worked part time, usually when he was thrown out of the house, fired from somewhere else or had run out of money. His work was excellent so Durry found a way to fit him in if he could. He had a weakness for the displaced and lost, believed he could always end up the same. He thought it was almost his duty to assist those who didn't deserve it or usually appreciate it. He knew not everyone knows who they are so it was hard to ever feel let down. Handouts were nothing personal.

The other two men, Roger and Doug, were full-time and had each worked at *Broken Furniture* for four and five years, respectively. Even though Durry had a college education he had always been drawn to the trades. He understood the men and appreciated their skill. It was crucial to understand the world through service and the ability to create, he thought. All things had to be created and it was a great satisfaction to try and figure out how. He thought that upon this idea all other things were allowed to happen. Everything was considered, no matter the time or how small.

Durry didn't run from city life but was weary from it. He tried a job in Chicago and with that got to see many other places where people bunched together and built huge cities. In his twenties it was all new. Like anyone, he was taken with the possibility. But he soon realized that no one had

57

roots in those towns. Everyone was from somewhere else. But people acting like they belonged. Some did but most didn't. Then there was a really bad year. First, a good friend died. A few months after that his wife let an old boyfriend go too far. The friend he had known from just after college. An artist who gave up after a failed relationship. A neighbor in his building found him on the floor in his pajamas inside the front door that was ajar. His legs were together and his hands were at his side and he was face up. Features beginning to distort. Durry was haunted and moved by the image, actually glad he hadn't been the one to make the discovery.

As sad as it was it wasn't nearly as upsetting as what his wife had done. After drinks on some Friday in the city she and an old lover got undressed back at his place. Durry didn't find out till long after. He found out by knowing what questions to ask. It was the gaining indifference between them that made him realize.

So after such a year he was changed. As the matters in Chicago were being settled he knew he wanted to live somewhere else. He had always liked the amazing landscape about four hours south. He also loved California. But everybody was there. He tried to find work out there anyway but nothing surfaced. He had a couple of anemic phone interviews that turned into nothing. They never even called back. Durry ended up laughing about it and decided to visit Perry. He had visited his brother and sister in law during holidays and wanted to see if he might also be able to make a home near there. An unlikely choice compared to everything he had been doing.

He quickly found a small house he could afford. He'd never owned property before but it wasn't a tough decision because the mortgage was less than half of the rent he was used to. He was amazed how many trees came with the price. Gigantic, beautiful trees. Trees *no one* deserved. He felt very fortunate. There wasn't a lot of money. The divorce didn't really bleed him but he hadn't worked in a while. Certain people at the last company were upset he was leaving. There was even some yelling. But life in Chicago was all over.

He also didn't know how difficult it would be to make money in the Engadine area. It was a small town surrounded by other small towns. He worked with Perry briefly at the electrical supply business but knew this time he wanted something of his own. The job with Perry paid for stuff for the house. A new lawnmower. He had to have a gas trimmer. Even drapes had to be purchased. He didn't want the local women thinking he was a tasteless bachelor.

Since he bought in the middle of winter a lot had to wait till it was warmer. He worked on the little house for months. Every day he found new things wrong with it. He had this way he inspected everything that gave away the entire scope of what needed to be done. He went over everything rigorously. He wanted to uncover anything that might be hiding. This was the way he approached most matters. He started with what he could see then worked backwards to what it was dependent on and what that was connected to and so on. If it was too big to grasp at once he came back to it after it had steeped. The overall approach prevented small things from turning into catastrophes. With limited funds he knew he had to use only what he had. Just working hard to prevent surprises was usually enough. You also had to keep it up. But that first year there were some surprises, not entirely unforeseen just against the wager.

Using the electrical supply and another job as seed money really, he started the shop almost seven years ago. There was work right from the beginning. It was hard for Durry to get used to the response he got just from repairing furniture. Many people drove long distances just to get there. He made a niche as a refinisher. He loved saving something from going in the trash. In that area family heirlooms held almost

59

totem status. Their importance was not diminished even in a neglectful state. These he carefully repaired and refinished for the families that would hand them over as if they were dropping off their grandmother at the doctor's office. In truth, maybe some things should have been thrown out. Everyone thinks what they have is so valuable and old that it sometimes embarrassed Durry to hear. In fact, only once did he ever work on an object that was an authentic and valuable antique. The rest, well, were not antique. But he knew that to those paying it made no difference. Only the fact that they cared about the items so much made them invaluable. Durry soon recognized this and turned every thirty year old antique table into better than new.

He worked alone for only one year. His hands became rough and in the morning were stiff until he was up for almost fifteen minutes. That was the unpleasant side of the work, it was all using the hands, gripping everything tightly. All the repetitive motion became a burden. He never had that many aches before. But he loved the work and working for himself. The money was also good.

He hired Mike first after seeing the great quality of his work. His attention to detail was close to his own but more relaxed. Or more tense, Durry couldn't decide. It was damn good, though. But Mike wasn't reliable. He was so tortured. He wasn't comfortable in any situation for very long. He would twist around and fidget till whoever he was with was relieved when he left. Mike knew this and it made him even more self conscious. Durry had a way with the cast offs though, and could get him to work for longer periods than he normally would. He did this by speaking calmly and acting unaffected, giving Mike the ability to direct himself by showing a confidence in him. Mike often made Gwen uneasy but Sandy liked him, of course.

Doug was hired about six months after Mike. Then came Roger. Each of them liked the company and had no intention of going anywhere else. They knew the way they were treated and paid wouldn't be found in other places. It was hard work but a good job. The boss was real unique. They had profit sharing and kinds of insurance they really didn't fully understand. They each made at least six hundred dollars per week with two weeks' vacation and also sick days.

Sandy and Gwen liked to stop by the shop but it made Durry uncomfortable. He was a different person at work and didn't like people he cared about to see that. He just couldn't be as hospitable as he liked because of his focus. An abrupt social call really broke his rhythm. And it was hard to get back. Frankly, he always found it irritating to entertain people while at work. He had only one desire during the day. People who came to see him seldom regretted it because he bit his lip and fought hard to be positive and gracious even though he didn't enjoy the casual drop-ins. He was sure the tension showed, though. If nothing else he purposely directed the conversation.

In Durry's mind the business was always revising itself. He saw it as something that was always in motion, never a completed work or arriving at one select destination. No, it went easier if it were treated as a process and not an end. Too many challenges crept up with no notice for it to be something fixed. He liked that it flapped in the wind, same as nature herself. It had taken time to learn this but when he did it changed everything and let in the light. It would probably add years to his life as well. He suffered before giving up control but after it was as if another like himself but not himself had stepped in and taken over. He liked that second self which had saved him. He liked not having the madness that possesses so many other business people. He understood matching the wind.

School would let out soon and Sandy would argue with her mother about coming to work at the shop with her uncle for the summer. Sandy made her mother drop by too many

61

times. Durry got used to it and almost thought he could hire her but it wasn't realistic. He was just responding to her great desire. As an owner it was hard to refuse that much desire. All she wanted to do was help and be near her uncle. Durry suggested she wait a few years then maybe she'd find better work. She told him he was just trying to get rid of her and was siding with her mother. He said it just wasn't the right time to be working. Go to school and have fun in the summer. She rolled her shoulders and hissed. It hurt Durry not to give her what she wanted but even to him it was ridiculous. He was sure she would see that later. It was true she didn't have many friends to occupy her time. Her way was unlike most others and hidden from them. Even though she held it out all the time few understood and so she was alone. Her action was too bold and this trait creates prejudice almost immediately. Durry thought of the police. Almost any behavior separate from the mob gets noticed. Good can look bad. You can get picked off. Durry worried for Sandy and himself because of that. Worry to change. He would sooner worry himself to death than change. He just wished more peace for the girl.

Durry leaned out the back door with Roger for a cigarette. As far as Durry was concerned he didn't smoke. But there he was, smoking. He found this particular lie he told himself amusing. Mostly because no one else knew he thought this way, he had been able to keep the habit from those who'd judge him.

"You finish the Cotter table?"

"Yeah," replied Roger.

"Good, she calls every other day. Somethin bout a family reunion," Durry said.

"Just the final coat."

"So when, tomorrow?"

"Tell her Friday, two days. Can she wait till then?"

"I'm sure. Finish it next though, just in case."

62

"I will."

An older man carrying a wicker picnic basket walked past them through the parking lot. The picture was so out of place. He didn't look like the type who had any business carrying something like that.

"Probly found it," said Roger.

"Sure looks glad," replied Durry.

"Off to somewhere."

"Has a collection hidden close by."

"Goin to a fancy lunch," Durry continued. Roger snorted and threw down his cigarette, went back inside.

Durry stayed to finish his cigarette and look around. It was a hot sunny day. He often thought the really warm days early in the season were owed to global warming. Because he didn't care for the winter at all anymore he decided he would embrace global warming. He had been to Florida and hated it. He might not ever be ready for California. Hawaii or something equally as remote seemed too unreasonable. No, the warm climate would have to come to him. Global warming was a good thing. Shorts on Christmas. He urged the earth not to hold back the heat anymore. Just a little warmer, he thought. Get my region lukewarm then let winter happen to everything up higher.

Inside Roger yelled something at him.

"What about Valanar?"

"Who?" Durry tossed the cigarette and came in closing the door behind, cutting off the natural light.

"Valanar. The shelves he wants us to do at his place."

"He woan be back for a week, maybe."

"He really went on vacation to do that?"

"Does it all the time."

"What?" said Doug.

"You wouldn't believe it," said Roger.

"Went on vacation to git ideas for the names of streets for his subdivision," said Durry.

63

"What, really?" said Doug.

"Yeah, he goes different places to get these ideas of what to name the streets in whatever area he's building. He says part of the arrangement with these towns is that he gets to name the streets. Says he likes them to be original, though. Not Valanar Street or Maple Street or something. It was pretty weird when I first heard it too. He calls em street naming trips, doesn't even take his wife. Considers it business."

"Fuckin weird," said Roger. He started to sand the table he and Durry talked about.

"Hell, I'll name his streets for him," said Doug. "How bout Jack Ass Road!"

All three laughed. Mike wasn't around that day.

"What does he want us to do again?" asked Roger.

"Go to his house and re-do all the bookcases."

"When he's gone is the best time for that," said Doug.

Durry shook his head. "He wants to be there," he said. "Lately, everybody wants to be there."

Roger and Doug shook their heads then continued working. Durry went into his office to make some phone calls. Then he thought he'd walk up the street for lunch.

Someone was slamming on the bay door in back. Durry poked his head out of the office and Roger was pointing. Durry exited the service door.

"I didn't think you could hear me," said Gwen.

"You just never tell me *what* you're doin."

"I need you to refinish these coat trees," she said.

"Just these two?"

"That's all I have."

She already had the coat racks standing on the pavement in front of the bay door. Durry looked them over. They were in good condition, just dull from time.

"It doesn't really matter when you finish em. Not a big deal."

"Won't take that long," he said.

64

"Whenever."

Durry took the trees inside. Doug and Roger's eyes followed him and the new objects across the floor before looking back to their work. Gwen waved to the men but waited for Durry just inside the door. The guys didn't see her wave.

"So what now? Do you think you're on vacation?" said Durry when he returned to where she was standing.

"It feels like it. Let's get some food. I know you haven't done anything yet."

"Was gettin ready to, then your bangin on the door interrupted me."

"Eatin by yourself is so sad," she said.

Durry rolled his eyes. "Alright, let's go." Durry waved to the men working. Roger nodded as he sanded. Those two usually took lunch later in the afternoon.

Gwen started to get into her car.

"What're you doin? Let's walk!"

Gwen conceded slightly embarrassed then shut the car door and joined Durry in stride. He loved Gwen almost the same way he loved Sandy. Even though there wasn't a woman in his life he felt he belonged. They didn't temper their contact because they couldn't come to terms with their apprehension. He loved Gwen for that. Sandy was just a girl, didn't have such thoughts yet, anyway, but he loved them because they gave and gave and gave, and they were women, and that was the best kind of friendship for a man. Because Perry was involved it kept it all simple, crossing the line couldn't happen. Durry was just glad as hell the girls embraced him. Their affection gave him a family. It would be a damned unpleasant life otherwise. Who knows, maybe he would have come across something else. He didn't think it could be any better, though. The odds were against it. Durry calculated everything in terms of the odds. What the numbers said. He knew the numbers were against happiness. So, what he had he treasured and would never intentionally fuck up. He knew just how to handle himself so it might all work for a long time. Or forever if it had to.

Gwen and Durry walked to the other end of town, deciding on Dairy Queen. For a fast food place it had a surprising number of old trees around it that made it appealing. Durry ate chilidogs whenever he was there which alarmed Gwen.

"Why did you get that?"

They sat outside in the shade at a round table but with no umbrella.

"I like em," Durry replied.

"You're gonna stink up the place!"

"I like chili."

"Chili in this weather!"

Durry shook his head. "Why don't you try your burger there?"

"Well, I guess they do look good," she said.

"They're really good, leaves a taste in my mouth I can enjoy the resta the day."

"Okay, now that's disgusting!"

"It's just lunch."

"Who wants to smell like chili all day? I mean, my God that taste! It's that restaurant chili-in-a-can taste too, worse than if I made it at home. Not a lot, though!" She made herself laugh.

"I had no idea it could go this far!"

"Oh, you're out with me. If I'm gonna have people talkin bout us havin lunch together or have to listen to Perry about it then I'm gonna have fun along the way! I guess everybody's used to our family now anyway, so.... Still, that stuff would burn a hole in my stomach goin down and comin up! Aren't you going to be indigested? I guess you'll just be aroun ol' Doug and Roger but what if a customer comes in or your sister-in-law? You don't want to stink like that all day!"

Durry dropped the hotdog and starting laughing. "I have absolutely no appetite now. You've killed it! I was all set for a chili dog and now it's ruined! Now I have to overcome this guilt before I can enjoy it!"

"Well, you shouldn't eat that stuff. They're for kids, burp and fart all day.... Kids love that! But as a business owner you can't do that to yourself! You have to be prepared!"

"Prepared?"

"Yeah, have good manners in case you meet someone. A customer or someone, right? You know that! God!" Gwen was holding her burger in front of her mouth with both hands. Durry knew now she was really going to enjoy it. Since his lunch had been so berated hers was going to taste twice as good. He actually felt sorry for his hotdogs. She had some nerve chomping away in front of him after all that.

"I'm just kiddin, eat your chilidogs."

"I will, thanks."

Gwen smiled warmly while Durry shook his head. "Jeez," he said then took a bite.

"I know you don't tell Perry what to eat."

"I knew you were gonna say that."

"Well?"

"No way. That's right. He and Sandy eat some very strange things. He's lucky I don't lock the bedroom door!"

Durry snorted.

"What kinda stuff does he eat?"

"Oh, God, I don't even want to picture it while I'm eating. Just some really horrible things."

"Name one thing."

"Canned ravioli."

"That's gross?"

"It just stays in his system a long time."

"Like how?"

"We're done talking about this."

"I think its nice that you don't want me to smell."

67

"I can't stop either of you."

"Nope." Durry laughed.

After a moment: "I'm a little worried about what to do with Sandy this summer. She's outta school before long and I doan know what she's gonna do."

"Whadaya mean?"

"Well, what am going to do with her? She's too young to be left alone all the time. If I did she'd end up down that river in another state! She's so adventurous that she scares me. So there's no way I can leave her by herself all the time, you know?"

"You might have to take her to work with you sometimes. She could come with me sometimes, too. Maybe she could do some team sports or somethin? I don't know."

"She doesn't have a lotta friends, either. Not a lotta interest in what most other kids do. Maybe you're right, I'll just have to take her with me when I can. Perry can't take her et all. I might even drop her off with you once in a while. I don't wanna do that to you very much, though. Its nice of you to offer but you need to work."

"I think she'll be fine. We'll just have to work around it."

"Come to think of it, she does have one friend who's in some sort of swimming league this summer."

"She might like that. I think she'll like that. Try it out. I'd even go with her if you wanted.

"She might. Anyway, thanks for offering to help. It's a relief."

"Of course, no problem, you know that."

Durry didn't want to return to work after lunch. He wanted to take a nap under those trees. His stomach was full and the conversation had been stimulating.

He and Gwen walked back to the shop where she got in her light blue car and drove away. It was always hard watching her go.

68

4

Perry drove to work in the F-150 without a thought in his head. He figured that meant he was happy. Nothing to worry about meant he was happy. Damn he liked the sound of that. It was about six-thirty and he was carefully slurping the hot coffee he made before he left home. He didn't like making the coffee but he was not going to bother Gwen about it either, not on a day he had nothing to feel bad about. Gwen showed him how to make the coffee just the way he liked it. Sometimes the benefit of having a wife was simply that the coffee didn't suck. He tried working it out a thousand times, but it was the smallest stuff that held the answers for being married. At first it was the sex and the fear of being alone. That's what drives people to marry he reckoned. If only one person understood me, and all that crap... Then later it was the understanding that he couldn't escape. The feeling of being willingly stuck. Now as the years passed she was so much a part of him that there was a lot more to run to than to run from. He again thought it was great not having anything right off bringing him down. There were quite a few days he didn't have to drink shitty coffee from the gas station like everybody else.

He rendezvoused with Allen at the shop about seven, killing a little time with Susie up front before finding a chair to make a couple calls, see if some jobs were ready. He sort of took the initiative when it came to customer relations. Owners are so inundated with owner crap that they fail a lot just getting to work. Perry knew this so in order to have an actual job to go to he hustled on the phones usually to find out right away who was going to be ready. Customers also liked the frequent contact for the most part and he didn't have to rely completely on Allen for what was going on, pestering him like a kid about what needed to be done.

Allen and Perry rode together in Allen's van over to a restaurant that was opening up about thirty minutes away near Belm.

"Your wife ever tell you she doesn't like the sound of ol Butz in the mornin, Allen?"

"Even you. I been wonderin when you were gonna getta aroun to makin that joke."

"Just layin there."

"Yeah."

Perry smiled and finished the rest of his coffee. Allen looked at him irritated because he didn't bring any.

The restaurant was more of a roadhouse on a piece of busy asphalt. The place used to be a buffet style restaurant and now looked like it was going to be turned into a steakhouse. Perry thought it looked pretty weak. Maybe somewhere for people to go who didn't really know how to cook a steak, or even have an idea what a good steak tasted like. Probably going to serve that frozen garbage with the instant kind of potatoes to a bunch of hill jacks in roomy denims. Perry thought it was beneath him to have to work in a place like that. Money was money.

Allen and him went inside with the new owner and he showed them around. The plumbing would all have to be updated for what the guy wanted to do. It was a pretty substantial job that might take about a week. Most of what they were going to need they had in stock. There might be a couple things to run out for but mostly it was all on the truck or at the shop.

The owner explained again what he wanted done and there was some talk about it costing a few more dollars than was originally discussed but the man didn't seem that concerned and turned them loose to begin work.

70

there for my goddamn chicken basket. Then the time would come when I couldn't afford anymore chicken and I'd have to end it and the last person to see me alive would be the fuckin chicken guy.

Perry laughed as he chewed. Probly never happen. I'm never in a mood to kill myself. And who knows what's waitin. Hangin out with a buncha other didn't-mean-to-do-its.

Perry finished his meal and took an inhale of Coke by the straw, started the van and got going back to the job.

"Gone long enough," said Allen.

"Only forty-five minutes."

"What'd you bring me?"

"Burger, here."

"Yeah, I'm ready to stop."

Perry had a smoke while he leaned against a pole in the kitchen.

"We're makin good progress. Gonna be bout five days, though," Allen said examining the room.

"Next job's waitin." Perry blew out smoke, also surveyed the room.

"Who's sayin they're ready?"

"Fruit stand. Remember, pipes froze over the winter."

"Small job, then what?"

"Looks like we're gonna git that bid for those houses."

"Oh yeah, how do you know all this?"

"Cause I call everybody."

Allen nodded and took a bite of his sandwich.

"This guy seems nice though, how much we getting for this?"

"Could be almost four-thousand."

"We gonna need to buy anything else?"

"Maybe, we have it."

Perry snapped the cigarette butt to the kitchen door. He then used a five gallon pail to hold the door open and got

73

back to work. Allen wadded up the food wrapper and tossed it toward the five gallon pail.

The men worked till six then decided to quit. They could easily pick up the next day where they stopped.

They left most of the tools and supplies on the worksite without any concern but cornered away. The building would be locked by the owner who certainly had no reason to steal anything. They told the man they'd see him in the morning and he nodded from a meeting with the asphalt guys or landscaper, they didn't know.

Perry and Allen drove without much talk just leaving behind the day.

Perry thought he might stop for a beer on the way home.

"You know how everybody thinks everybody else is the asshole..." said Allen.

"Been wonderin bout that lately, too." Perry's tone added a deeper meaning which wasn't investigated.

When they stopped, Allen went into the office and Perry got in his truck. It was still surprisingly light after moving the clocks ahead an hour. In winter darkness smothered the day unmercifully early. The joy of summer and longer days were almost reason to cry.

There was a little bar called Stim's on the town square back in Engadine Perry would have a drink at. It was about seven on a Tuesday. The real characters, especially during the week, showed up between nine-thirty and ten. Downright weird and entertaining creatures that Perry had no idea where they were from or how they made a living. One night with Gwen he witnessed the whole lot in its strangeness. The point of no return drinking, the swearing, the mired speech. Maybe years ago but he couldn't be that anymore. The way they waited each day for the release quantity drinking leant. Then, right in front of you, losing their minds, traveling away. It was only pretty if you were onboard, otherwise it was a sick feeling. Someone screaming about how fire ants

74

ate their dog and another that his car could talk and told him not to pay for insurance anymore. Things like that. During the day you might meet one of them and there would be no indication of that kind of behavior, usually only malaise or exhaustion. But at night that woe begotten soul would dance unfettered under the painlessness of alcohol. The silliness was the sick part. After the nine-thirty mark, a man once advised Perry about his weed and brush problem over at the house. "Spray that shit with *Dirt Nap* and kerosene. You'll never have anything growin there again. But don't let the neighbors find out you're sprayin stuff with kerosene. Oh, man! You'll hear about that one! Warden'll be at your place with a ticket. So do it at night! They won't catch you!" He then roared in wild happiness. "If you don't wanna use kerosene, use hot water. It'll open the pores on the leaves like on human skin. You know, so the poison can get in. You can almost see it dyin right in front of you!"

"You're serious? What's this Dirt Nap stuff?"

"Dirt Nap. Can only buy it at that little hardware store over there or on the internet. You know, the internet. You ever get on that thing, no shit baggin there!" Perry felt as if his own mind got legs for disappearing too.

He thought about what the guy said and even tried just pure kerosene on a few square feet behind the garage. It worked, though he had been anxious to see the weeds die right in front him, they didn't, took about three days. Actually finding a product called Dirt Nap scared the hell out of Perry. Somehow, discovering its actual existence meant he was inhabiting the same world as the one who told him about it.

At home, Gwen was in the kitchen cleaning up. "Where'd you go?"

"Stopped at the nut house."

"Stim's?"

75

He told her that he and Allen might have a drink on the way home, which ended up being half right.

Perry came up behind her at the sink and gave her kiss on her cheek, grabbed her ass, unusually saucy.

"Yeah, went to Stim's. Had a drink, left. Started gettin the willies thinkin bout what might be comin in later. "That strange? Couldn't wait before now just wanna leave."

Gwen knew already that he had long ago changed but was always pleased to hear an affirmation.

"Sandy's been waiting for you in the TV room. Sittin in there by herself."

"Fix me somethin, okay?"

5

Sandy's new friend was a golden-haired girl who was either very quiet or throwing a fit. Sandy thought the girl's outbursts were funny at first but then later just wanted to help. She knew she shouldn't feel sorry, either, but did sometimes. Also, embarrassment. When her friend had a tantrum, especially in front of adults, Sandy blushed. She believed the girl just needed a friend. She was going to get one like it or not. Someone to also stand in her corner. If she knew she had someone who was with her she would have to calm down. Sandy suspected being afraid and being angry were pretty close. Her young brain knew they were just about equal.

The girl's name was Tera. Her mother and father seemed like the kind who wouldn't have a tempest for a daughter. They felt like they weren't the kind either. But moving a few times had really set Tera off. They didn't know exactly why. They originally came from a small lake town in rural Michigan where the man of the house worked for a large lumber company. For years he smelled like fresh cut wood when he came home from work. He had no idea how nice it was to breathe him in. Even though he worked in the front office he spent a good deal of time in the warehouse, mostly supervising the unloading of railcar deliveries. He used to tell stories of strange insects that had hitched a ride from wherever the logs were harvested. One summer it had been black widow spiders. Tera squealed at their mention. Immediately she thought of them in her mouth, crawling between her lips. She shook and shivered to rid herself of the thought. Her father said he was sorry and put his arm around her. Her mother just stood in the corner of the room with her hand over her mouth. If she'd have known what her husband was about to tell their young daughter she would have tried to prevent it. But the girl loved her father and down deep delighted in the grossness of the bug stories.

"Where did the spiders come from, dad?"

"We think they rode in all the way from California."

"California," Tera repeated.

After a moment: " How did they live all that time?"

"Well, it was warm all the way across the country. Nothing really disturbed them. They never got squished, maybe just got bounced around on the train."

"What'd they eat?"

"Other bugs, each other, I guess."

"Ewwwwww!"

"Please, Dan, she's going to vomit!"

"I'm not going to vomit, mom!"

"Well, still, maybe I am!"

Tera's father smiled tentatively. Tera breathed him in as he stood in front of the big window that provided the best view in the house of the lake.

"I'm not gonna throw up dad..."

Her father sniffed. Their home was really just a nice size cabin on one of the wild lakes in the county. They could easily afford it on what he was making. Tera's mother worked part time at the miniature post office just for something to do.

Even at seven Tera knew her life was very well constructed. Then they moved three times in two years and it broke her heart. Her father was more anxious and her mother reflected a new sorrow. A sorrow not from loss but from longing. Though the woman never spoke of it to her daughter it was there in her face every day. Tera only felt anger and thought her mother was pathetic. Hated her for not trying harder to go back to the way things were. Hated herself for allowing it to happen and disconnected from her fa-

78

ther because all he had once meant to her was now confused. Their new life wasn't bad, only no real water nearby and a strange new house.

"Do you hate everybody?" Sandy asked.

"Yes," said Tera.

Sandy came up beside her as they were going into school. "I hate everybody sometimes too, but I don't think like you."

"You have to be quiet now, so everyone doesn't know. I don't wanna talk to them."

"Were you mad this morning? I saw your mother."

"I just don't wanna talk to anyone."

"I usually just talk to myself. Sometimes people hear me and think I'm acting like an old person. You know how old people talk to themselves when they're in the store or somethin?"

"Do you *wanna* bug me? I don't talk to myself! Who's gonna answer if you just talk to yourself... I don't ever watch *old* people!"

"They can be anybody. There's an old man at McDonald's who's always moving his lips but there's never any sound!"

Tera almost laughed. A teacher heard some of the conversation and imagined what kind of future waited for the two little weirdoes. Thank God they're bright, she thought, or they'll end up marrying real dipshits.

At lunch the two girls sat across from one another. Tera's head was lowered and she had the usual negative expression.

"My mom likes your mom," said Sandy.

"You're so lucky you get to bring your lunch," mumbled Tera.

"I have to. I can't eat that shit. I'd kill my mom!"

"What!"

Sandy exploded with laughter. Tera dropped her spoon on the floor then burst out laughing too. She covered her mouth with one hand and aimed her knife at Sandy with the other.

"You can't say that!"

"My dad says that word all the time. I didn't think it was okay for a long time either."

Tera just looked off the point of her nose at Sandy.

"My mom says you're taking swimming lessons this summer, are you?" asked Sandy.

"They are not lessons! Its like a club. Its at the high school. But I don't wanna do it. I don't wanna see anybody."

"My mom thinks I should do it with you. My dad didn't think so because he said we'd have to be givin that little bitch a ride all the time. I told him you're not really a bitch. I told him we're friends. My mom thinks I should go swimming with you. I don't really want to because its indoors, but I might do it just as a surprise. I know my mom will be surprised if I do it."

"My mom doesn't make my lunch because I told her I'd throw it out the bus window if she did. She made it a couple times anyway then she found out I got in trouble with the school for throwing my lunch out the bus window. I *told* her. She cried when she found out I threw away my lunch. She said she won't make my lunch anymore if I didn't want her to. Now I have to always eat this shit!"

Sandy laughed hard holding her sandwich with her arm fully extended above her head. Each girl then shared every cuss word they knew.

It was getting incredibly busy at the nursery. Gwen found herself asking that Sandy take the bus more and more lately just so she could get to work earlier. She would rather start sooner than stay later. But that strategy seldom worked all the time either.

The home builders had been working most of the mild winter and were ready for landscaping. Residential customers were also doing an enormous amount of planting this year. Bret theorized it was because so much money was on

80

its way down from the larger cities in the north. The cost of living had gotten so high in those areas and people could buy a much larger home for about the same price. These home-owners were also used to spending on improving their houses. It was a new kind of demand that Bret didn't fully understand. He almost equated it with lust because it seemed to be no more than heavy emotion. That kind of customer usually filled him with dread; he could predict that their satisfaction would cost him a lot. He also realized it was important to them that they push you around, almost revenge for not giving them the merchandise for free. Were they devils? Were they here to stay? Now he had the regular competition and these dogs from the city beleaguering his top line, too. They added the unnerving expense of wanting it all perfect. Bret began to send Gwen to work with some of these customers at their homes. Gwen's patience would far outlast his own he knew. And if she brought in some new business he'd have to find a way to compensate her. He hated to pay more but felt he should, a little.

Gwen arrives a half hour later than she wanted. Just looking at Jill behind the counter irritates her. Her plodding mind, her unbusy brain. Gwen was surprised at herself for feeling contempt for Jill. It wasn't like her to have a barrage of so many unkind thoughts. These days a lot of her thinking had become spoiled. The pressure of work was taking hold. She decided to try really hard to control it and not be over-powered by something from the outside. That was it, really. Wishing a co-worker or bad driver would croak on the spot didn't bother her, it was being controlled by something from outside.

Jill then rattled off people who had called for Gwen and the one she needed to get back with right away. Gwen nodded while Jill talked. She stood in front of her register reciting information scribbled on pink message paper.

81

"Thanks," said Gwen. Maybe she wasn't unlikable after all.

"You jist have to call the Thomases right away. They were confirming your appointment for this morning."

"Okay." Gwen felt the contempt immediately return.

After organizing phone messages and going over a couple account files she slipped away to her unofficial office in back. She wanted quiet while she talked with Mary Thomas. It was always better not to be overheard, by anyone. Mary gave her directions and was looking forward to seeing Gwen about ten-thirty. Gwen refilled her coffee cup in Bret's office then went back into her own office to put down the mug. She said hello to one of the Hispanic employees coming out of the men's room and was reminded about that first cup of coffee she drank.

As she was pulling up her jeans in the restroom she glimpsed her vagina and pubic hair and contemplated how much power it had anymore. There are many more important things than sex appeal she told herself. The idea was disappointing, however. According to Jill at least her ass was still doing a job, difficult catching the patrons.

Gwen made it to the Thomases just before ten-thirty. She didn't find Mary irritating at all. Bret was off *again*. Then she thought he just didn't want to cope with what he presumed would be an assertive woman. Who did? Even other women didn't care to, really. Gwen centered on the money.

The two of them drank coffee and wandered around the yard. Mary had a drawing she'd made for herself on the computer that Gwen could swear had been done by an architect. Maybe Bret was right on some things. Mary slurped her coffee and pointed to different places in the yard. It was May and the flowering hedges were just beautiful. Gwen now thought she could get the account easily because Mary seemed to trust her. Nothing had been discussed yet about a budget.

Gwen got a copy of the plans for the landscaping and Mary told her she could just use that to generate some pricing. Gwen suddenly realized how crass the whole sales process was and that a certain part of her had turned kind of disgusting. So this was chasing money...

"Bret needs to dig deeper," she said aloud in the car driving back. She took her time, went the speed limit. The scenery was amazing that time of year. She stopped at a filling station with a small café and bought an egg salad sandwich for lunch which she then carried into the restroom with her. She did that sometimes without thinking. Buying food knowing she had to use the restroom then having to take it in there with her. She just thought it was gross to have food anywhere near a public toilet. Whatever... it was wrapped up tightly and overseen by her protective gaze. *No germs shall penetrate!* Danced through her mind as a black and white banner. A little goofy today, she realized.

She then became distracted by her pubic hair again while pulling up her pants.

"Looks good to me," she said standing and facing down. She touched the dark hair and smiled. *For a good time call...*, she thought then snorted. She washed her hands in cold water smirking at herself for a second in the mirror.

The rest of the day was easier. Something in the first half had been overcome. Gwen knew she was changing and wasn't sure how she felt about it but like so much that involves work life it always needs to be done, romancing you away. Many times it didn't lead to a better self but that is something that must be found out. Having exhausted all other options now to discover what you are to become on the great other side. Many good people have lost everything because of the transition while some merely scooped up their dreams as easily as rain filling a birdbath.

The worst example of a person getting destroyed means they have no recall of the human being they once were. This is the greatest loss of any. Nothing as valuable has ever gotten gone. Gwen eye-balled the game as much as she could then.

Her mind acted out this play during what felt like an uplifting afternoon. Am I becoming someone I don't like because of all this or is what I am becoming normal and necessary for my family's survival and what I am is totally acceptable by everyone, now I am the same as them.

She felt a little insane. Knowing she could never be that ogre who lives for the money while also knowing she could never be totally happy without touching it once in a while, tearing away a piece. Most important was her family, they would have to see any change in her as positive. It never goes extremely well with something like this but at the worst there might be a bit of growth with the sacrifice of a little humanity. Life might bring it back again if we really need it! Gwen almost laughed as she was loading baby shrubs into someone's trunk.

The grocery store was this sort of magical place now. It was six o'clock and the produce was rare art and the dairy section, including the cheese, and down the way all the juices, were a gift from God. Gwen shopped for dinner with the expectation of a child on Christmas Eve. This is just the greatest stuff, she thought. Am I the only one who has even noticed that? The relevance of the answer disappeared from her mind as she watched all the yellows, reds, greens and oranges. What would you like to eat tonight family! There are so many luscious items to choose from! You should be grateful for whatever I decide to prepare but I'll make sure its one of your favorites, anyhow! Gwen selected pork ribs, decided to make Caesar salad and potatoes, even felt she must mix her own barbeque sauce. She searched for the ingredients meticulously, garlic, unsulphured molasses, cinnamon, everything raw to go in.

84

The Heavenly aspect of the market made her forget all about time. It was now past six-thirty. Those at home were probably in shock she imagined. Poor starving family, angry too. Well, for a decade everything has worked perfectly. Now they would wait but hopefully be elated at the end. Such great food. All the sharp tastes! My darling girl waiting for me! Hopefully she hasn't ingested a poor substitute for supper! Such as block blue cheese with Italian dressing like before. My God, the amount of such rich cheese! She said it smelled like feet but tasted good with the dressing. The dressing covered the feet smell. Once she even ate strawberry preserves right from the jar. She said the big chunks of strawberry are what made her actually feel full. She said the chunks made it a huge meal. It made Gwen sick to imagine. But by the time she finally got home Sandy was doing her homework and feeling fine.

Perry was looking out the window when Gwen pulled up the drive. The sun was out later as summer approached. She was anxious about Perry and preparing dinner.

"Just comin home whenever now, aren't you?" he said. He had come outside and met her beside the car.

He knew how busy work was for her.

Gwen smiled timidly and began to haul in the groceries. Perry also helped.

"Well, what's all this?" he asked.

"Did you guys eat?"

"No, bin waitin."

"Okay, good. You hungry?"

"Of course! Perry calmed down a little. "Got home a little later tonight myself."

"Really?"

"Yeah, just ran over on this one." Perry casually looked inside the grocery bags, stirred packages with his hand.

"What about Sandy, where is she?"

"Upstairs. She wants to bring that friend of hers home from school but I said no."

"Perry, its great she has a friend. Let her bring Tera home sometime. You'll see how happy she'll be. Or maybe you wanna keep er all for yourself."

"I don't know about that, but I do like knowing she's there if I need her to be."

"Yes, so let her have a friend. This summer you're probably going to be seeing a lot of that girl and her parents." Suddenly, "Put on the grill, will you? I got ribs and a lot of other stuff to cook!"

"All on the grill?"

"No, but I'm gonna be busy and don't wanna have to remember to tell you to get it goin."

"Got it." Ribs thought Perry. What is she trying to do?

Perry started the grill, which turned out to be a great reason to start a beer. He went outside to the mild spring air to drink a cold beer and light the fire. He started using wax starter bricks because there wasn't any petroleum smell getting caught in the meat anymore. He bragged about this to a guy not long ago though and immediately regretted it. The guy represented that it was less masculine to deny the fire of a gasoline-like start. Perry might now be a fag. Or worse, others would follow and also become fags. Probably one of the biggest reasons of fag creation from how it was taken. Fuck him, he can call me a fag, at least imply its an effeminate thing, and I'll still do it because it tastes good that way. Perry then realized that the food tasting good was more important than people thinking he was gay. Secretly, Perry knew he would *rather* be gay than to have the food taste bad. Its always about the goddamn workmanship, asshole.

Gwen quickly put together the ingredients for the sauce while Perry pondered evermore into the maturing coals. He loved the high-pitched searing sound, almost their muffled

86

screams, and the white-hot edges. "God, I need another beer. This is too fucking great!"

Inside he got that drink. "You need some help?"

"I did, but I'm okay now. Got the potatoes boiling and the sauce is done and also the ribs are in the pot. Don't know how I did it all so fast but its done. Just puttin away the rest of the groceries now. You wanna fold these, maybe?"

"Can....yeah."

"Where's Sandy, you say?"

"What? Still upstairs."

"Haven't seen her yet. What's she doin?"

"No idea. You always know more than me anyway."

Gwen smiled. Perry didn't mean it to argumentative. It was sort of a mild confession at his lack of interest in his daughter's life. "You should know the same as me." It was a risk but she said it anyway.

"What do you mean? No, you know what, I'll go and get her. You just keep lookin after that sauce ma'am." Perry was so horny he wanted his wife right there among the potatoes and empty sacks on the floor.

"Sandy!" No answer. "Sandy!" No answer. Perry was going to climb the stairs.

"What!" Sandy stood at the top of the stairs with a pencil in her hand. "What're you doin! I hear all kinds uh things down there."

"Are you comin down er what. We're havin dinner soon. Let's go!"

"Alright. I already ate but alright."

"Ate, whud you eat?"

"A pear." Perry was able to make this out even though she was now in her room.

"Well, come on. Maybe your mother needs help."

"Homework, that's what I'm doing. Being a good daughter, you know. I have to do things for myself sometimes. Not always everything else."

87

It all went unheard because Perry was already long gone from the bottom of the stairs and had since felt up his wife, drank half a beer and was now outside thinking how weird it was the fire liked to make dead bones sound for mercy.

In her room, Sandy put the pencil in the holder on her desk then capped a blue ballpoint pen, putting it in the over-stuffed holder also. She shut her spelling book and started lazily down the stairs.

"What's goin on? Why we eatin so late?"

"Hello, Sandy. Where have you been?"

"Right here, where do you think! Why're we eatin so late?"

"You want ribs?"

"I don't know. I ate a pear."

"Just a pear? Maybe somethin else will be good?"

"Yeah, I'll have a rib."

"Just a rib?" Gwen held out her arm for her daughter to come over. When she did she squeezed her next to her.

"Yeah, just a rib, mom." Sandy laughed

"Help me put the plates out. Let's just eat at the breakfast table, okay?"

"Yeah, mom."

Gwen went back to working on the salad. In her mind she cheated because she used bottled dressing instead of mixing some from scratch, keeping with the evening. Just one little shortcut.

After a half hour in slow boiling water, Perry removed the ribs, dry seasoned them and lovingly placed them on the ready grill. The ribs, his substitute lovers for now, how they would make it together perfectly. He took a big swallow of beer. He realized he hadn't had one cigarette since Gwen came home.

"We eatin soon, mom?"

"Yeah, Sandy, few more minutes." Sandy sat at the table looking bored.

88

Perry suddenly came in with the ribs and shoved them on the table. "Eatin in here? Good," he said.

He immediately sat down and Gwen came right behind him with the salad and a bowl of extra barbeque sauce. She went back for the potatoes then stood by the table for a second trying to think of anything else.

Mostly they ate without talking. That night's meal long anticipated. But the chewing sounds began to amuse Sandy.

"How's your homework, Sandy?" Gwen asked.

"Fine." Sandy became preoccupied looking down at her plate.

"Sorry for the time tonight," said her mother.

"Eatin this late is okay with me. When I'm older you'll *never* see me again."

Gwen jerked backward. "What does *that* mean?"

Sandy hadn't meant to hurt anyone with what she said.

Gwen took Sandy to school in the morning. All desire to begin working early evaporated. She knew exactly what was most important. Though Sandy wasn't aware of any kind of revelation. Her mother to her felt like business some days. Humans could all feel like business. But today Gwen was warm next to her daughter and even if Sandy couldn't pick up on it she was sacred. Her mother was only business to her lately but Sandy was sacred. This distance made Gwen evaluate herself as a mother but then she just realized that it always went that way. Nothing can act to pull things apart more than time. They all swiveled on time, as if a holy mason had made it a chisel. Buildings to brick, brick to chards.

"What kind of day do you think you'll have today, sweetheart?"

"A good day, mom."

Gwen smiled at her in the passenger seat.

"I don't think it did your father any good to eat that late last night."

"Why?"

"Seems like he's having some trouble getting started this morning."

"He liked the ribs and he kept touching you on the butt."

"He gets like that sometimes."

"He loves you, though."

Gwen smiled. "I think so."

"He does, mom."

"Even this morning, you think?"

Sandy didn't answer.

"Was he screaming at you for more toilet paper?"

"Yeah."

Sandy laughed.

They were almost to the school.

"How's Tera?"

"Just fine."

"What about you this summer, what do you wanna do?"

"I don't know. Thinking about swimming."

"With Tera?"

"Yeah, maybe, if someone doesn't kill her first."

"Well, if you want to be part of that class, try to find out when it starts and what days and all that, okay?"

"Okay. Its indoors. I never thought about swimming indoors. Where's the sky? Just a roof. No air, only chlorine. How am I supposed to feel like I'm swimming?"

"Is Tera your friend?"

"Sometimes."

"Is that why you might want to go to the high school?"

"The only reason, yeah."

"Whatever you decide. I think it only meets three times per week for two or three hours. You might like it. I'll worry less about you if I know where you are. And I think it would be good if you had a friend, even if she is a little odd."

Sandy giggled. How did her mother *know*?

"You decide, Sandy. I'll pay for it and a new suit if you wanna do it. You can finally test your strength against other kids. Then you venture outside afterwards. I think it could be great."

Sandy didn't reply but had heard her mother's words.

"I guess I could swim, mom."

Perry hardly felt like working that morning. The women thought he had some kind of health trouble but really he just woke up feeling pissed. And he might have had too many ribs. His sore rectum was testament. So he just wanted to relax. It was Friday and the tail end of the restaurant job. He stole a little time at home after the girls left. Something he wasn't used to. The whole house seemed so peaceful and a nice place to be. He had to let his guts settle down. No coffee now. *But how the fuck am I going to wake up!* Perry pacified himself with a glass of water and a vitamin, some toast after that. He sat on the porch for a few minutes and felt like he was the biggest slouch that ever lived. Still, he reluctantly rose and went to the sink in the kitchen for another sip of water. He was still deciding whether to make coffee to take with him. After looking out the side door at the grill he started the coffee maker. It was comforting just to make it. *It'll rip my guts out later!* Perry inhaled deeply the last of his stolen morning. *I am out of time. I have to get to work.* It felt so good to fuck off for once. Allen'll look at him funny but it would all pass momentarily. He had enough Brownie points to get away with it and then some. Not like the other place. *They almost caught me at the electric supply! That was damn close! So I sold a few things to contractors. It was a rush and I'd do it again! Owner made so much money off me anyway. The prices I charged guys in a bind more than made up for it. Nothin flowed down here in the way of electrical supplies unless I made it. I got drunk on it, I admit, but its what the market would pay. I took my commission in a way I*

91

probably shouldn't have but just feelin good for a change was worth it. The books were so fucked up when I got there. I finally thought I caught a break. They couldn't prove a thing. And I might whine about the shitty health insurance or what little I was makin but back doorin that shit was bad ass. I mean I felt like I had a twelve foot dick. Some of those guys still ask me for stuff when I seem em at different job sites. 'Hey Perry can you get me some copper?' I miss it like hell. Now I'm just this guy's honest John. I wouldn't ever do nothin to ol' Allen. Sonofabitch is way too nice. Just a nice guy who works as hard as me. When the boss is only another swingin dick except you, you don't fuck with him. That's how I see it. And its still all about the work. Either do it right or cut off your arms and act stupid. God I wish I could sell some more shit! Allen's all right but I don't feel like I'm really made to be just a helper. Maybe that's just what I'm supposed to be in this world and to hell with what I want. I'm still damn lucky I never got popped for the bullshit over at High View. I don't know if Gwen would have left me over it. She's put up with a lot more than that before. I don't want to see...

Perry's coffee was ready so he filled his regular stainless mug and took off. The truck rode more smoothly that day it seemed so he put in the Allman Brothers, listened to *Please Call Home* taking very tiny sips to get just a buzz.

"Where you been?" asked Allen.

Perry was embarrassed but also resentful. "Couldn't get otta the bathroom."

"Oh."

"Gonna finish in here today." Perry went into the ladies room for a look.

Allen didn't look at him.

Perry appeared again then went back outside for some tools. Allen was smoking a cigarette near the back of his own truck. "Waited for you this mornin."

92

"At the shop?"

"Yep."

"Sorry, jist couldn't get goin this mornin."

"You ain't never been late before."

"Try not to."

"Call the office next time."

"Were you worried."

"I didn't know what happened. I had to go, get here."

"Sorry, you never need to worry, though."

"I feel like your fuckin auntie or somethin!"

"Shut up, I got work to do."

The men worked through lunch, making up time. Perry intended to finish the restrooms that day. Allen had struggled with installing the new lines for the bar. Too much concrete to cut. He used a subcontractor and just ran it past the customer first. It was an extra nine-hundred to open a trench.

"Do you have any idea what you're doin out here?" said Perry.

"Fuck it. What a fuckin mess. How the hell did you get outta this?"

"Boss said so."

"Every fuckin job I leave somethin out. I gotta slow down on each one. Its gonna kill me if I don't start payin attention."

"I'll bid em."

Allen did not say a word. The idea was too great. Too great to contemplate then. "Might have to."

Perry stuck out his lips. "You think about the money too much. Hard to concentrate that way. Like you say, every time there's somethin." Perry headed for the kitchen.

He's right, thought Allen. I'll have to at least let him figure time on one or two. Damn he was right. Now if he can just show up on time. If the fucker can't show up on time doesn't matter how good he is, won't be able to depend on him.

93

Perry looked around the kitchen and started cleaning up. They'd finished in there the day before. Both men always left the worksite spotless. They never wanted to hear they were a messy crew. The work could be exceptional but there is going to be some problem with it eventually. When that happens you're not as good you thought you were. Being a pig was something that could be controlled. When mistakes happen, no need to look sloppy too.

Perry helped Allen with the rest of the bar and together they got everything done near four-thirty except clean-up. They took a break outside.

"You think we'd finish on time?" asked Perry.

"Nope, can't believe it. Got into more than I thought on that bar."

"See how you're always worryin bout the money?"

Allen nodded and worked on his cigarette.

"You see how those tornadoes clipped that whole row of trees in half," said Allen.

"Yeah, heard about it, haven't been down that far to see it. The other night I heard."

"Wednesday, big tornado destroyed that area. My wife couldn't wait to see it. So we had dinner last night and went down. Unbelievable. It's like they always say about those damn mobile home parks. They were everywhere, you know, those trailers. Trees busted clean in half just like somebody put em over their knee. Must have been like that for miles. Just this strip right down the middle of a valley. We followed as long as we could by the road. Sometimes it would dip in away and we couldn't see anymore. But I'm tellin you, it was amazing how it only followed that one valley."

"Hmmm." Perry shook his head.

"Jumped over the road at one point and then started down the same valley but on the other side! Couldn't believe it. Made you wanna shrivel up and gag."

"You just saved me the trip." Perry smiled at his boss.

94

"Didn't you watch the news?"

"Yeah, looked bad."

"*Really* bad."

Perry endured his boss' attempt at closeness like any employee. He ribbed him a little then smiled, put out his cigarette, the official end to any matter of conversation and on back to work.

The men cleaned up and were ready to leave by five-thirty. But the owner had still not arrived.

"Knows he's got to pay today," said Allen.

Perry widened his eyes in agreement, but partly to mock.

"You did good, get outta here. Have a good weekend."

"You don't need me for the walk through?"

"That I can handle."

"See you, then."

Perry got in his truck and pulled away. Allen had gone back inside the building. Probably to reach the customer, Perry thought. He debated whether he should pick up his check at the office then or in the morning. Banks were almost closed anyhow. Fine, tomorrow.

Perry drove through old downtown Belm, hurried to get through. Another small depressing town. Just as many occupied buildings and unoccupied. Nothin wrong with em just empty.

After town was the road back to Engadine. Home. He went the speed limit to enjoy the scenery. He wondered if his wife enjoyed this time of year. All the great trees. Cars were on his ass the whole way.

He stopped at Stim's for a six pack. It was Friday so all the bar stools were busy. They'll drink tonight till they split open, Perry thought. They'll all be half dead and wish they were tomorrow. Perry folded over the paper sack with his beer and went back outside, daylight.

He didn't feel like going straight home. He wanted to celebrate. No real reason. Spring maybe. His wife maybe, or

95

how horny she made him. Hard to say. *Its kind of a combo, you know?* He thought about picking up Durry at his shop to join him but Durry didn't drink. *I like it by myself.*

Perry had a favorite spot along the river that mostly only fishermen knew about. You parked in a short turnout then had to walk through the woods a ways. Most were too lazy for the walk and would rather find something where the water was right next to the road. Great if you like tourists or other assholes. *No assholes tonight, please.* He found his usual spot and sat down with a deep sigh. He put his arms on his knees and looked around, soaked up the calming scene. As he sat on the sitting mound beneath a great ash he opened a beer and took a sip. There was still another hour of good light left for the world outside but in there was going to shadow. The water moved silently and the birds were near finished chirping. He decided to give the river another new name. It just didn't make a sound.

At home Perry's mind continued to be sedate. Though only his body tensed coming through the door, centered in his chest. He was late and slightly buzzed. Happy is how he'd tell it. Gwen said there was something left for him in the fridge. Activating his guts with food felt like it would disturb the harmony achieved in the dark woods. But the appetite arose and squelched the debate. He ate alone still by the river. Somehow the table in the kitchen was by the water. The moon now settling on the dark surface and leafy branches reaching for their handout. Then above him his daughter working quietly upstairs on something for school. His wife bathing in the shower in their room. The faint squeal of the pipes conjured an image of her. He thought he might finish his reheated meal and slip into his evening routine without anyone saying anything and maybe even get into bed later with a loving wife who had no memory and wanted him only because he was the man she needed to be with. If that didn't

96

work he'd just tell her he was feeling so happy. He looked up at the ceiling from his seat and listened to the lines like they had a message. He gave a soft grin.

"Dad, are you hiding from us?" asked Sandy now in the kitchen entry with her arms folded.

"No honey, I was just a little sick earlier today and was runnin behind. Went kinda slow."

"I couldn't think why you would wanna miss dinner. I tried to think of a reason but couldn't. I could tell mom might have thought of a reason but she wouldn't tell me. I thought it was probably not a good reason."

"Just runnin behind et work. It was the last day of a pretty big job and I was moving a little slow, anyhow. Just took a little longer, that's all."

"You okay now, I mean are you sick?"

"I'm okay. Feel fine."

"Good dad. Well, I just came for an orange and now I have to go back up."

Sandy produced an orange from a lower drawer in the refrigerator, waved to her father still at the table before leaving the room.

Perry stayed seated for another minute then walked his dish to the sink. He even rinsed it before placing it in the dishwasher. Fork and knife, too.

What a great feeling, head is so relaxed.

"You *must* be feelin good if you're puttin things in the dishwasher." Gwen came in the kitchen and stood in front of her husband by the sink. Her reddish brown hair was combed back wet and she was wearing a fuzzy pink robe. Now different parts of his body were activated by this picture and an appetite was summoned again.

"You all done in here?" Gwen asked.

"Thought I might have a chocolate milk chaser."

"Go ahead, have your chaser."

97

Perry found a glass in the cupboard and filled it from the half gallon container on the top shelf of the fridge. If his wife weren't there he would simply have freed two or three glugs from the carton by mouth.

Perry drank the milk looking at his wife.

"So what is it, a little TV tonight?"

"I thought so, yeah," he replied.

She took his hand and they went in and sat down on the sofa together. Gwen leaned into him and drew up her legs while he found something to watch. They kept the room dark and he had the faint taste of chocolate milk in his mouth. They settled on a program and undistracted again, still felt like part of him was on that riverbank. All good vacations leave an impression for a time, he thought.

"It's Sandy's last week of school next week," Gwen said quietly.

Perry ran his hand along Gwen's leg then underneath her robe and they made out on the sofa. Some idiot on TV was talking about religion, war. They chose a better work area on the story above in bed.

6

Sandy's teal bathing suit went very well with her hair and eyes her mother said. Sandy said it was the same color as the sky. They both agreed it reminded them of the color changing paint of a low rider. Sandy said one of the Latin kids' fathers dropped him off in a car that could jump up and go back down again and had some kind of paint that changed color. Gwen said a boy at work had a car that was similar. So Sandy liked the teal bathing suit even more because it was tied to something that was supposed to be outlandish. It was for a while held up against purple which was eventually ruled out because it was too close to the color of her fading bruise.

Sandy did as her mother requested and discovered the days and times swimming class met at the high school. So on the first Tuesday after school let out Gwen went with Sandy at eight o' clock in the morning to the first session. There were supposed to be basic skills tests to determine which coach or leader you would end up with. The leaders at the sign-up a week before looked to Gwen like college or older high school students earning money for the summer. There were two girls and two boys all about eighteen Gwen figured. To her they all seemed like babies. The girls' sleek breastless bodies, and the boys' muscular and hairless. Not a fat cell stored among them and each armed with dangling whistles and stop watches from around their necks. Depending on skill and age level the children were divided among the four. They would then train and compete among the other local summer swim clubs. The program was believed to have been conceived by bored high school swim team coaches who would otherwise have the summers off. It

99

wasn't that costly and the schools lent their facilities that also would have been dormant for three months. Parents got one more venue where they could enroll their kids either to cheer them on or leave them on deposit.

Perry said it was for parents who were too afraid to control their kids so they paid someone else to do it. They were really cheering the fact that the kids finally listened to someone in authority. Most parents were failing at raising children or believed they were so assumed paying someone had to be better. Perry said he knew what he was talking about because students never shot at each other till the last ten years. Upon hearing this when waking that morning Gwen only stared at her husband, he then winked, rubbed the round of her stomach, rolled out of bed and walked toward the bathroom, letting out gas.

Gwen didn't know if the kids were supposed to get changed in locker rooms or if they should arrive in their suits. Anyway, she put Sandy in her bathing suit and flip-flops and gave her a towel to drape over her shoulder at home. In the parking lot she noticed most of the other kids were also in their suits.

Sandy walked slowly from the car eyeing all the other swimmer hopefuls. It was her first time participating in an organized event. She would only be in fifth grade next year but she knew of kids who had been playing some kind of organized sports for years by that time. She was surprised at how much she liked the thrill. She'd have to see though, maybe she wouldn't fit with any of this either.

"Sandy, you all right," asked her mother as they stepped inside the building.

"Yeah, mom." Sandy might as well have landed on the moon. She just kept looking around at the structure and occasionally glancing at one of the other kids. It was only then she became aware of the cacophony of flip-flops and voices in the vast corridor. The approach piqued everyone's

100

excitement. At this time Sandy determined that it wasn't important about the competition only that she got to swim. And if it had to be indoors she could live with it because of the competition. For three hours every other morning she'd hardly be aware of time going by.

Gwen also started to feel they had made the right choice. It would just be something different to try that Sandy may or may not care for. Gwen believed Sandy would like it though and would try to spectate as she could.

"Mom, I think we go that way," Sandy pointed.

"Yeah, I think so." Gwen now saw the open double doors leading into the pool area. They were met there by two of the leaders who showed them where they could suit-up if they had to and leave their towels and shoes. Most kids anxiously had their parents put away their extras and got to socializing at the water's edge. The other two instructors were there introducing themselves and getting to know some of the kids. Gwen felt herself smile inside. She was going to leave Sandy with these people and go to work. *Sandy doesn't want me watching her practice for three hours anyhow. Some of these insecure parents would make this their life though. I'll have to do my best to act as if what I have to do doesn't take away from the fact I still care for my daughter. But give the kids some room.* Sandy's need to express herself was widely known and Gwen had to imagine other kids shared the same need. *These grown up baby athletes will certainly help them with that.*

"Sandy, do you need me to stay?"

Sandy's mother's voice seemed like it was coming from a television. "No, mom."

Gwen half smiled.

"Look, its Tera, mom."

Gwen looked which direction Sandy's head was turned. Tera walked right up to Sandy where they spoke three inches

101

apart. Tera's mom, Darling, came up to Gwen with her arms folded.

"It looks pretty well run. The kids already seem to be loving it," said Darling.

"Why do I feel like I want to cry then?" replied Gwen.

"Because you have to let someone else look out for her for a little while."

"Look how cute they look together in their suits," said Gwen.

"I know, Sandy's suit looks totally slippery."

Gwen laughed. The girls were still talking but starting to walk away.

Sandy suddenly came over. "Tera's suit is tangerine, mom. She likes hers too. We're gonna go swim now."

"You go swim. I'll see you at eleven."

"I can get them, Gwen, you have to work," said Darling.

Sandy and Tera walked toward the pool.

"Are you sure? I can do it."

"Yeah, absolutely. I can drop her at home or take her to meet you at work, either way. Its okay."

"Okay. That would really help. Just take her home if you can. I'll tell Perry. No, Perry's at work, its Tuesday. Shit!"

"I can take her home with me. She and Tera will be fine. I can bring Sandy around after you or Perry get home."

"I'll get her from your house. You have already done enough."

"I don't mind, really. It actually gives me a pretty full day." Darling laughed. "I'll be calling on you some days, too, I'm sure! Don't feel like its all one way. But I don't have a job right now. Its great to help where I can. Go crazy, you know."

Gwen laughed again. Could this be happening? She wondered. A person who could actually help. "You're twenty minutes from us, though."

"Like I said, I'll be calling on you some days, too."

102

"This is so fantastic I can hardly tell you! You should start a service!"

"Maybe, but for now I'm happy to do it."

"Thank you." Both women watched their daughters. "Tera's hair is already so *blonde*."

"She's always been like that. Just a little sun and she's got what cost somebody else four hundred dollars."

Gwen couldn't stop laughing at this woman. "Do you think they'll end up in the same group?"

"I hope so. I think it would be great," imagined Darling.

"Well, I hate to, but I've gotta go."

"I'm going to stay for about an hour then do some errands till eleven. That's the plan anyway. Don't worry about anything. Call me when you're leaving work and I'll drop her off by the time you get there."

"Okay."

"Does she have any clothes to change into after this or shorts or something?"

"Shit! I forgot to do all that. This is new for us, you know? I thought about that driving over."

Darling jumped in before Gwen's guilt became insurmountable. "They're the same size. I'll give Sandy some of Tera's shorts and she'll have an outfit to play in. Don't worry so much, okay?"

"Oh my God! I'm falling apart because my daughter has swim practice!"

Now Darling laughed. "It'll be okay, mom. You have someone on your side. Sandy should be charging for therapy. Tera doesn't like anyone these days."

"So you're paying me back by helping?"

"It's a deal!"

"All right. I like it." Gwen smiled at her friend. "I think I want to give you money for food now."

Darling just looked at her.

"All right, all right, I'm going."

103

"See you this afternoon."

"What's your husband doing these days?"

"Still sellin lumber."

Gwen went over to Sandy and told her goodbye. Just then the sound of a leader's whistle ripped through the air. Sandy nodded at her mother and so did Tera. Gwen gave a little wave to Darling on the way out. Gwen knew she had to be forgetting something else. Work was going to be shit.

The whistle got everyone's attention. Kids' voices trailed off as one of the leaders began to speak. She did role call with only five names going unclaimed. Bringing the total to about thirty participants. The kids sat beside the pool listening as they were told how they would be broken into groups and the skills assessment exercises they must perform. The two female leaders received the smaller children and the young men received those who were older.

"We're going to separate you by age for right now," said one of the female leaders who said her name was Diane. "I want everyone six thru nine to stand over there with Cassie, everyone ten thru thirteen to stay here by me and everyone fourteen thru seventeen to go over by Rob and Peter."

Diane put her hands on her hips during the shuffle. Kids began to whisper as they separated. There were also some questions. Sandy found out she could remain with Diane because her birthday was in July when she would be ten. Tera was already ten so they would be able to stay together. Other friendships did not fare that well, inferred from the groaning.

"How are you today?" Sandy asked Tera during the commotion.

"I'm okay."

"You didn't fight with your mom yet?"

"Nooo."

"Okay."

104

After Sandy's psychological assessment Diane blew her whistle lightly bringing everyone to order. "I want you to introduce yourself to everyone in your group. Many times you will be working with a partner so I want you to know everyone in your group. You can do this now."

Sandy actually stood up and introduced herself to the seven that were in her group. Everyone else remained seated so they got Sandy's rear end beside their heads while she bent over to shake hands. The little talk show host in low-rider blue. But it was truly painful for Tera. She was almost wincing when looking into the eyes of her classmates. She either wanted to scream or run away or hit someone. Sandy knew it would be hard for her and clearly saw the agony in her expression.

"Okay good. Now I'm going to show you some stretching exercises I want you to do every time you come before going in the water. Also stay away from eating a lot of food before you come. No one likes barf in the pool!"

"Oh, man!" exclaimed Sandy.

"Ewww," said another girl.

The boys in the group just looked concerned but the older boys in the other group laughed.

Tera just smirked.

"Better not vomit on me," mumbled a girl.

Sandy turned around and looked at her. She was the only black girl in the program so far. She wore a soft pink one-piece. Quarter panel pink Sandy thought. Its what all the chicas were into in these days. Sandy enacted a commercial for pink bathing suits in her mind. Eventually Diane's voice squeezed out the image. The sound of the other leaders' voices boomed in the enclosed pool.

"I want you guys to call me coach or Diane, okay."

"Okay, coach."

Diane looked at Sandy and nodded too.

"Also some common sense rules," began Diane. "If one of you does feel uncomfortable or agitated because of some food you ate, let me know. I don't want anyone sinking to the bottom from cramps. Also, absolutely no running while you're at the pool. This is my biggest thing. This concrete and your skin don't mix. It's the number one injury poolside, scrapes and cuts from running and slipping." Diane scanned the kids' faces. "All right?"

"Yes coach," came a unanimous reply, save Tera.

"Another thing, if you think something is going wrong with you or with someone else put your hand in the air. If I don't see you put your hand in the air yell my name. This can be a loud place and echoes a lot. So if by chance I don't see you, yell out! We can't have enough eyes and ears!"

"Yes coach!"

"Okay, we're going to do some basic exercises in the pool after we stretch. These exercises will help me understand where you are. If you sink to the bottom you're going to go with Cassie. If you are intermediate you are going to stay with me. If you're a superstar you'll go with Rob and Pete."

"I wanna go over there," mumbled the black girl.

Sandy again turned around and looked at her.

Tera just was staring at the ceiling. She then reached behind her and pulled her suit from her crack. Sandy almost laughed then thought how she needed to do the same thing.

"Okay, everybody let me show you how I want you to stretch." Diane went over to a pile of aerobics mats then requested everyone join her. Each child took a mat then knelt down on top of it after returning to the same area.

Diane came back over as well and started with a leg stretching routine. "Have any of you ever done these?" she asked.

The answers were a mix of 'yes coach' and 'no coach'.

"Its so important to stretch your legs and torso and arms." Diane was in front of the class contorting herself.

Sandy began to see how you could easily barf. Tera was stretching but not whole heartedly. Her hands wandered around pulling at her suit.

"Nobody likes the warm ups but its all necessary. I won't let you in the water without warming up. So please spend ten minutes each time doing your stretches. Once you're in the water you'll feel much better."

The black girl was just sitting there, legs extended, arms behind.

"What's your name?" asked Sandy.

"Trista," she replied.

"Does anyone have any questions before we go in the water?" bellowed Diane.

One of the boys raised his hand.

"Yes?"

"Are we goin to race?"

"Yes, you are going to compete with other clubs during your six weeks."

The boy looked away.

"Yes?"

"Will we ever be going outside?" asked Sandy.

"Yeah, a few of the other teams have pools outside. Do you like to go outside?"

"I do."

"Okay, let's head for the water!"

The four boys and three girls plopped themselves in the water without even testing it. Anything was better than sitting still. The rest of the time was spent performing basic swim exercises. Treading water. Various strokes. Swimming underwater. Sandy set a new nine year old record for time underwater. Unofficially. It just seemed to Diane she was under for a long damn time. Tera undertook these tasks but really preferred just floating on her back the rest of the time.

107

At first Diane thought she had a rebellion taking shape then realized Tera was just off somewhere else. She's obviously intermediate anyway. The day was mostly to root out the drowning potentials. All the Myrons and the Berthas who would quickly settle to their deaths. Life is weeding, separating, and one lunge ahead of the thresher.

Diane was tempted to put one of the boys and Trista in the beginner group but decided to wait till after one more session. She wasn't sure if they just couldn't follow by example or if there was a lack of ability. So she wanted to wait and see again to be completely fair.

Sandy splashed around near Tera while Diane worked with the others.

"Are you nervous?" asked Sandy.

"Not really. Its just so loud."

"Please stop pulling on your suit."

Tera laughed. "Why?"

"Becuz, you make me think of doin it too."

"What's wrong with it?"

"Because I start to get nervous because you're nervous. It just works like that."

"Okay, I won't pull on it anymore. I'll just let it stay there cutting my butt apart."

Trista heard and paddled away.

The boys were grouped together while the fourth treaded water to Diane's stopwatch.

"Are you in intermediate?" asked Tera.

"Yeah, I think that's what she said," replied Sandy.

"Good, so we're together."

"I hope so."

"Did my mom leave?"

"I think a long time ago," said Sandy.

"Good."

"Don't be upset, Tera. You do a good backstroke."

"I mean *good* because I'll be too nervous if she's here."

"I know what you mean."

"All right, guys, big day today. I think everybody did very well. If you've tested and I haven't told you otherwise, you're with me. Jon you can go with Pete and Rob tomorrow. All the switches will happen tomorrow. You all did a great job today." Diane wore a sincere smile.

"Do you think Diane's a racer?" asked Sandy.

"Maybe."

"I'll give you five more minutes in the pool then everybody out and wait for your rides. Don't forget your things in the lockers!"

Tera got out but Sandy floated around till the five minutes expired. She imagined how nice it would be if there were no roof over the pool. The sun above, light chasing around on the opalescent bottom.

7

Darling picked the girls up as promised. Her errands had taken her past eleven by six or seven minutes. The girls stood talking in front of the school when she showed up. She apologized then tried to run around to the other side of the car and open the doors. But Sandy and Terra had already done this, hardly noticing that Darling felt ashamed being tardy. It was about how much she cared. And she will really be made to feel sorry if someone were to forcibly make off with the kids because she was late. That, of course, is always the implication; if she loved them then she wouldn't leave them because doing so means she probably wants someone to take them. Darling discovered that she might have a subconscious desire to see Tera taken and sold by slavers but not that day, not with Sandy along. Darling then frightened herself by thinking that perhaps she did resent Tera or any child because of what she had been through over the last couple years. All the arguing and complaining, threats of running away… She was terrified that this might actually be true. *What's worse than a mother who resents her child!*

"So, how did it go today!" Darling appalled that she had spoken so loudly.

"Everything is fine, mom. We had a great day. We both love to swim," answered Tera.

They both still had on their bathing suits and were also wearing towels wrapped around their waists. They both seemed so relaxed and absorbed relating to each other. Darling was pleased to see her daughter display an even temperament. God, was she…

It had been so difficult lately and seeing Tera this way almost made her want to cry. *Do I have a chance of getting her back? Do you think my little girl could ever love me like she used to?* Heaven didn't answer nor did hell but she took no response as somewhat hopeful.

"Do you two want anything? I have to run into the store here," said Darling.

"I don't think so, mom."

"How about you, Sandy? Whutta you feel like for lunch?"

"Maybe egg salad. I don't care really. I'll eat almost anything," Sandy replied. The girls were still talking away in back. So well behaved, Darling thought. But she also felt like she was being ignored. And come on, what girl doesn't care what she eats? First she doesn't care then she sounds sexual about it. I'm losing my damn mind! Darling thought. I'm just gonna drop to my knees here in this lot and cry into my tire!

"Mom! Mom!"

"Yes, Tera."

"We decided egg salad, mom. Is that okay?"

"Egg salad is fine. Happy to make it."

"Okay, good." The girls went back to ignoring her. It wasn't so insulting as saying you don't care like before. But at least they're not eating anything like sluts and now want something definite even if they have to ignore me!

Darling left the SUV and walked toward the store. Nothing wrong with drinking at lunch she thought and once inside slung the six pack into the cart first thing. That's really the only reason she stopped. The girls' lunch was secondary. There was all kinds of food at home including the ingredients for egg salad. Even bread to make sandwiches assuming they didn't care if they ate the mixture right from the bowl. It felt good to Darling getting some of these terrible thoughts out. It had been a long time and negativity was stored up like soupy water in a bird bath. She thought she needed to get drunk and laid. Then she thought she could at least get drunk. Then she thought she might want a mas-

111

sage. And if she couldn't have a massage or get laid she would just get drunk and masturbate. That sounded like a good afternoon. The girls got to have fun and she would too. A couple beers and a good solo romp in the tub. She couldn't wait to get out of the store. Dale wouldn't be home till night so the laid part would have to wait. Besides, after being married so long it was less disappointing to just do it yourself sometimes. Oh, it was going to be a good afternoon!

Darling had kept the windows rolled down so the girls wouldn't get too hot. They were leaning far back in their seats almost listless playing some game about birds?

"Next practice is Thursday, right?"

"Yes, mom. You told *me*, remember?" said Tera.

"Just bein sure!" Darling giggled loudly.

Tera leaned up. "What did you get? Any food?"

"I remembered there is food in the house for what you want so I didn't have to get any."

"What did you get?"

"Just some beer for your father, he works hard."

Tera then leaned back not sure of her mother.

The house was atop a great dirt mound. It was a beautiful home near a lush woods and large pond.

"My dad had that pond made," announced Tera. "Then he colored it with something that wouldn't kill the fish."

"Oh," responded Sandy as she beheld the new color of water. The color itself wasn't unnatural only for the region. Usually deep blues and emerald were reserved for much larger bodies and the ocean. Sandy still thought it was exciting. It wasn't the usual muddy brown filled with algae. She knew somewhere inside was the muddy brown but through the mineral blue.

"I assume you both wanna eat now?" Darling asked.

"Right away, if that's okay Mrs. Ray," said Sandy. "I'm very hungry after all that swimming!"

They all stood in the kitchen. Mrs. Ray began a beer. She hung her head back and let the bubbles from the first sip expire in her mouth before swallowing. God it stung the inside of her cheeks but the pain was magnificent! She laughed audibly.

"I thought that was Dad's beer?" said Tera.

"I bought it, don't I get one?"

"I don't know, mom. Seems funny around here."

Darling laughed again. "You girls wash your hands and grab the eggs and mayonnaise from the fridge. I'm just going to stand here a minute."

Tera looked at Sandy. "I told you."

Sandy looked at Mrs. Ray carefully and then shrugged. "Where's the damn eggs," she asked.

Tera made a snot bubble.

"Oh, Sandy! I know your mother would disagree with your choice of words," said Darling.

"Disagreement for sure," replied Sandy looking in the fridge. She was worried no one else wanted to eat. She suddenly realized this wasn't her home and these people with their seemingly lax attitude toward food might let her die there in front of plenty. "Just need to eat, yawl."

Darling came over and handed Sandy the eggs. "You all right?"

"Oh, yeah, just some sort of headache from weakness."

"What?" Now she had Tera's attention.

"We'll fill you fulla eggs and then you'll be alright," said Darling smiling. She took another pull from the beer bottle. Close to the best bottle of beer she'd had lately.

"Tera, help Sandy. Get the pot for the water. You know where it is."

Tera nodded. *This is great.* Darling took another sip of beer.

"Fill it up to about half. That's good. Yeah, there... Now put it on the front burner on high. Let the fire do the rest!"

113

Darling realized she was having an out of body experience. The girls were fine, could make their own lunch. She'd maybe help during the mixing to save more work later.

Sandy used a spoon to place the eggs in the water once it was boiling. Immediately two of them cracked open and white ooze came forth. The fresh egg cooked off to drape the outside of the shell. Sandy watched, a little nauseous but marveling.

"Sandy, does your mother let you help her cook?"

"If I want to."

"Ever make boiling water?"

"If it has fire I can do it, Mrs. Ray."

Darling ceased more questions.

The girls finished their lunch while Darling had another beer. She asked them if they wanted to stay inside or go outside. Both wanted to go outside.

"Am I here all day?" asked Sandy.

"I told your mom I'd bring you home when she called. So yeah, you can stay here. Its no problem."

"That's great!" Sandy felt she seldom got to go anywhere new.

Darling told Tera to change and find something for Sandy too. Both girls ended up in khaki shorts and t-shirts.

"Now be careful near the pond. And don't get all muddy." Darling inspected the girls as she was washing the dishes. "I don't want you going near the stream in the woods. Its too far. I'll never hear you back there."

"It's a river, mom."

"Yes, do you understand me?"

"Yes, mom, if we're going to die do it where you can hear us," said Tera.

"Well, I don't want you to die, just be careful."

The girls escaped through the back door out the kitchen and down the flight of wooden steps off the deck. Tera made

114

sure her mother wasn't looking before entering the garage through the service door.

"We're going to need this," said Tera. She handed Sandy a BB gun.

"Are you sure?"

"Yeah, I have to find the BB's, though. Its too dark in here."

"Are you afraid to turn on the light?"

"Kinda, yeah. Just turn it on, though. I can't see a thing in here."

Sandy walked over to the door that lead into the house and flipped all the light switches she found.

"I was banging into everything," said Tera. "Okay, here we go!"

"You better be quiet."

"Okay, we're outta here!" Tera whispered loudly. She twisted the knob of the service door and trading Sandy the ammo for the gun hid it with her body. They slinked along the edge of the garage in back then turned right around the corner till they got to the front, figuring Mrs. Ray was still in the kitchen with only a view to the rear.

Darling had finished cleaning up after lunch and even scrounged a little egg salad for herself. Not enough for a sandwich, though. Sandy wasn't kidding, she could eat. Darling smiled. What a nice girl, she thought. So good for Tera. *Tera. Tera almost put me under. That girl could be positively evil. Two solid years of sulking and being plain mean to me. The screaming at each other and the guilt afterwards had almost gotten too much. Waking up in the middle of the night having dreams of divorcing my child. My marriage was fine but its this child. If she was put here to kill me or make me stronger then that's what happened. I nearly wanted to die and I couldn't find any more strength. My husband hardly ever caught it and if he heard he would*

115

coddle me in some way that made me seem like I was over-reacting in the first place. God that was it! So irritating. He caused it but she blamed me! Hardly fair. But here I am, keeping it together and trying to act normal taking her to fucking swim practice like nothing's the matter! Maybe nothing is the matter and I'm just weak. Maybe I had to get through hell like anyone else. Another sick test like every-body else gets that makes life a drag sometimes. Its just the damn guilt, that's the hardest to shake off. It gets in there and in the absence of anyone else doing it, punishes thor-oughly all by itself. Makes you weak and restless and sick in your soul. I don't want to be sick anymore. I better have another beer. Its my day to celebrate. Finally I'm broken. I can't keep it in anymore. From here I'll either be lost for-ever or in some way come back. I don't think I'll come back the same though. Wounded and with a twitch. She took a drink from the fresh bottle. Beer is so good today. Her mind played with her some more: *My husband, whom I love more than anything hasn't ever let me down. Its just the way everything went. I was actually ready to move. That is what I have to make Tera understand. I was ready to leave that desolate place. The winters were so hard. To a child all that snow is a blessing but as you age it can help sink you even lower. White on and on.... Desolate cold and white six or seven months per year. You think you can handle it, you tell yourself that but three or four months in, after New Year, you think you're going to die. Its just so stark, whatever—how can a soul find happiness? I tried for so many years, it just kept getting worse, my soul was so unhappy. I almost wanted to vomit it out and leave it out rather than endure any more bleakness. And so we accepted moves out of that place. Now we're here, and there's so much more sun, less water than Michigan but more sun. It seems so anyhow. The winters are much milder and don't last nearly as long. The pressure is off here. Some people said traveling lower would*

116

do that. Take the pressure off. People seem friendlier, not depressed like during winters up north. We were even going to have another child. We were thinking that we would. But then the first transfer came and the change in Tera and I didn't think I could handle a baby anymore. It wasn't the right atmosphere. It was a shame because I would have loved a boy. A boy and a girl. Hard to say, my pipes might not be frozen yet! She took a drink of beer. *Feel like a man* after work she thought. *Wanna scratch myself and burp. We really have landed in a good spot. Dale made the house wonderful. There's plenty of room inside and out. And I know those girls are going to misbehave. I can see it in Sandy's eyes. My little one I know about. She's so damn mean I don't worry about her as much as I should. But the other one is not mine. Please don't let anything happen to her....* Darling pushed away the bottle. She resolved to hunt for the kids in an hour.

Sandy observed how perfect the path was from the house to the pole barn. A perfect strip of dry dirt cut about three feet wide slightly covered in fallen grass. The vegetation on either side was waist high on the girls.

"Are we stoppin here?" Sandy asked.

"I don't think so. Don't you wanna go to the pond?"

"What's in there?"

"Neat barn isn't it? Just my dad's stuff, a tractor, a lotta tools. Not a lotta places to play or sit, though."

"Yeah, I wanna go to the pond!" Sandy shook the box of BB's. They traveled past the pole barn on the same cut path.

Tera was carrying the gun like an old soldier. The butt in her palm and the barrel against her shoulder. Sandy walked steadily behind, could hardly wait to get her hands on the shooter.

Down the hill toward the pond Sandy heard a quick rustling. Something dashed past the girls up the path. They

117

both turned to see a scared red fox running away. His fur was long only in patches, seemed mangy. Sandy thought he might be sick. "Its because he's still losing his winter coat," said Tera. Sandy was relieved. "Remember those weeks of cold?"

"No."

"Well, some of the animals are finishing their winter coats now like raccoons too."

Sandy was very pleased. This girl knew things. "I didn't want you to shoot it."

"I wouldn't have."

"Whutta you think he was doin here?" asked Sandy.

"I think he might have been drinking water or trying to eat something. Usually they hunt at night. I don't know, maybe."

The trail ended almost at the water's edge, before cattails and water grass. Tera moved around to the left toward a tree. "Bring the BB's," she said.

Tera twisted the barrel opening a hole where the shot was loaded. Sandy poured in the tiny BB's while Tera cupped her hands underneath. They figured they'd loaded about fifty shots. Tera twisted the tip of the barrel closing the loading port and cocked the gun. The sound of all those miniature ball bearings rolling inside.

She shot out across the water and Sandy saw the spray go up toward the center of the pond. Very cool. The water droplets sparkled in the sunlight.

"Did you see the mist!" yelled Tera.

"I saw it spray!" Sandy realized she had patience she was not even aware of. If she had been with Durry or her father that gun would be in her hands and already fired off most of the fifty.

"A couple more and I'll give it to you," said Tera as she cocked the gun. It was a small lever action not really made to resemble any popular rifle, like a lot of them do, and only

118

moderately powerful. Sandy understood that as long as they didn't get hit in the eye there would only be a sting. Not that anyone was going to get shot.

Tera put another shot across the pond. It made the same cool mist. This time they heard the BB strike the growth on the other side. It made a dry sounding *whap!*

"Did you see it skip!" exclaimed Tera.

"I heard it hit the other side, too!" Sandy was close to pushing Tera's face in the mud and absconding with the weapon onto a new adventure.

"Can't she see us down here?" asked Sandy.

"That's why we're behind the tree."

"Will we really get in trouble?"

"My dad said the gun is mine. He asked me if I could use it when he's around. My mom doesn't really know about it."

"She'd be upset if she knew."

"We wouldn't be out here." Tera looked out over the water. "Find a frog, Sandy."

"Oh, you can't just shoot a frog!"

"I don't wanna shoot it, I wanna make im jump!"

Tera patrolled the shore, kicking around in some muck to scare one up. Sandy helped half-heartedly, just wanted the gun. She didn't know if it would taken away soon.

"I can't believe the water is this color," said Sandy. "How did your dad do that?"

"He just put some stuff in it. Found it on the Internet. It came UPS."

"Was it a little or a lot?"

"Well, a lot, I guess. Big pond, maybe."

"It's a weird color. There's no other water aroun here this color."

"I know."

"And all the plants and fish are still alive. That's amazing. It makes you think about what else to color."

Tera still kicking green clumps on the shore.

119

"There's gotta be a frog or toad in here. Frogs are hard to find even though they're so big. Toads are everywhere even though they're smaller." They both thought about this for a moment. "You ever seen a frog?"

"I didn't know there was a difference."

"*Big* difference..."

Tera fired another shot across the water. This time it struck close to the opposite side. They heard the same *whap* though the growth.

"That noise is a frog," Tera whispered.

Sandy quieted her mind to listen.

"That's a croak."

They both started toward the sound on the other side.

Tera placed a shot near where she thought she heard the sound coming from. There was a low splash and a gurgle.

"Frog jumped in the water. He's out deep. He's safe now. I probly woulda shot im," said Tera.

"I knew that's what you were going to do." Sandy was disappointed. "You can't just shoot im."

"I say I'm not going to but then I want to."

"Lemme see it for a while."

Tera handed Sandy the gun. The BB's rattled in the magazine. Sandy quickly gave it an inspection then aimed it over the water. They were in full view of the house. She was sure Tera's mother would be watching. The moment was too big to miss. She cocked the gun and fired then looked for the mist. "That's the coolest," said Sandy.

Tera squatted and twisted her hair, getting it to her mouth.

Sandy cocked the gun and fired once again.

"Hit that rock right there," said Tera.

Sandy aimed and shot.

"Whoa!" yelled Tera. The BB ricocheted straight back. They could see it travel. "I shouldn't have told you to do that."

"I shot at it anyway. Did you see it bounce right back? Wonder what my mom would say if I lost an eye?"

"Let's go toward the river in back," said Tera.

The girls started up the path to the barn under the watch of Darling standing on the deck at the house. "Everything OK?" she yelled.

"Yeah!" Tera yelled back. She wasn't sure how well she was hiding the gun. She tried to put it behind one leg as she walked. "We wanna go to the river!"

"Please stay up here, Tera." They were talking across fifty yards but the sound carried.

"For an hour, mom. I wanna go!"

Darling couldn't think of another reason but fear to keep the two up close to the house. It was still hours before Sandy would be ready to go home. "I'm going to come find you in an hour!"

Tera just waived at her mother. Sandy stood there torn. Tera plodded a new direction and Sandy went behind. Tera always kept the gun on the opposite side out of view. Now there were two bodies in the way.

The way north didn't have much of a path. But at least some grass was trampled in a narrow line to the edge of the property. After the high grass and a few more trees the Ray's lot gave way to farmland and the soybeans that had begun to sprout. Tera looked behind for Sandy who had stopped a few paces ago with her back to the trunk of a seventy-foot white ash. Tera watched her there. It was getting good 'n hot. The sun threaded its way through the atmosphere down to the rich green surface of open leaves and a dancing dry field. Sandy looked out across the beans and at her friend. "What's out there?"

"We have to walk through this field and the woods to the stream." Tera pivoted her torso and pointed behind. The wind blew her hair over her face. She gently moved her head

121

and wiped the hair from her eyes. The muzzle of the gun on her shoe.

Still at the tree: "Nice day isn't it?"

"Nice day," replied Tera. She watched the air separate locks of Sandy's hair sending them out and up. "Windy out here."

"I like the wind."

"I like it."

They started across the soybean field to the next woods. The trees that farmers let survive along a path of water. Sandy suspected if it weren't for agriculture the earth in the area would be blanketed with trees to the horizon. She had never eaten a soybean and couldn't imagine they were much good.

Darling watched the girls for a while cross the field. *Why did Dale show her how to use that gun? If I make it through this day...* Beer alone in the kitchen looking out the window at her daughter and her friend and their gun was such an utterly helpless situation that she actually felt pretty good. I'm ready and sunk down, she thought. *If anything happens I'm here, be waiting.*

Approaching the woods Sandy saw an entrance into a world she had been imagining. It was going to be tough to leave once there. The independent afternoon caught her by surprise. This might be my only chance, she thought. If I can find the way I might not have to return. *Oh, damn, my little game. I don' want to be alone, though. Who would be with me? My little game... I'd miss the love in the faces of my family. I won't ever be able to leave this windy, yellow world, I guess. Not so bad. Might trade it for a hint of what's beyond, eventually. I can never leave, though. I thought I would be disappointed. Instead I feel calm. I know somehow the only thing I'll ever find is flat water to take me a mile or two.*

122

The field withdrew and leafy silver shook before them in the drenching light. Sandy felt the sting on her forehead from all the sun. The girls entered the line of woods that held the river at a natural opening through the undergrowth. Inside the wind subsided and they were shielded from the blowing heat.

Neither paused but kept going because at every step was felt the tension of tiny bent branches on their bodies. Tera used the gun to sweep away the bothersome ones right in front of her.

Just when the urge for a real brisk hike became appealing, it was over.

"Is this *my* river?" asked Sandy. She stood in front of the quiet moving water trying to see if she might recognize any similarity from the land near her home.

"Its *my* river," said Tera.

"Its so beautiful but its narrow." Sandy had her hands on her hips. The air smelled just like sweet flowers but she couldn't see any. Nothing but green forever. She couldn't remember ever smelling flowers when there weren't any in sight.

The girls walked in the direction the river flowed. Tera seemed to have a place in mind. Sandy followed along still not sure if it was *her* river.

"See, it's a beach," said Tera swinging up the gun to point.

"How many times have you been here?"

"Only with my dad before. But he started his job and I couldn't come back here by myself. Wasn't happy enough."

Sandy smiled. "Cool beach. Did you find it?"

"My dad and me. We were walking along. He said snakes were gonna get me. It made me angry."

"My uncle always says that. I say I'll catch the snakes. He always says they're gonna get me. I usually end up getting afraid. I never thought about getting angry."

"This beach is great, c'mon."

They took off their shoes and socks together sitting on the bank. Sandy stuffed her socks into her empty shoes and Tera hung her socks on a small branch.

"I'm leavin the gun, I think. Do you want it?" asked Tera

"Fire one shot."

Tera cocked the gun and pointed it toward the water and fired. Sandy saw the copper ball fly then the spray. What a kick, she thought. Tera left the gun on the ground near her shoes.

"I'm glad I have on shorts," said Tera beginning to wade out. She sort of drug her feet stirring up the mix of silt and sand making up the barely submerged peninsula of earth that fanned out into the hobby river about two-thirds of the way across. In large patches though it was free of the water to make the dry brown island beaches Tera had discovered with her father. Today Tera saw that many of the *islands* held lots of stones making it too uncomfortable to sit down or stand in bare feet.

Tera hopped on one of the islands and kicked around the sand. "Not a lot of rocks." She pointed her toes and moved her leg from side to side through the sand smoothing an area. She sat down and closed her eyes at the sun. She was leaning back on her arms, left hand touching the water. She would gently raise a couple fingers to better feel the moisture. She thumped her feet on the beach.

Sandy saw someone who liked it all as much as she did. She waded out across the sticky silt to the beach island. It was like walking over cheesecake. One at a time she dipped her feet back in the water to clean them, bending over using her hands on the stubborn stuff.

The river was wide enough not to have the trees on both sides shutting out the light. Above most of the water was blue sky in many places. Tera made her plot look like quite a destination.

124

Sandy smoothed a spot looking carefully for rocks. She looked at Tera. "Your foot is bleeding."

"How can you tell?"

"I can see red."

"Sand isn't stuck to it?"

"Some sand and blood."

Tera drew up her leg and examined her foot. "Every time I take my shoes off I step on something." Her eyes narrowed and her mouth widened. "Its from something on this beach! I thought I felt somethin when I was clearin away my spot." She extended her leg again looking queasy or disgusted. "I hardly felt it though."

"So its okay?"

"Yeah, really nothing. Justa lotta blood." Tera bulged out her eyes and croaked.

"Jerk. Don't get hurt or we'll have to go back."

"You don't wanna go back?"

"Red is a warning."

"Is that why its red?"

"I think that's why." Sandy tapped her feet anxiously.

"Don't worry, if it were bad we'd have to go. I'm always getting cuts somehow."

Sandy nodded looking at the foot. She couldn't see a cut at all from where she was sitting. Must be a scratch she thought. Just bleeding a lot. Mom says nothing bleeds like the head. *I'll have to mention bout feet, too.*

Tera tried to relax but was preoccupied with her foot. She rubbed it in the coarse sand. "Its like an itch that stings," she said with a puzzled look.

"Put it in the water. Rinse it off and let it dry."

Tera did what Sandy said. She looked at the foot. Just a small flap of skin cut back at an angle. She played with the flap then looked under it. She actually did feel better as her feet dried.

"What time do you think it is?" asked Sandy.

125

"Maybe three. Maybe four."

"I have an uncle who can tell time with his hand."

"How?"

"I don't know. He counts his fingers or something."

"You mean like five o'clock for one hand and ten o'clock for two hands."

"I don't really know."

"You didn't help us at all."

"I think its about four."

"We goin up yet?"

"Not yet."

The girls lingered on their island, leaning back on their hands or sitting Indian style or walking the perimeter. Tera forgot about her foot. They both knew traveling was no good that day. It would take too much time and Darling was already on edge. Sandy's mom would be coming soon.

Sandy became aware of the birds. "Where do the birds sleep?"

"In the ground. Or up in the air, while they fly. Horses sleep standing up, birds sleep in the air."

Sandy laughed. "You don't see em on branches anywhere during the night." She thought a moment. "I'll say they all sleep in the ground."

"There would be a million holes then. They sleep in the air."

It was much more intriguing to believe they slept while flying. "Okay, for now they sleep in the air. I just can't believe it."

"You never see them. They're above you. Then in the morning they're always coming down from the branches. They're always above."

Sandy thought how great it would be to sleep in flight.

"God keeps the air clear of everything else so its only the birds. Planes are too high, doesn't matter. But there's nothing else above the trees to interfere."

"You believe in God. I wouldn't have thought so."

"Why, because I'm mad all the time?"

"You are mean to a lotta people but I usually feel fine around you."

"I never used to be this way. I'm glad you still like me, too. I also believe there's something out there. Even though I'm not happy all the time I know there's more than me. I know that besides me there's a lot going on. That's why I feel better around you because I forget about myself and we always find something else going on. I don't know if what you and I do is important but I stop thinking about myself and start having fun. The stuff we do seems important to me."

Sandy knew her friend was revealing a lot. She didn't know if what they did was important either even though it could seem so at the time. She didn't know if the things they did had any meaning at all. She thought that she might pray for more meaning in her life. She thought she might pray that Tera would find more meaning too. A sudden thought almost departed before she could grasp it.

"Your face is so red," said Tera.

"Is yours?" Sandy looked Tera over.

"I've had my back to the sun today. You've had your front to it. Gonna get wrinkles!" Tera laughed.

"Wrinkles? What does that mean!"

"You've never heard that?"

"No."

"Too much sun makes your skin old and you get wrinkles when you're young."

"Now I have another thing to worry about."

"You would actually worry about it? I was just kidding." Tera put her foot in the water.

"It seems like I *should*."

△

127

"You always hear something you should probly worry about. Usually bigger stuff comes along though and you forget!"

Sandy was still a little too concerned to forget. "I love the sun. I don't wanna worry bout it."

"I think its only if you sunbath a real lot. Like for years." Sandy was staring at her. "Do you fidget while you're lying in the sun?" Tera asked.

"Sometimes. But I don't really ever just lie in the sun like I'm on a beach. Its too boring."

"That's what I mean. You're safe. If you hate it, just lying there like a dog, you're okay."

"If I can't do what I like to do…"

"You have a weak spot…"

"What are you talking about?"

"You have a weak spot. You like freedom. You have to have freedom. That's why you like me!"

Sandy wanted to swim away.

"You think you're weird too. I know you do. So you're here with me. People are afraid of you, aren't they?"

"It doesn't make me feel good."

"I think everyone else is crazy for not wanting what we want."

"I think the *same* thing."

"In Michigan I didn't think about myself. I sure do here."

"I just imagine."

Tera splashed her foot in the river.

"I wanna swim," said Sandy.

"You can't here, its too shallow."

"We can't find a place, either."

"No, we're late already. My mom might even come down here."

"I *do not* wanna go back," Sandy said.

"It is just perfect out here."

"Its probly five now."

128

"Shit."

Sandy sprawled out on the sand completely, like someone who couldn't get out of bed. She stretched her arms up behind her head. She felt the rocks poking her back. "Do you wanna go up?"

"Yep."

Tera stood up knocking some of the sand loose from her shorts. She stood over Sandy casting a shadow. She hung her head so that all her hair covered her face. "All right, I'll get up."

"How did your face get so red?"

"Is it my face or my forehead?"

"Everything."

"Well, I'm pink. I've done it before."

They crossed the open water across the silt bed extending their arms occasionally for balance, still a bit languid. Tera's cut started to sting again.

Their shoes and socks were waiting for them and Sandy immediately sat down on the bank. Tera leaned against a tree holding up a leg. She was hoping her feet would dry quickly. "Aren't you afraid a bug will run inside your underwear and disappear?"

"I don't think anything could live up there," answered Sandy with a snort.

Tera groaned nervously jiggling her head back and forth. She was struggling to put her socks on over damp feet while leaning against the tree on one leg.

They started their walk out of the woods to the bean field. Their speech almost inaudible through the brush and growth except for laughter sometimes. Tera wasn't impeded by her cut. It felt better once she had shoes on. They each found holes again in the vegetation to slip through emerging in the earthen field. The afternoon sun seemed double hot on Sandy's burn. She pressed on her forehead with the back of her hand testing for rawness.

129

The slope of the newly planted bean patch was slightly uphill this time. Tera held the gun lowered with one hand and it swung as a pendant with her stride. The girls were marching slowly. There was enough light to drown in.

"I feel stuff in my shoe," said Tera.

"Look toward the tree."

Tera raised her head. "My mom."

Darling was standing under the big white ash watching the girls come closer.

"She's got the phone in her hand," said Tera.

"How does she look?"

"Not sure. I know when she's furious. She doesn't *look* mad. Always worried, though."

"Can't really hide the gun."

"What if I drop it?"

"She's already seen. She saw it when we were leaving I'll bet."

"I could shoot her in the butt."

"Do that after I'm home."

Neither could laugh at what would normally sound funny.

"Well, you're both alive, I guess."

Tera and Sandy looked at Darling.

"Didn't know what to think. Didn't know when I'd see you." Darling was utterly relieved. "Is anyone injured or shot or been bitten?"

"Not that kind of excitement, mom."

Darling looked at the girls, looked at the gun. "Sandy you alright? No near death experiences to report?"

"No, Mrs. Ray. Had a really good day. I feel fine." Sandy smiled.

They were both tired Darling saw. Sandy's face completely fried. If that's all that's happened today its okay. The rest of her still looks intact. Oh, thank God.

"Tera, are you still going to carry that?'

"Yeah, mom."

130

"I can't believe I forgot sun block. Too much to remember, I guess. Or baseball hats."

"We're not wearing baseball hats, mom."

Darling realized she didn't want to argue with her daughter while she held a gun. "What did you shoot?"

"Not much. The water."

I'm afraid they're going to hurt each other and they're shooting water, Darling thought. Well, that's perfect. God, they're getting bigger but the gun stays home next time. I don't need it. Not with someone else's kid. She rubbed her forehead. "Let's go up."

The girls were surprised to see it was almost six as they stood in the kitchen. Darling poured tall glasses of cold water. The girls stood at the sink and drank each glassful in a swallow.

"I called your mother, Sandy. Told her you were going to eat here. She said she would just come get you. Then I told her I'd take you home."

"Okay."

"She said she'd have your dinner waiting."

"Do we need to go?"

"Tera will also come."

8

Darling write this, who are these people? Dale thought. He leaned above the kitchen table supported by one arm and the other hand held the note. He didn't recognize the names she had written, Sandy, Gwen. Then he remembered Tera had a friend from school. So that's where they are. Dale didn't drink much but he stared at the single bottle of beer in the fridge long enough to raise the electric bill by a dollar. He popped it open then watched outside from the large window in the kitchen. His eyes moved from a point in his own lawn straight to the long waving grass after that to the bean field to the woods hiding the river. Looked like miles, probably only a few football fields. Seven-fifteen and bright like middle of the day. I love these summers he thought. For what seemed like the first time ever his nostrils filled with the becalming aroma of new cut lumber. Must go all the way through my skin by now I bet.

Darling rode up Gwen Toolering's long drive anticipating shrieks and calls of child abuse. She also had the most peculiar sensation of warmth. She prayed up that drive that these were her friends. She wanted to claw her mark at the highest part of a tree she could reach. The silver SUV stopped rolling directly in front of the porch. "Thank you Mrs. Ray," said Sandy. "I had a lot of fun." Sandy looked at Tera then opened the door in back where they both sat.

Perry sat on the porch with a smoke, almost sullen, and then something inside him rose. It was nice to have so many women around. The kid's mom had nice hair, big curly dark. Who could tell what the real colors were anymore, it was either just dark or light to Perry. He found it in him to lean forward in his chair but did not stand. Not enough of an opportunity to warrant throwing himself in it. *Huh, the kid looks blond, though. Well, there's no way to explain everything.* Sandy appeared and he felt like a boy on the playground again. He wanted to tease her until she had to throw rocks to shut him up. Tickle her till she was fighting for air. There was a constant itch to bother somebody or love em, whichever.

"Hi dad, why're you out here?"

"Hi Sandy. Why's your face all red?"

"It *is* not. Why's yours gluey and smoky?"

"What did you say?" Something cut a taut thread in his brain.

"Girls had a whale of a day. Sandy's a little burnt. Such a nice day they wanted to be out. I'll pay for the lotion," said Darling. She was out of the truck talking to Perry across the hood.

"She'll be alright. My mom used to use lard," Perry responded. When he spoke of his mother he pictured his aunt. "Keeps it cool and brings the moisture back." He looked at Sandy whose eyebrows were stretched high. He smiled with a kidding glance to Darling.

"Well, they've been busy..." Darling started.

"Sorry, was on the phone," said Gwen coming outside. "Oh, God... Sandy I've told you about sun block. You'll be thirty and look like sixty. That cute young face will look like buckskin." Gwen walked right up to Sandy, almost pinned her against the truck and held her head with both hands like she was examining round fruit at the farm market. "Sandy! Does it hurt?" Gwen pushed the skin on her daughter's forehead to see the white finger prints.

"No it doesn't really. Put some lotion on it. Be better tomorrow."

"Hopefully tomorrow." Gwen looked at Darling who was crossed between ashamed and embarrassed, still without her Dionysiac bath.

"Man, burn my kid up," said Perry with a screwy smile, lighting a cigarette.

Darling realized that Gwen was not upset. "I am sorry, I should've…"

"Oh don't worry. It just means she had a good time. Do you think she listens to *me*? My daughter listen to me just once about how to be a little more careful outside? It's a fight for sure. No, don't worry." Sandy went to Tera's window and they began whispering to each other.

"Its so nice lately they wanna be out, you know? And they roam! They roam and your mind imagines all kinds of things!" Darling deflated after revealing her anxiety.

"They did that to you! Roams like a boy! Roams the river! Can never be sure if I'll find her floating by or what might happen. Can't stay in the house. That's my daughter. Oh, its endless!" Gwen and Darling rode down the moment. "You want anything? Anything?"

"No thanks, Dale'll be home. Wanna see how his day went. Glad we came out though. Decided we probly outta give er back. Worse for the wear but had a jam-packed day these two. Still's more in em too, guaranteed." Sandy turned around to flash the onlookers a smile. Perry leaned forward enough to stand up. He waved on his way inside.

"Listen, her uncle's birthday is comin up in a week or so and we wanna have a party. Not a regular party but like a big barbeque outside. I'm even thinkin at his place. He has a house big enough and a lot more room outside. I just have to tell im that's what we're doing," said Gwen sneaking a laugh.

"I think we'd like that a lot. You just tell me when. And how much you need us to bring… That sounds really good."

"Now listen. Durry is a real good guy. But he's single and he's kind of artistic. So anyway, tell as many people as you can about the party and I'll give you the address. I don't

134

think he'll get mad but I wan him to meet as many people as possible. He has an appreciation for unusual things anyway."

"Really?" Darling was fascinated.

"Oh, yeah. He's sorta new here too. I don't care who comes. I want everybody. Tell em bring meat and liquor. If not that'll piss everybody off and there won't be enough. Come to think of it, people are good about that. They'll bring stuff. Just tell as many as you can. Tell em the same thing. Have em invite anybody they want, just bring somethin."

Darling didn't think the idea was crazy at all. She wanted to find out more about people around there too. "Okay. I'll tell people. The ones my husband works with. I can do that for sure."

Gwen nodded eagerly, like a salesman right before the deal is struck.

"What does he look like? ...Just curious," said Darling.

"He's alright. Hot when he was younger. Now just sexy and sort of earthy." Gwen snorted, smiled genuinely.

"Well, for a good cause then, huh?" Darling returned the snort. Perry returned to the porch. "Perry comin?"

"Wouldn't miss it," said Gwen. She really wanted to laugh. "I'll call you real soon after I talk to im. Or I'll see you at the high school. Oh, and thanks for everything today. Can't believe you had her the whole day. I'll have to figure out for Thursday how its gonna work. Just put her where I can, but I think this swimming could be important. I just think so."

"They seem to love it, too. I'll help anyway I can. Don't ever think you can't ask, okay?"

Gwen definitely felt she was taking advantage. "Okay, you asked for it. I'm gonna have to plant your whole yard probly.

"I wouldn't take it, but your earthy-type brother in law maybe..." Perry heard this and immediately suspected them both. He was sitting on the porch again with his arms and

135

legs wide. Had yet to light up. He momentarily pictured both women naked. Then he put Gwen's clothes back on, left Darling's off, quick glimpsed his daughter's face and everyone was suddenly dressed to their necks. Ice in the bathtub instead of new love tonight he thought. Upon noticing, Gwen thought she actually liked his strangely rambling posture.

"Well, I've filled your mind with enough probly. Say hi to Dale. Sorry we kept you from him tonight. Something so simple and look at all the time it took. Going to be an interesting summer."

"I hope so," replied Darling. She circled back to the driver's side and got in. Gwen put her hand on Sandy's shoulder for her to stand back. Sandy ran up to her father on the porch.

"You know when I went inside a minute ago...?" started Perry.

Sandy just looked at him.

"I ate the resta your dinner." Sandy reached out quickly for his face but he blocked her arm. "Was good too, filling."

Sandy sat down in another chair a few feet away, perpendicular to her father's. "Mom'll make me somethin," she finally said.

"Not of what we had, kid."

"Don't be mean to me, dad. I could get shot and I'll only remember how mean you were today."

"Whoever shoots you is meaner. That's what you'll be thinkin about." His daughter looked at him with passive irritation, knew she'd been upped.

"Being nice gets you shot, is that what your tryin to tell me?" Sandy's expression was a clean blackboard.

"Stop bein so nice and the bullets whiz right by. *Bastards* never get hit. Lookit all the assholes. How many of em are there?" Sandy was going to answer. Her mind racing between what the inside of a butt looked like and what she knew he meant. "Plenty, plenty uh assholes."

136

Gwen was now hearing some of Perry's speech. She was waving to Darling. "See you Thursday!" she yelled.

"Remember, a little bit meaner and you won't get a surprise. Nice people are the first ones to go. Nice people die and the bastards live, live long. Hard beats soft, young lady. I'm afraid its true." Perry leaned back in that same sprawling way, sure the audience must be marveling.

"Perry, can you please stop that. She doesn't need to hear so much negative. No one's getting shot and hard doesn't beat soft or your life would be very different if you know what I mean." Gwen spoke as she ascended the three steps to the porch. "And stop swearing at her. Look at her. She's burned and tired and probly very hungry. She hasn't had anything to eat yet. And did you tell her you ate her dinner?"

"So, do you hear *everything?*" he asked. His limbs were no longer so confidently strewn. "Damn." He looked over at his best cat who was burned, pathetic but hilarious, with her now woebegone aspect. "Well, I don'no know…" was all he could manage rubbing his head.

Durry loved Saturdays, didn't really care to work. The words of those self-help books like a chant in his mind. 'Self-employment means unlimited dedication.' Whew, hew, hew, hew, hew, hew, sounds from a banshee. No fuckin way. It should mean choosing the hours you *want* to work if it means anything, he thought. And so, since he'd been doing it a while, and there had been plenty of Saturdays in the past and there would be plenty of em ahead, he'd be free for this one. *Yeah, orange juice and bills this morning, isn't that some kinda work? Damn, it might be. But grateful it's a sunny day. The weekend weather gamble. Fuck if half the time it didn't just pour or more than half the time it seemed when you're really looking forward. Forecasts here just as nagging as Chicago's, more intemperate than a heartbroken*

137

woman. Chicago was an exciting town though, he reflected. Now I'm in the country. *Funny, I don't long for the big city. Knew I wouldn't. Still get that middle a nowhere feelin here, though. And the women... nothing goin on. Everybody's married, go to church on Sunday, raise the kids... I'm havin a hard time with all that. And that's it. That's all anybody does. No mystery in their lives, only mowin the grass, survivin on vittles from Miser-Mart. I can smell that place even when I'm not there. There's this signature odor comin outta the back... seared processed meat. Processed into a whole nuther food group. What food group would that be? Along with water flavoring packets and calcium impregnated orange juice.* The women thing was tough. Nothing much single past twenty-two in such a rural area. Sex and love, love and sex, what else was there to do as a teenager? He believed everyone hooked up out of boredom and so they wouldn't have to be alone in a place that could feel so cut-off. But his soul loved the simplicity. The cities were so distracting, constantly screaming, "Look at me, look at me!" He didn't want that anymore. Opportunity was great and money flowed, flowed, flowed. The journey was within now. He had to believe that. Relying on the outside and its guidance only left a soul empty and debilitated. A real woman may show herself eventually. *I could always advertise on the internet, maybe troll the bars. Could always travel and score a wife in some foreign country. The internet... but in person... Guess I'll have to make a move on one of my customers in the short run. Don't care if she's married, M-U-S-T G-E-T L-A-I-D!! And now that lonesome pitiful part, folks...* Durry took a sip of his orange juice. Can't have everything, he reasoned. *I'm still lucky because I know what I want. I'm not broken anymore from booze or love. I've got this great house with all the trees. Got the motorcycle, need to fix up the garage window though or it's gonna be taken.* He looked at the bike as part of his healthcare. Clearing the

138

head was invaluable. He didn't think Gwen knew about the bike. She'd just worry. Sandy would drive him nuts to go for a ride all the time. Perry knew about it though but didn't care, said he had the way he wanted to die all picked out and it wasn't going to be getting skinned alive on the asphalt. Durry tore a check from the checkbook, shoved it in the correct envelope then licked the flap. I don't know how I want to die, he thought. I don't want to die in a million pieces either. *I guess I don't want to die at all, be happy right here. Can't see gettin old an disappearing either. Worse than getting ripped apart around a tree on a back road somewhere, for sure. I'd rather get ripped apart... take my broken body, sprinkle it with cinnamon and nutmeg, wrap it in cheesecloth, let the turkey vultures have it. My birthday next week reminding me of death... like brown bits of grass and dust blowing up and down the road.*

Well, death was tomorrow. He finished his juice, thought he might want more. There were two more checks to write. It had been a good week, cleared about twenty-eight hundred after paying the men and buying finish. Now just bills pertaining to the house and his own compulsive spending. He was absolutely shocked at one of the credit card bills, decided to set it aside and pay it closer to the due date, absolutely shocked.

After paperwork he had more juice. It was not from concentrate or had vitamins pumped in, only loaded with pulp. He couldn't figure out why men needed to constantly mess with everything. Not only was food quality going down, he reckoned, all sorts of diseases were on the rise. When he was much younger he speculated that the only thing wrong with the country was that it allowed anything for profit, as long as it was legal. There were still plenty of ways to produce a product that didn't have consumers' best interest in mind. That was unthinkable to Durry. *How could you offer a product that wasn't thoroughly beneficial? Or at*

139

least undeniable benefits over some negative? The civil war was over so what atrocities can a man wreak upon another? He would always be asking himself if he were adding to or taking away from the collective. Much in his view took away. Restaurant concepts based on taste that becomes addictive but food with no nutritional value. So many foods like that he thought. *That's why so many fat chicks down here in the hills! Keep em plump and at home with that grease and sugar.* Two of his own weaknesses. *Damn sugar! Forty pairs of pants. Each bunch fitting by some sort of tidal schedule. With the belly out, these three pairs fit, with the belly in, these two pair. After turkey and mashed potato season might even be at the store buyin a new size.* He wasn't opposed to exercise either, had mountain bikes, loved to run. Though he did realize people down here thought jogging was for gays and the mental. But he didn't care. They were against anything new. They tried to kill you when you were on a bicycle too. No one rode bicycles except children. If you were on a bicycle on a regular road you would almost certainly be grazed by someone upset at you. *Why were people angry at bicyclists?* Durry didn't know. *Must be something new for an adult to want to have a little fun in public besides getting blitzed and grabbing his friend's wife's tit.* Durry often wondered how he could feel so at home in a place where he noticed so many aspects that didn't fit. He supposed with less to be distracted by a lot just stood out. *I'll get on a plane from time to time for a new perspective but I can't think of anyplace else I'd go to live, the budget being what it is. A female might shore up that feeling of poverty, deflect it.* He really liked brunettes. Natural dark hair down the back... He finished his second glass of orange juice, heavy pulp still stuck to the inside of the glass. *Tits, I like tits, don't care so much anymore though bout size. Known great girls with nothin, known terrors with big ones.* Midwest girls were also the most beautiful, he

140

thought. *I've traveled everywhere, been to Europe, all over California, nothing like husky farmer's daughters. If you get em young, they have everything. Later they seem to age pretty well and love kids. Get em young* rolled through his mind flattening all other thoughts, way too late to have that kind of feeling again. He turned away from the window overlooking the backyard holding his empty glass, hauled it over to the sink to keep the other dirty dishes company. *No reason to clean every day, just more gonna be used later.* He rinsed away the pulp, too hard to scrub once dried, went to look out the front window. *Have to mow, fix the siding, do something about the gardening, shop for food, do laundry, some research on the web for work, dust, dishes, spray for insects, empty the dehumidifier, buy stamps, get some exercise, check the oil on the bike... That's it, I'm just gonna go riding. The rest can wait. Too much to do. Everything to do is the same as nothing to do. I'm going to the post office after I check the bike, stuff the letters in my pants, go for a nice ride after. When it cools down this afternoon I'll mow. I hate mowing. Tedious, vain bullshit. Let it grow. Let it reseed itself like alfalfa. Have to cut it, though. Others will think badly of me and it'll make the house look like shit. Gotta keep mowin. In the summer its mowing, in the winter its shoveling. Generally, its bullshit.* He recognized how much little kid was still inside, complaining about chores. There was a man in the mirror, a boy inside. He hoped he would always know that boy. Durry bitched a lot but his house was pretty well run. The paint outside always in good condition, never flaking. Though he hated mowing and pulling weeds it was usually done before anyone could say he was unmindful. Leaves raked regularly in the fall and their respective trees carefully monitored for proper health.

Durry ran a load of laundry while he took care of the dirty dishes. The washer and dryer's proximity to the kitchen made it almost a requirement to initiate both tasks together. I

141

need some help around here too, he thought. The sun was already drenching the area and he worked quickly so he could get out and enjoy it. He put on wrinkled clothes that were already condemned to the dirty clothes heap then went outside to the garage to check the oil level on the bike. If it wasn't exact he could be fifty miles away with the little red light flashing, the motorcycle's sensors telling the engine to shut down. It happened once to him before, ended up pushing his ride along the road to an elegant farm house owned by a local doctor. Scared the shit out of his wife but the doctor was very accommodating; let him use the pole barn as a place to work. There was also a telephone and tools. Though the tools were certainly not those of a professsional or even an enthusiast. Durry was disappointed that a man of such learning had an inferior collection. The oil bag plug on the Springer needed some coaxing. If it was pulled too hard it jerked out then black oil spatter everywhere. He put in half a quart knowing it was time to get it changed anyway. A little golden fifty weight would hardly make the rest new. He stood back and looked at the bike, still very much in love with it after three years. He wasn't obsessed like so many, didn't spend a lot buying custom parts or wash it every weekend, or every month. He rode when he could, usually suddenly, when time opened up. He had a small collection of destinations that he thought worthy and would go out to discover the new beauty of the land and the sweetness of the air in an afternoon extrication on two wheels. Durry stood outside the garage looking in thinking how he was his own best friend. Only when women he liked peeked at him from a distance was this uncomfortable. A grown man seemingly so content under his own management. He knew there were jokes about him... must be gay, etc... He was always willing to take on another passenger but so seldom did a woman who fit ever want to sit down. He didn't expect much anymore and if by some accident something got start-

142

ed or grew legs it would have to be freer. Two had to simmer like a coal fire, glowing to the thick middle until blood hurts as it moves around. Blood like coal once lit will go for an age growing by little coaxing and with both underground no amount of water to ever call it back.

Inside, the wet laundry got tossed into the dryer. Durry walked around the house a little more seeing if there was anything else on the list that could be done before he wanted to go. He got into some jeans, boots and a t-shirt for the ride, cleaned the bug grease off his favorite sunglasses. He locked the back door on the house and started toward the detached garage feeling very fortunate to have what he had. He felt that way a lot anymore before a ride. On a bike there was always a chance of not coming back. Just too small and too light against what's out there. Farm boys still blow those two ways at full speed.

It was late morning and the humidity turned the earth into a hothouse. Only the bike could make sense out of heavy boots and jeans so the walk was slow to start her up. Any extra energy turning directly to sweat. Durry decided on the route he was most fond of, toward Rising Sun then over to Madison. He loved the foliage near water and seeing the Ohio at least gave him a similar feeling of bigness he missed in Lake Michigan. His cell phone rang, he saw it was Gwen. He wanted to answer but his mind was already clear. It was almost like stealing when he would disappear and not having to feel guilty about turning down somebody else was a much better way to leave. The phone at the last moment could only be something to make him question.

Gwen was surprised there was no answer. She thought she called late enough in the morning so that Durry would be inside for a while. She imagined the inside of his house and wondered what he might be doing. Then she imagined the outside and decided he was probably doing yard work and left the phone indoors. "Durry, I have an idea for your birthday. You're going to like it, I promise. But you need to call me soon. Are you doing alright? Where are you? Well, I hope you're doing okay and having a great day. Remember, call me! Bye." Gwen hung up the phone at her house feeling anxious. She didn't know how it happened but she had actually gotten the day off. Sandy was at swim practice and Perry was also working. Spring was almost over so the big push at the nursery was leveling off. The time alone was a Godsend. She was able to eat her breakfast slowly and shower late, to look into some personal items away from work. It wasn't that Brett had some strict policy to discourage it but people were just *everywhere* and her mind could hardly spare another conduit to carry something not business related. Her job had gone supernova with ever increasing duties. She was technically general manager but without the plaque and pay. While she was on the phone with Perry the other day a couple approached her on the other side of the counter and just started in about how one of their grandkids was mauled, possibly killed by a black bear near Belm. They could easily see she was on the phone; between them speaking directly at her and trying to hear what Perry was saying she wasn't able to discern either conversation. Did the bear eat the kid?

It was Darling's turn again to pick up the girls. Gwen almost wished Sandy could stay at their house once more for the afternoon. She really needed to see Charlie, make an appearance. Then she thought she might see if Charlie could meet for lunch. Might have to bring Sandy but they both liked each other so there wouldn't be any conflict. As she thought about it she wanted to spend time with Sandy anyway. She poured another cup of her good tasting coffee and dreamed of more time.

⌂

144

Durry pulled into the filling station and gave one final loud rev before shutting the engine down. He was still quite pleased by the choice of pipes he'd made. Old people and children didn't run and hide but they knew he was there. He stood next to the bike watching carefully to make sure the tank didn't go over. Some of the less updated pumps didn't always shut off automatically and would overflow in an alarming gush. Such a treat to watch gas pour over the paint and leather and sizzle off the motor and exhaust. As Durry leaned over the tank opening, watching, he heard what sounded like birds from behind but none natural to him. He looked around and across the street were two teenage girls with their backs against a building that by the sign was an insurance office, though probably closed from the high weeds growing in the lot. The girls had spaced themselves about ten feet apart and were dressed in black clothing. Each had one leg raised with a foot on the red brick wall. Facing toward the street they made sounds like birds and cats. Durry's first impulse was that it was creepy then he suddenly laughed to himself and soon was turned on. I can't take much more, he thought. I might be turned on if there were two goats lookin at me like that. Perversion could just drag him away. For many years he had managed to avoid going where his base impulses wanted to take him. But he still fought with his mind. It was hard for him to accept he wasn't twenty years old anymore. Since there was no one at home sometimes it was tempting to bring just anybody. He also made an effort to stop doing that several years ago. Falling in love with ill women was worse than any period of celibacy. He believed there wasn't anything more harmful and during the last one almost wished he was dead, right up to the moment she proposed to him. He sometimes thought about the agony he went through during the following weeks. If he told her no then he would again be alone. But he couldn't say yes because the only things he liked about her

145

were her breasts. Far from enough. She was the most dishonest woman he had ever known. She didn't know herself one bit and never even *tried* to know him. But she was beautiful. And it was nice just to have something beautiful. He knew he should have let her go soon after her capture but fear gripped him along with vanity and he closed the door to any right thinking and developed the whole damn thing into something synthetic. The years went by and she ran around but he'd take her back because she was so damn beautiful. He remembered once when he hadn't seen her for a while because they were going through bad times how he had forgotten or never quite noticed what height of beauty she stole. When he got a fresh glimpse of her in the parking lot that day he had to have her all over again. Weak bastard, he thought. The line, *what a way to go*, was the only thought for his head.

At eleven-forty Darling pulled up with Sandy. "Do you want coffee?" asked Gwen.

"I will," Darling replied over the empty passenger seat. Tera and Sandy cheered from the back then hastily exited the vehicle and ran behind the house. The women paid little attention.

"Sit here old woman and I'll bring it out." Gwen pointed to the wicker chairs on the porch. She smiled and turned to go inside. Darling gave a muffled laugh and picked out a chair. She sat down and leaned back like she'd been on her feet a hundred years. Had her arms covering fully the arms of the chair.

"How'd it go today?" asked Gwen returning.

"No one drowned, even from that poor remedial group she's got goin over there in the corner. So sad. You just wanna snap your fingers and make those kids better. Anyway, the girls did fine. They get along almost too well. It's not like they have to help each other in the water a lot but they

146

seem like they have known each other a long time. Makes me worry less for both of them. Two's always better than one."

"Coffee," Gwen said holding out the cup.

"Thank you." Darling sat way up and reached for it with both hands.

"There's milk and there's sugar. Just let me know."

"Black is good today." Darling sighed deeply then blew on the dark coffee. She took a good sized sip even though it seemed too hot to Gwen. "I'll tell you, watchin those kids in the pool is so relaxing. Other than the echo from all of em yelling and the coaches whistles. God, those things split your skull right open. But the kids respond, don't hardly see any problems." Darling sipped again.

Darling seemed like she was deflating. Gwen waited till she sat back again before talking. "No, I think we made a great decision puttin em in there. What did they work on today?"

"Well, they stress doing those stretches which I remember hating but also know they're really important. So they stretched for about half an hour then they get em all in the water, our kids' group anyway. Some of the other groups practiced certain strokes out of the water standing up. I think it was more stretching, really. I think I was busy looking at the tiny butts at that point."

Gwen laughed surprisingly hard, had to watch her coffee.

"You know, jealous of all the little girl butts and wanting to smack all the little boy butts. That advanced group had the tightest butts! God! I thought about my old flat butt and couldn't imagine anyone wanting to smack *it*! Damn depressing." Darling smirked and watched Gwen for a reaction before a sip.

"Well, yep, that *is* interesting. Hmmm." Gwen took a sip. "Speedo butts or regular trunks butts?"

147

"I saw only trunks but my mind fit em with Speedos!" Darling stunned herself. "I am so sad!"

"Mmm-hmm. Yes, you are." Gwen felt a large smile growing. "One horny old woman."

"It was just so beautiful. I'm so sorry. Our girls could have been drowning and I'm busy thinking about such awful things!"

"Is awful the word you want to use?"

"The most distracting things!"

"Well, you're enjoying yourself a little too much over there. Thank goodness its my turn comin up."

Darling laughed. "Obviously I'm unsuited." She lowered her head feigning shame. "Been living too long in the hills. I think I believe everything they say now!"

"Find you one night camped out with all those teenagers—dancin round a big fire, them in black Speedos—feedin you Oreos, rubbin your feet. When they catch you won't be a big surprise. Have to say I had an idea all along. Was a good woman just really depraved. Kept those boys tied up during the day, foot rubs and I don't know what else all night! It was like Lucifer was workin through her, officer."

Darling's mouth hung open in astonishment. There was a bit of a silence. "Oh, I like yours much better!" Both women laughed. "More coffee please…"

After their laughter Gwen went in to refill their cups.

"Boy, that was great," said Darling upon Gwen's return. "Took that gray away…" Darling looked far off, across the field to the neighbors place nearly three hundred yards distant.

"Dandelions… You see em?" Gwen pointed to the lawn on the south side of the driveway. "Perry cuts their heads off every week and the next day four inches of stalk comes back." Gwen looked out and shook her head. "They come back," she said softly.

"Never noticed."

"Well that's what livin out here does to me. You start to see a lotta different things. Things I've missed all my life. Nothin was ever quiet enough. But I see it now... sometimes..." Gwen looked at her cup.

"I think you have all those dandelion heads hidden somewhere."

Gwen smiled and leaned back. "What about the girls?"

"They're doin their voodoo now."

"Haven't heard a sound."

"Doesn't really mean anything, does it?"

"Nope." A pause. "But in a minute I'll look, anyway. Don't know why I do it. Guess as long as she's here figure I'll look out for her."

Darling smiled. She saw how much Gwen loved the girl. Made her envious.

"I've been through a lot with Tera but I'm starting to feel better now. Dale hardly notices. That's alright, he has worries at work. I've always thought he's given me more than I thought I wanted. Its not a lotta money but its good money. And I see now the wealth you talk about. Great big dandelion heads..."

"There's just somethin catches somehow. The fear gets bigger but stays deeper. So damn big it would have to. Plow you over otherwise. Yeah, so big you have no choice but to run it off. But you watch it pop up all around you. Someone dies, loses a job... maybe gets real sick. Anyway..."

"And so you think about dandelions?"

"I think about dandelions."

Both women leaned back, cast their eyes across the field.

"What about Durry's party? How's that goin?"

"I've told so many people... I'm gonna be in big trouble..."

"Why?"

"Still haven't told the man."

149

"Oh, my. You *are* dead. You mean you're going to have this blowout at his place and he still doesn't know?"

"Nope."

"Nothing's gonna change?"

"I'm set. Nothing changes. It's the way its gonna be."

"Well, I hope he's a nice man."

"The best. Repairs furniture for a living. Can do all sorts of amazing things. I'm always buggin him for leftovers. He just laughs at me."

"So he's pretty laid back?"

"Pretty.

"He and Perry have trouble sometimes. I can understand that though. Perry's not nearly as easy. Oh, no, no."

"Why isn't he married?"

"Well, he was. She got with somebody else. He's a love though. I think women are afraid of him. Like they won't measure up or something. But I can tell he'd be amazing. He has a strong way of thinking but I like that in a man. He's aggressive without being too rough."

"Listen, I just calmed myself from the last thing we were talkin about."

"So he's just out there lose in the countryside. Runs his business. Hires great guys, talented. Has an exceptional eye. He could be gay I guess but he's *just* inside. Has a deep sensitivity. Whutta they call that? ...artistic. Well, that's what he is. You get the feeling you're takin a big chance gettin to know im because there's so much there you have to be willing to commit. Cause he'll pull it out of you. The questions keep coming. And he's interested. Really interested. Not just makin conversation. He listens... and I can't believe I'm saying all this... guess I'm totally in love with im."

"Well, all right!" Darling hollered.

"Don't you have those, though? Those guys who just do it to you? Yeah, you're in something and there's no chance. And you hardly ever think about a chance but they just get

150

ya... in the front and out the back. You could talk to em for hours. Fills up that lonely side you have no matter how much you love your family. I'm not ashamed. I think it takes a lotta people to keep us all going. Sleep with one man but maybe love more. I think its good. I like that."

"It sounds really good. And I think I know what you mean. Its just been a long time, if ever, since I met a man I wanted more than Dale. That's okay, right? I mean it's the best. I don't ever worry or have to look around. I mean he's good and loves me back."

"Yeah, I don't mean to sound like we all are unhappy it just happens by chance or luck. You have something even more just because that's life. Something just came around. I guess I was lucky enough to notice it. But I'm never torn. Then it wouldn't be so amazing anymore."

Durry found Carter Road east toward highway 56. Many of the trees so heavily shaded were still shaking off the night's dew in the wind. So much sometimes he'd check the slit of sky above to be sure clouds hadn't formed starting the rain.

The sound of the engine, the wind, the flying dew all stimulated thoughts away from regular life. The men in the shop working so hard. Their aching joints and bombarded noses. Doug opening up the palm of his had last week with a chisel. How he calmly kept it elevated while everyone watched the blood flow down his forearm, drip off the elbow. Mike who looked at the hand said, "You cut your lifeline in the middle." And Mr. Sota who didn't want to pay his bill because he felt he should be allowed terms. "Who gets paid right when they finish a job? Nobody," he barked. He already had his son back their truck up to the open bay and was asking the men for help loading. Durry for some reason let him take the restored dining table in exchange for a promise to pay in two days. The old bastard thought it was a competition. It made him feel he had put some effort into winning if he could get terms. "Nobody pays *me* right away," he said in the end. Durry thought take the fucking table and we'll see who's the worst fool. It was mainly to get the obnoxious sonofabitch out of the shop. If he didn't pay his ticket there were other ways to collect. A bug then slapped him in the face so hard he jumped. Can never see those monsters coming he thought. *Damn if the impact doesn't almost bury them in my skin sometimes. And what the hell were they? Go crazy trying to imagine what kind of animal. Or insect. Animals and insects are different, right, zoologically? I look for their disembodied parts on my shirt and face but never find anything. Terrible that they explode against me and I never even know what species. But if I knew I'd probably be more upset because just the fact that they are so big limits the possibilities to a more frightening class like wasps, giant yellow-furred bumble bees and other uglies with lethal daggers. Daggers. How many daggers? And nothing yet gone in. Would one ever be perfectly lined up like a tiny spear waiting there in the air?*

He stopped at a roadside grill south of Rising Sun on highway 56 where there were three other bikes parked in front. The building made of low-grade wood white-washed on top of a hard dirt lot. Perfect, grease to go. He went in and sat down at the counter near the strangers, two men and a woman. The burly woman's skin seemed lose, too big to cover her carcass. Typical hog types, fitted bandanas over their skulls, arms and necks full of blurry old tattoos mixed with some newer and more crisp drawings, always hearts, flames and Japanese characters. It must be so hard to come up with anything original anymore Durry thought. A whole world with the same idea, perhaps hopelessly slighted by the human condition. Friendly people though, willing to talk and tell stories, many times buzzed too, or pretty recently. The men kept their sunglasses on while they ate, crumbs clinging to their extra long outlaw style goatees. It was strange to Durry that although he had little desire to mimic them he always felt more comfortable around rough characters. He wondered how that part of him got in there. He just knew his psychic stomach spit more acid in the presence of the suit-cladded.

Since Durry was alone he initiated a dispassionate detail of the things he'd seen that day. Told them which direction he was going. It started out dispassionate. By the time he got to the part about the chipmunk he was a little too excited.

"Why do they just run out and stop? Usually I can miss em but he was too close. I didn't even think about swerving. Felt the vibration of his crushed bones through my frame. I wondered a few minutes later if I coulda swerved, missed im. Maybe I wanted to hit him, you know, subconsciously, murder something. Feels good to kill I'll bet. Bug spray on a spider or a rabbit in the garden with a .22. If you can do it clean the guilt's shorter."

One of the men started to laugh. He took off his sunglasses and rubbed the bridge of his nose. The other one began to wipe his mouth then flicked at his goatee in an upward motion with the back of his hand. Durry observed this instructing his brain to be tolerant. It was just the thought of what would fall on the plate. After all, what Durry could lay on the unsuspecting required a form of forgiveness as well. It was mostly work to behave and not make an adult's mind begin to short. Some he could just bury and they didn't make a sound but many could get upset. He watched as they crashed, quite disappointed by how little it took.

The woman wanted to engage him now that she knew he was off center. The men were not really interested anymore and would avoid eye contact. The husky gal with the loose skin had something to say. Durry looked at the wrinkled skin between her tits. Tan and lose, framed in the "V" of a black

153

leather vest. It was still a woman's cleavage and yes he *was* aroused momentarily.

"I can think of a lot of things I'd like to kill," she began. The two men looked at each other then at her. The men were still sitting between her and Durry but she just looked at Durry. "I know what you mean, though. If we could just kill something sometimes we might feel better. I hate the deer that come in our yard and I wish I could kill em. They eat everything, everything. One day I was so mad I found a hatchet and thought I could just hit one. But when I went outside they both took off. And there's always more than one comes outta the woods. Pairs they say. I know that because that's what they told us when we got our motorcycle certification. If you see one look for another because there's always at least two. Did you know that?"

"Yeah, because I see deer all the time," Durry responded.

"So they're always out there. I don't know what to do." Her eyes were almost pleading.

"I asked if you wanted me to start killin summa those deer but you said no. Now you're tellin this guy you wanna murder some deer. I can kill em... you can kill em if you think it might calm you down." He smiled and took a drink from a glass. *The husband*, Durry thought.

"I don't remember asking you to kill em. When did I do that? Anyway, how you gonna kill em? Shoot em up close to the house and put a bullet in the kitchen... I don't want that either. You never know when they're gonna come out. I know in the evening a lot but where you don't know. I just look out and there they are. Sometimes I see em comin up to the house but they don't bother me then because they're not eatin anything. I don't know." The woman twisted her lips into a sideways "S".

The husband rolled his eyes and took another drink. The other man continued to appear indifferent, having a cigarette alone.

"I'd kill em I guess, if I saw em. But I *don't* want to shoot the house," the husband said to Durry. He wished for some reason the husband hadn't spoken to him.

Durry looked at him while he thought. "Put some kinda chemical around the property. Gotta be somethin they don't like," Durry said.

"Maybe," said the husband.

"Nothin that *kills* em though," added the woman. Her eyes darted between her husband and Durry.

Durry's food came and he just wished they would all leave. Nothing will come of speaking further he thought. He also didn't want to be the only one eating since they were already done. Silence befell the group as each glanced at what was on his plate. His eyes stayed front, pulled a napkin from the dispenser.

"I'll kill em all for you...your spiders and rabbits and all your deer," the man said with the cigarette. He looked out and exhaled.

Durry put pepper on his lunch with a big smile.

Gwen savored the time sitting outside with Darling. They drank too much coffee, certain topics of conversation became tired but being able to relax in the daytime smelling the sweet air away from responsibility was almost a vacation. She would have to see Charlie another time, a little bit of a relief. When she was around Charlie there was always the question of whether or not she had been a good mother. The anxiety wasn't deep but the thought always formed at the sight of the girl. If Gwen was misguided she wished to know another day.

Sandy never played with pink dolls molded out of genetically perfect plastic. She and Tera were sketching plans for a new rabbit cage at her father's workbench in the garage. They left one door open for more light in addition to the incandescent lamp above where they sat. The first draft looked a lot like a house boat. The second version a tall slender birdcage. The design they were finally happy with came as the black wax pencil was only a nub. They were tired of drawing and thinking so hard, decided to find something cold to drink in the kitchen. Neither girl had listened to Darling and just put their shorts on right over there suits after practice. The elastic in the suits was starting to pinch in certain places and they made efforts to get comfortable as they walked.

"Where's the bathroom?" Tera asked.

"That way," pointed Sandy opening the refrigerator. She put a container of fruit juice on the table then two glasses.

Tera's bathing suit landed next to Darling still sitting on the porch with Gwen. "I can't wear it anymore, mom."

"Okay, so lemme see you."

Tera came all the way out the front door.

"So what do you have on?"

"Just shorts."

"Are you okay with that?"

"Yeah." Tera didn't understand why she wouldn't be okay. She pursed her lips at her mother. Darling knew the look well and found herself recoiling. Tera returned inside.

"So she's made herself comfortable," said Gwen.

Darling picked up the suit and started to laugh.

Durry was soon the only customer sitting at the counter in the restaurant. It felt right. Not a lot after hours lately that got done with company. He wasn't feeling sorry for himself as much as his mind was just getting used to being alone. It can be kind of a sick feeling but that can be overcome. He told himself at least he wasn't in prison or unable to travel as he pleased, laid up or something. He could still visit people, see freedom, the opposite sex. He was brave enough for the silence. He heard things anyway. In the quiet much awaits

156

including madness. He talked to himself more than anyone he knew. But he was a problem solver. He pronounced his thoughts in broad daylight to hopefully assess them better. To interrupt how he understood his world she would have to be very merciful. He thought about an American woman with mercy. He couldn't imagine anything so it was back to hope and dreams. And so he lived in his dreams and all the outdoors was a dream, the only place he truly found God away from all the empty vessels that preached their version of faith everyday in town, put their accusing epigrams on signs in front of their churches above information about a fish fry. Durry had a constant and recurring thought of falling onto a tall spike that cut his vertebrae so cleanly that he'd be dead in an instant. He'd lie there, dreaming, arced upward, belly-button toward the sky, totally at peace. He almost wanted to cry at how much peace. Then it was over. The life of boldness and bravery had ceased. He was only happy. He thought about his solitary form hung on the spike and thought about perfection. He was sentimental about his blood dripping down the pole under him. He thought about the color of the sky and it was usually overcast. Quiet. Quiet skies as the world had shown him. The best always happened under a quiet sky. The people who had loved him saw him and instantly knew he was at peace and they felt an unexplainable joy. They cried softly because somehow the universe revealed knowledge that it was all okay. It wasn't that he had fallen and died in a terrible way but that now there was such peace. It was a reminder that all the rest was so much blank paper. As he rode he thought God kept him living quietly so that he may find something out, the world, the blowing wind. That voice that came when he was rubbing his temples, picturing the spike. When he stood there in the dark bathroom of an empty house urinating, looking out the window at the 10pm light wondering what his neighbors were doing, waiting for them to pass in front of their win-

157

dows, just to see someone else out there. The words happy negative came to him. He would go on to be the best happy negative person he could be. He believed that for anyone who actually used their brain there weren't a lot of other combinations. The cursed, the quiet, the enlightened, had a responsibility not to behave as greeters in the family dining industry. There wasn't a lot to the feel-better-about-yourself audio tapes without an excited thirst for understanding. The force behind the curtain loves the chaos. There is a wet longing maw to every uttered word. And with that can come a prediction about the future by only studying all the tribes.

It was one of the loveliest stretches of road he had ever found and if it weren't for traveling fifty miles an hour in the open the humidity could almost choke a person. Durry turned his head perpendicular to the wind to hear the sound coming out of the pipes. Still dull because of the rush of air but thumping nicely. He thought if he ever did get a tattoo it would only be sun and water, nothing but light and waves. He thought the guy would laugh at him, the childlike rendering. Where was the intricacy, the explosion of color, the attempt at recognition? But there was nothing to that. Light over water couldn't be captured by anything else. Ahead a turkey vulture's enormous form hunched in the lane with his back to Durry. As the motorcycle came near he drew his five foot blackened wings up like two great weapons, holding them there. The bird bounced on its legs then the wings started and he was heavy in flight. When Durry reached the place the bird had been he saw the road kill that was being feasted upon. Not high above the vulture swirled, joined by another and another. Durry turned to see them landing again.

The girls finished their drinks and now had their heads down in their arms on the table. The empty beverage container between them.

158

"Whose gonna build it?" asked Sandy.

"You'll have to find someone."

"I don't think anything we drew is gonna work." Sandy had turned her face toward Tera to talk then turned into her arms again and sighed loudly.

"You need someone to fix it. Just so he can't get away. How bad do you want a rabbit do you think?"

"Pretty bad. I told you the last one got eaten. I was never so scared in my life. When I looked at him I thought he exploded. I didn't know he'd been eaten. There's all kinds of animals round here that'll eat a rabbit my dad said. Then he said *he* might eat it if it weren't mine. I don't know why he does that, it makes me want to be mean to him."

"You don't think something will happen to a new one?"

"If the cage is built right, no. I don't think I know how to do it. I will kill anything that kills my rabbit."

"What if I kill it?"

Sandy sat up, startled. "Why would you kill it? You know how sad and mad I'd be. Why did you say that?"

"I'd kill it to eat. They've always looked pretty good to me." Both girls were sitting up now, intensely looking at each other. Tera licked her lips slowly, arms straight at her side.

"I would chop off your head and throw it in the trash." Sandy stared ardently into Tera's eyes.

Tera put her head back down burying her face in her arms then turned slowly and looked at Sandy with one eye. Sandy could see she was grinning.

"Yes, you need to hide because I see you." Silence and Tera with one eye. "My poor bunny, and what kind of sauce would you prepare?"

"I'm learning to like garlic."

Sandy shook her head with incredulity but was entertained.

159

Long after Rising Sun Durry was beginning to move east along the river toward Madison. He saw deer constantly and thought about that woman in the restaurant and her dilemma. The creatures to Durry were magnificent. The desire to manage them stemmed only from a desire to harm *something*. That was done by those who like it. All sacrifice outside wartime must be done for enjoyment he thought, wishing though it would still be despised. So two distinct capacities for waste emerged. But to be consistent at something you had to practice. To excel at a sport you had to appreciate it, even love it. There had to be some enjoyment. These were only the facts and they filtered through his brain on that road like the noisy pieces in one of those children's games when turned upside down. It was easy to drift out riding on the motorcycle, wind and vibration, without talking everything was inward, much like when mowing grass. But at high speed the tendency is very strong. Durry found he had to be careful to pay more attention at times. It was becoming easier for him to just sail down the road, looking around, forgetting about the danger of inattentiveness. It took less than a second for the road to dive in putting a rider on the dreaded lip of the road. If you could control your fear you had an equal chance of making a good correction. But if you were startled and your steering too hasty the ground would behave like it was rising up. And there would be a great big meeting with pavement and dirt on the shoulder. It happened all the time to anything on two wheels, getting back on the road after passing the lip. In martial arts they called it a takedown.

So with the reminder that too much drifting possibly meant a takedown Durry made a renewed effort to stay in the moment. Do not get hypnotized by the vibration, the strong wind and all the sights. Instead he vowed to find what level of trance was workable. With no trance it was possible the experience would be no good at all. Being unaware of falling asleep was similar to falling into thinking without thinking. It was that place he had to find. He watched a man on his front porch look through a telescope wearing a bathrobe and holding a beer. When Durry turned the direction the telescope was pointed there were only woods. Maybe it was birds he was watching, or animals. It could have been the changing sky, certain planets maybe rose during daylight only visible with a strong lens. Maybe he was watching a young couple make love in the forest on a Saturday afternoon. Large trucks in their fury on the two lane passed by and he'd swing to the outside near the lip not to get caught in the huge amount of air they pulled with them. It felt like the bike could get sucked under if the truck were going with a tailwind. Passing on a curve he could read some of the monikers on their trailers like the idiotic "Service Is Our Pleasure". It was hard to imagine what level of contempt the owners had for their customers to patronize them so completely. To Durry it read, "We're so used to hearing you bitch that we're totally willing to put up with it". Durry then began to think of a slogan for his business. What about "come dig the fumes with me". The ride was just getting better and better. The river was just spitting distance away and the light was landing on the water and coming through the foliage in a tear-jerking way. He saw pick-ups and beater cars along the way pulled off in the weeds whose owners were undoubtedly fishing. Outlaws without any permits. All that was necessary to catch a fish was bait and tackle. The time the line was in the water was enough license. Unregulated fishing in the river probably meant everyone would depart with an unfair amount of carp or shad or suckers. Durry immediately saw the suckerfish enjoying underwater river-bottom casinos without ever having too much of a run. Poor gamblers with constantly moving lips who expectedly turned it all over, perpetually gaining then losing more. Suckerfish. Optimism without any real insight, born to be

161

taken. Someone had to finance the infrastructure of river world. They had his sympathy. Durry downshifted for a coming turn, a backfire like a shotgun blast stirred him fully conscious, not uncommon for a carbureted bike with modified exhaust. He actually loved the way the bike sputtered and banged to a stop. There was some Japanese word he was once told about that expressed an appreciation or acceptance of imperfection. He learned of it from the guy he bought the house from after starting lists of improvements to be done before the closing, at the seller's expense. Many imperfections, sometimes actually part of a perfect design that otherwise would not allow for an object's ideal effect. A predicament certainly at odds with an entitlement society and only embraced by the more humble who could be said to have no choice. All that everybody worried about seldom helped he thought. When did worrying ever justify the energy it took? His only worry was not living full enough. He usually got jealous around those who traveled a lot. He was afraid they were closer than he was to a full life. Nothing else bothered him so much. People who had monotonous stressful high paying jobs didn't worry him. But those who got to see much of the world on the company made him envious. After all, to see everything and not be required to pay was a great trick and he wondered all the time if he could do it.

The sun poured ceaselessly down and he thought about his girlfriend Sandy and what she had been doing while he was stopped at Elky's Grill on the edge of Madison above the river. Elky's had a veranda where patrons could sit outside and just soak in the view, eat at one of the tables at the other end or just sit in a white wicker chair and look out from an elevated position to the river valley. The expanse of green was so lush but with an occasional cutout for some industrial structure. Business gathered at convenient shipping points, always had, Durry understood. The Ohio had to be one of the most used he thought, at least at one time. He wasn't sure it was true anymore. Probably Los Angeles and New York were the most important for international trade and now maybe trucks had replaced the big river as the best way to move goods around. Less traffic on the river meant less chance to ruin it but then it occurred to him what had already been done. Sandy wouldn't even be aware, he knew. And she'd keep him from worrying about any of the stupid shit that had been rattling around his brain all day. He knew it was weird and lucky to have a friend in the girl. It was only lately he wished he had a daughter of his own. As detached as he could be he was beginning to think he was missing out on a reward so big that it would be a tragedy to forego. He sipped his pop there on the veranda, a few other people occupying tables on the other end. He glanced at his bike, saw the skull etched in black on the primary cover, made him feel sexy but not wicked. He went inside and tried to buy cigarettes, the hostess told him they didn't sell any and offered one from the pack in her purse. He smoked the non-filtered sitting in the same seat as before. A little bit lonelier though because he wanted to know a girl better who smoked such bad-ass cigarettes. He smiled, laughed to himself, thought about pussy, continued to smoke until he didn't think about it anymore. He wanted to be shot from a cannon across the road, across the river, into the distance, maybe grab a fucking bird as he went, a white line of smoke kept him visible so everybody could see him go, somersault through the roof of a river boat and land in a plush red chair wearing a tuxedo and a smart-ass grin in time for a new hand being thrown down.

Sandy stood facing the open refrigerator eating cheese. She didn't care for the cellophane wrapped flat kind because it could taste like orange construction paper so she broke off chunks of mild cheddar and popped them in her mouth. Tera

163

alternated between head up and head down still sitting over at the breakfast table. She'd yawn or sigh to help ensure she got notice.

"You want some?" asked Sandy.

"Don't feel hungry."

"Okay." Sandy had found sliced hard salami and would push a piece in her mouth while chewing a chunk of cheese. She liked the two flavors together but was not going to have a formal lunch with slices of bread and plates, just there in the cool of the fridge eating from packages. Tera was something like family now so the impulse to keep her entertained was more moderate. She can suffer with the rest of us Sandy thought while chewing an especially delicious mouthful of cheese and salami. She knew that without company there she would be squirting mustard directly in her mouth on top of what she was eating.

It was now mid-afternoon. Gwen asked Darling if she cared for something to eat ages ago, the two just preferred to talk. Sandy had appeared closer to one-thirty wondering what to do about lunch, she told the girl to make something for Tera as well. Meanwhile, Gwen got to talk about relationships, religion, government and business, especially the nursery trade. She did her best during the business topics not to alienate Darling. Even though she might have understood clearly resentment at being shown she was missing out was something Gwen didn't want. I hate it when people do that she thought, throwing around their ideas on money without thinking how its going to be heard. Offending people was easy and it was so much harder to keep them right there with you or bring them up for any period at all. She then saw why it was so much easier to just shove ideas at someone and rattle off your thoughtless views before they showed signs of resisting. It was a rather savage communication tool and was employed but almost everyone. How interesting she thought, we all seek acceptance so instead of working hard trying to

164

keep the other person right there with you and risking possible rejection anyway, why not engage in a sneak attack, hit them with your stuff before they can wiggle free? Actually it shows little development on both sides. The starting point for human behavior could at least be counted on. Because of similar construction all the way across artful conversation can be made or abandoned. Those always wanting specifics will continue to be disappointed in a world that slowly rotates from a fixed position rather than zooming across the stars in only a simple straight line. Gwen smiled and took a carrot strip from a tray she had put out anyway. Where my thoughts lead she mused. She didn't think she had come upon anything substantial just a touch of reinforcement for what she already believed.

"I'm afraid I'm terrible with plants," Darling said. "I'm embarrassed to tell that Dale does all that. He picks everything out and plants it. It usually looks great. If I looked after everything they'd just die. I have this idea that once its in the ground its on its own. I know you have to water, fertilize, all that. I have no idea. And *forget* about picking weeds, I'd just as soon have a bare mulched area than have trees and bushes and a buncha weeds." She laughed in light of her confession. "How do people learn all that? I guess its like anything else, you have to study. I guess I just don't care to do it. Now maybe if I got paid I could figure it out. Funny how getting paid might make you learn a lotta stuff! I guess I don't care otherwise! I know you think I'm nuts..."

"You *are* a nut. What do you do over there, just satisfy your husband?"

"I am pretty good at that. So yes, I guess that is my job!" Darling took a second to study Gwen's expression. It was one of surprise and curiosity. "He likes it, I get a good response."

Gwen reached for her iced tea and when she was leaning forward asked, "Well, whutta you do?"

165

Darling produced a laugh that sounded like a choke. "I don't know, I'm just not afraid. I get up there and express myself."

"Oh my God." The depth of Gwen's intrigue increased. "So, you like it on top?"

"Oh, yeah."

The 'yeah' sounded too much like a grunt. Gwen was smiling though. She thought it was good to know someone who was healthy sexually.

"I also have an enthusiasm. I usually don't think that I'm with the same guy, I think about the experience. Of course it has to be with the right guy so you can forget yourself but after that it just kicks in and usually both are happy. Is this too strange, am I making any sense?"

"You have a huge job, and you're good at it. I'm jealous you get to practice more. I think sometimes if I could just clear my head everything in my life would be better. Same old shit. But I can't, it seems like I have to worry about too much. But you've had the opportunity and I like hearing that its possible. Even with Perry, I'd like to whip his ass sometime, attack him all around the bedroom till he passes out." Gwen raised her eyes to Darling.

"Damn, hurt im…"

"The screaming turns me on!" Gwen leaned back and laughed facing upward. After a moment: "I can tell its different for you and I think that's wonderful. Perry and I have less bliss and more anger but we both love each other. And part of me showing how much I love im comes out in me wanting to kill im."

Gwen's matter-of-fact look amused Darling. She recognized no marriage was perfect including her own and just appreciated Gwen's honesty.

Sandy and Tera came out then found a place to sit.

"Dad's comin up, mom," Sandy said.

Gwen turned to look. Perry's truck was halfway up the drive. That's alright Gwen thought, I already got a whole afternoon. "What time is it?"

"I don't know, three," replied Sandy. Gwen had a watch but didn't bother examining her wrist. Darling leaned back and closed her eyes.

"Look at all these bitches on my porch again," Perry said coming up the three steps. Darling's eyes were still shut but she formed a smile.

"My lover," Gwen said shaking her head.

Perry realized it'd been nothing but women all afternoon. "Let's not use that kinda language, Sheila," Perry said. Darling's eyes opened.

"Sheila isn't here and lover isn't a bad word," Gwen responded.

"I know you're tough from sittin here all afternoon sharpenin your claws and I love all you ladies but I just gotta sit down awhile."

Darling didn't think that she would like Perry but now thought she was starting to. At least she didn't want a nap now.

Perry was going inside. As he went past Sandy gently grabbed his forearm until she was just holding onto the tip of a finger. Perry kept going toward the door. He eventually returned and sat down on the same lounge as Tera but next to Gwen's seat. "So what have you horrible broads dreamed up today?" he asked.

"How our husbands can get us to do anything they want," answered Darling. Gwen shook her head because of Sandy.

"Yeah, dreamin," said Perry. He looked at Sandy. "What about you little girl, how was your day?"

"Good, dad. I'm glad you're home. Now you can see Tera."

Perry looked at Tera. He admired the blonde hair. "Who's crazier you or my daughter?"

167

"Me, I'm sure," Tera replied. She felt very vulnerable sitting right next to the man. He seemed incredibly brash while she was still caught up in her apprehension. Perry could see it, didn't care, had a swallow from his beer, shortly then lit a cigarette.

It felt like the best smoke of the month. He wanted to spread his arms wide and lean back and relax but he knew the girl would freak out if his arm got into her space, so he kept his right bent at the elbow while it rested on the lounge back. He also had to switch the cigarette from his right hand so the kid wouldn't get cancer. Lotta work tryin to please everybody Perry thought. The smoke eased any misery. He was glad everyone was there but he also wanted to throw his wife on the floor and fill her ass full of splinters while he made her growl with her head back. He looked at Gwen. "Howdy," he said with a goofy grin.

"Howdy," she said back.

Darling looked back and forth between them, trying to get an idea of what they had.

"Perry, we're havin a big party for Durry next Saturday *at his house*. It would be nice if you didn't have to work that day but if you have to lemme know and just tell me when you can come. I could use you that's all." Gwen now braced herself for the impact of the announcement.

"Big party for what? *His house*? Oh that's right, its his birthday. Wait a minute… what date is that? I can't remember my calendar."

"His birthday is really on Friday but that's no good for a real party so we wanna do it on Saturday."

"Who, you two?"

Darling made an innocent face.

"No, you and me," Gwen said. "*Over there*."

"Yeah, alright, I feel like doin somethin nice for the sonofabitch." He took a sip of his beer. His little white hiney stickin way out there.

168

Gwen had her first non-sexual orgasm. "Really? You'll help!"

"Course I'll help. Whutta you think? Can't be a bastard all the time, makes hair grow in weird places."

First the girls then the women looked at each other with disgust. "Okay, alright. Well, do you think you can get off?" asked Gwen.

"Probly. Even so, I can put in only half a day if it comes down to it. Be done by twelve or one. That work for you?"

"It'd be nice to have you all morning too but I understand and not gonna bother you about it. Do what you can do, okay?"

"Yeah, sure. I've been wantin to git out to his place anyway. Take a look at what he's been workin on. If I knew a single girl I'd bring her with me too." Perry smiled before a drink winking to Sandy. She showed no reaction.

"I want you to tell everybody you run in to. Most everybody, I mean be careful, just invite people you think will add to it. You have to remember, its at his house. I don't want too many crazy people or jail birds or meth heads. You know what I mean. And tell em to bring a dish. Bring something, food and preferably drinks. You and I are going to pay for most everything else."

"Like what?" he asked.

"Well, everything to tie it together. Definitely burgers and dogs, and all the stuff that goes with that. A lotta drinks. I might make potato salad, all kindsa things. I'm not going to spend our savings, just make it nice." She looked now at Darling. "I really think I can do it with only a couple hundred. That buys a lot of the kinda food I'm thinkin of." She gestured with her palms up.

Perry shrugged. It was apparent he was thinking about something else. Gwen was watching him. "I think I know how to get some people over there." His eyes never met Gwen's as he said it.

169

"Perry just watch yourself. I don't want…"

"I'm just gonna make it fun, I don't have to watch anything." Gwen was still staring at him. "And Darling, is that it, Darling?" She nodded. "Make sure to bring your husband, I'd like to meet im too. I already met blondie." He turned his head toward Tera. The girls shared a spooked expression.

"Sounds nice, mom, havin a party for Uncle Durry. He might like a big party. Yeah, I know he'll like it."

"I think so too sweetheart, thank you," Gwen said. She had been feeling rather uninvolved when it came to Sandy lately. Their past closeness impaired due to a different schedule. She knew neither loved the other any less. Sandy was making her own way this summer and Gwen was proud.

"What about drinkin, he doesn't drink?" said Perry.

"It doesn't bother Durry. He knows other people are gonna want to. I'm sure if somebody goes too far you'll escort em away. Right?" said Gwen.

"If you wanna say escort em that could be about right. Or somethin like that." Perry had a devious grin. "Drunk or sober won't matter which," he finished.

"This is just something I wanna do for him that I know he'll appreciate. He's always over here when we need an extra hand. And he does that because he loves us and I wanna do somethin big for im." Gwen felt her throat tighten and her eyes water. "It might be something no one will believe." She leaned back and took a breath. Caution had already lost to anticipation.

"Well, after all this is over I gotta go to Lied." Perry knew no one would know what he was talking about. There weren't even questions just looks. "To Kentucky. I've gotta go to Kentucky."

"I remember but we haven't even talked about that," said Gwen. And I thought I was goin, remember? I mentioned I wanted to go. You don't have to go all by yourself. I wanna help."

170

Perry purposefully brought it up while Darling was present to make it easier on himself. He could tell it was working because Gwen's grip on the arms of the chair didn't match her even voice. "I was just gonna run down there and pick that stuff up. Need to get a van or somethin like it. Didn't think you'd wanna run down there in that."

"I don't care what we take to ride in, you know that. You don't want me to go. I know why, we'll talk about it later." Gwen felt twelve years old, left out of some activity by a brother or sister again. She wanted to go inside and pout. *Oh, I'm gonna torture him for this, bringing it up in front of Darling too. I will peel his skin off.*

"Mom, I thought we're all going. It was gonna be all of us," said Sandy.

"It will be; your father will need us to help carry all the stuff."

"Well, when are we going because I have swimming."

"After swimming Sandy, after swimming." Gwen managed a smile, turned toward Darling who had been sitting quietly.

"Sounds like Perry wants to do the robbery by himself." Darling took a sip of tea after the comment.

"Its not a robbery," Gwen said. Perry looked at Tera for her reaction. She had begun to fidget. Sandy was smiling with her hands in her lap. She sometimes liked that her dad seemed crazy and she was thinking the excitement of robbery would be worth the deed. She stood up to go over and smack Tera on the knee then sat back down. Tera didn't see her coming, didn't expect it. She gritted her teeth at Sandy. The women had been watching; both managed a breathed chuckle. "Perry's family is from there and I guess they left some stuff for im."

"You mean in a will?" asked Tera. She was watching her feet as they went back and forth.

171

"No, I think it was like one guy told another guy and eventually one of em let us know," interjected Gwen. Perry laughed.

"Is that what happened?" asked Tera turning her head to look at Perry.

"Just about right. I don't think anybody thought of it for a long time. Doesn't matter, I've got everything I need right here. This stuff I'm sure gonna be extra, where the hell to put it all," Perry answered. Tera let out a sudden loud belch. Sandy stuck her tongue in her cheek and shook her head.

"Out with it," said Perry. He began patting her back, laughing. He liked the kid. She was more contrary than *he* was.

"So do you know what any of it is?" asked Darling.

"Well, listen, its me and Durry's stuff, Gwen can have whatever she wants, I just wanted to take a look cuz my uncle's gonna throw it out," said Perry. "Its probly nothin but a burn pile if dust'll burn. In this sorta deal might find one thing good. I'm hopin to find that one good thing, you know, see what happens."

"Great Uncle," Gwen corrected.

"Yeah, that's right, Great Uncle. I guess I forgot all about im. Granddad's younger brother." Perry put his hand to his face. "He's still livin there…"

Gwen thought about mentioning that some of the things were supposedly left behind by his parent's but realized it wasn't the right time. Perry had enough to think about she could see. Fucking past comes and finds a new hole which can grow so large she thought. The irritation she felt earlier cooled.

"It'll be nice to see im," said Darling. "Nice he's still alive, right?"

"Never saw im when we were young, but yeah, its nice to be alive," said Perry.

172

Sandy completely agreed. She wanted to smack Tera one again. It was difficult not to enjoy bothering poor somber Tera.

The playfulness suddenly went out of Perry. He forgot the man mentioned his health was failing last time they spoke. Though he didn't really feel he owed his Great Uncle anything he viewed his levity as disrespectful. Perry was very superstitious about the dying and the dead. If it wasn't necessary to mention them he didn't. He felt strongly they should be left alone, not slapped down.

Sandy napped on the lounge where Tera and her father had been sitting. All the talking was over and since everybody left now she could hear the other sounds in the air which induced her drowsiness. She fell asleep believing she was blessed to have found a friend and being able to go swimming. She was also thankful for her parents and Uncle Durry. And anyone else who loved her as her mind's curtain closed.

"Why didn't you wait till tonight to talk about goin to Kentucky?" asked Gwen. Perry sat at the breakfast table with iced tea now and Gwen was swallowing vitamins standing over the sink.

"Because it was a good time. Your new friend looks trustworthy. I just wanted to remind you and I knew Darling would think it was interesting. Its just gonna be a short trip."

"You can try and tell me you're innocent. I told you before I was going and you didn't argue. You know I wanna go so I felt embarrassed."

"Is that her real name, *Darling*, or a nickname?"

"I don't know about any other name. It's a nice name, you think?"

"She's a grown woman. The kid I like. Tough little brat. I'll bet she can be wicked. Sandy seems able to deal with her."

173

"It does seem that you and Durry could have a good trip together, *alone*, but you'd miss me. I know I should be with you. You'd miss me."

"You can come and your daughter too. I can't talk to *Durry* the whole time."

"We'll all be together. You and *your* daughter too."

Perry laughed a little.

"If you think like that you won't see what you need to see. You might spoil your mind with such a suggestion and it would be just like loss. The opposite of resisting something bad. By thinking about it all the time you actually start to do the bad thing. Afterward, it will feel like loss."

"You don't have to imagine so much." He leaned back in his chair swirling the ice in his glass.

"Sandy's so quiet out there," said Gwen.

"She was sleeping when I went out to my truck."

"Her days have been filled lately but she's relaxed to it. She's slowing down sooner, like the rest of us tired souls."

"Sometimes I feel like a soul, sometimes I feel like a robot," said Perry. He thought about his daughter and wished anything but that for her. He wanted to be able to help but he knew when the time came all he would able to do is apologize. He envied children for not having to be aware of such things.

Durry thought about the river before him, all the rivers upstream, how they feed into each other, knowing the way downhill. Big and little veins, blood of the region, no different than how liquid got carried around his own body. Without water the land would thirst, maybe die, just like an arm or a leg gone dry. Blue squiggles on a map, the Walnut, Scioto, Big Darby, Deer and Kokosing bring fresh from above to float the valley, swell the shore of the main.

It was one of those afternoons that got more comfortable as it drew on. And being away from home Durry gave some

174

thought to staying where he was. He always did that, kidded himself he was lazy. He dreamt of luxuries, like stealing a few days, but seldom did, there was business to be done. The motorcycle he bought because it could make six hours out feel like a ten day escape. With the men to keep busy he knew he wouldn't ever let himself be to blame by not paying close attention. He believed all businesses without an owner present were failures. He didn't want to be a burden like that, deliberately going in selfish need.

The calm before the dinner rush was a golden time. Durry got a free refill and had the gall to bum another cigarette, she couldn't come sit with him though, got told how nice it was that he asked. Still no caress. He stepped back outside to let the day soak in triple before he had to get going. The second cigarette did nothing.

The wind at sixty shoved everything back. As he rode north there was that condition again he could never get used to, conciliation.

9

Gwen hung up the phone. *Where is he?* She went back to cleaning up the kitchen after a late dinner. She was still unable to reach Durry and was beginning to feel anxious. She knew she had to keep trying or it was going to have to be a surprise party. He's just *gone* she thought. *He's usually always available.* She liked that, a Durry who was close by, someone she could count on. She usually forgot that he was a single man who could without her permission go off somewhere. She wanted so badly to have the next conversation with him, conquering the awkwardness, smashing it apart making her comfortable again. She watched Sandy and Perry from the window above the sink play catch with a foam football in the approaching dark. Perry rested his beer on Gwen's trunk and flung the football with a cigarette in his mouth. Gwen laughed to herself as she usually did seeing Perry in those moments. He was never very athletic and the expression on his face when he was exerting himself could be comical. Gwen knew he was self-conscious, masking it with humor. It was enjoyable to watch, his exaggerated straining or disappointment at a bad throw. It was great that he spent time with Sandy but Gwen also wanted him to be serious. It would never happen she realized and lowered her head to wash a fork.

Durry stood up with the bike under him so he could pull the key to the shed from his pocket. The beam from the headlamp washed over the white building. The gravel he had just ridden over offered a calm cloud of dust. Durry took the bolt-cutter proof padlock from the hasp and slid open the stable style door. The hot motor and exhaust cracked and pinged in the sudden quiet. As always, he looked once more at the bike now in shadow before shutting it in for the night. The motion-sensing spotlight lit the foreground as he walked toward the door of the bungalow style house. He noted again how sweet the air smelled, it wasn't ever like some dessert confection, maybe a little spiced from the mix of grasses growing nearby he figured. He switched on the light in kitchen, the smell of the outdoors still with him, stuck on his skin. He found the plastic bag of fireworks in the dark laundry room and the miniature blowtorch on the counter behind the radio in the kitchen then went out the back door to the patio. He launched bottle rockets in the dark from a piece of PVC. It was soothing to follow the trail of sparks upward then hear the loud bang. He remembered visiting a customer's residence before and noticing all the spent .223 caliber shells mixed in with the loose stone of the drive near to the mouth of the garage. "He just stands here and shoots, doesn't he?" Durry asked the woman of the house. "Shoots here, over there, all the time," she pointed. "Shot a coyote, he was standin right there." She walked to the exact spot she believed her husband had stood. "Yeah, he gets a lot of em," she finished, looking out toward a nearby buckle in the land Durry assumed the coyotes sprang from. Durry didn't shoot animals anymore, not since he was little more than a boy, but certainly saw the pleasure in firing an assault rifle right outside the door. The crack of the Black Cats now was the only sound in the dark as the lightning bugs blinked their yellow butts along the perimeter of the yard. The smoke and noise usually shut every other critter up while it lasted. Giant moths banged into the floodlights above the stoop. Durry wished he could somehow aim at the moths and shoot them down as they flew. He didn't consider them animals which made them open for sport. He just kept launching into the sky. He gave himself a mild reprimand for wanting to kill the moths. Just then he found a plump spider along its

177

evening web, chased it down with the blowtorch. He lit another bottle rocket and after the beloved *pop*, sat in one of the two plastic chairs to look at the gray horizon, soon complete dark.

Inside he stood in the kitchen deciding whether to eat or not. It was too late. He drank a shot of cold water out of the big bottle in the fridge. The sudden cold made his throat clench. He pulled his cell phone from the light jacket he'd worn while riding to check messages. He smiled but was slightly alarmed at how many times Gwen had called. He listened to the messages and there didn't seem to be anything wrong, just wanted to talk she said. He didn't want to call so late though, not just to talk. Somebody would reach somebody tomorrow.

Charlie was real skinny. That was the first thing anybody noticed. Being so thin could give the impression of being sickly. Her skin wasn't gray and her body was usually healthy. Most didn't take the time to figure out it was her usually solemn expression and long narrow bones that made her seem older than she was and maybe infirm. Her long dark brown hair was without a strand of silver and at five foot six her posture always erect. Gwen and Gwen's family struck her as too bold or just more confident but she seldom felt that secure and so married a man who was also particularly reserved. Ross did have a warm heart and obviously cared a lot for his wife but when together the two of them could seem like figures carved from wood. He was three or four inches taller than she was with close cut dark blond hair and hazel eyes. When they went out one never got more than two or three feet away from the other, security and love overlapped or became the same.

Charlie, the name she preferred, became excited at the thought of going to Durry's birthday party. She had a hard time believing anyone would want to invite her to anything.

178

Its such a shock to be asked she thought, even by her own mother. Charlie dreamed of what she'd wear and who she'd see. The opportunity to interact with so many other people did anything but petrify her. Although she was apprehensive about inviting others *she* knew. She was always afraid someone would see her for what she believed herself to be. But Gwen said to talk to as many people as she could. There had to be someone who would be interested and not make me panic all night she thought. She knew she needed to quiet herself because so seldom did anything she was afraid of really happen. And she had been secretly teaching herself not be scared, feel alone or lost. The *lessons* were helping but she could still get overwhelmed, would have to try hard to remember what she believed and knew was true during those times. She really thought herself handicapped at one point, broken, vowed to find any kind of strength somehow, try to fix herself with no one else knowing. She wasn't sure what would happen if anyone knew the things in her mind, it only felt natural to dwell on them privately, too much risk and expense any other way. When she did reflect on what she was and all the action going on inside, it wasn't ever plain like people thought.

It was only six-thirty in the morning but Charlie was already outside sweeping the porch and watering plants. The weather so far, really only a few days after the start of summer, had been terribly hot. The heat didn't bother her but her flowers and trees needed lots of water. Anyway, she really just wanted to keep busy till her favorite produce guy opened at eight. She was always up early. Thought it might be because she was skin and bones. She scoffed at herself when she had an idea like that. *What difference does it make if there's a connection, howzit gonna help? I love waking up early, bed's an empty page, the day is what has to be filled, every day. There's a lot to miss if you don't watch out.* She pulled away some dead yellow leaves from one of the

179

hanging plants she was near, wadding up the leaves and stems in her left fist. She opened the storm door quickly in back and swung her arm over the trash can, then thought better to put the leaves in the outside garbage containers in case of bugs. She let the hose run in one of the flower beds while she went on sweeping. There was simply too much to be watered. Their monthly bill had tripled because of the constantly running sprinklers. She looked at the swept porch and thought it needed to be pressure washed anyway. Maybe soon. The plants were still getting their drenching so Charlie stepped inside for a sip of coffee. She heard Ross already in his office sliding paper around. They'd made a space for him in one of the bedrooms that had a desirable view. The eighteen hundred square foot ranch worked well for the two of them. They envisioned living there through the birth of their first child, should they decide, but then sell and find something larger for a family of four. Neither was convinced but the notion of new life in their midst was becoming more and more accepted. Ross' job for a large distributor seemed tremendously steady and Charlie's at the candle factory was probably something she could arrange to leave and come back to.

Charlie picked up the keys to her husband's company car. "I'm leaving," she said to Ross quickly leaning in his office.

"Okay," he replied with a touch of a smile.

"Be back way before ten. I'll pick you up."

"I'll see you soon." He was already turned back to his desk. It was still early Sunday morning, more chatter later.

The corn man as she called him was fifteen minutes away, directly east. He was just a belligerent old man who to her seemed imprisoned by his own farm but grew the sweetest tasting corn she could find. Normally she wouldn't let herself burn two gallons of fuel to spend three dollars but it was a seasonal treat that she craved all year long till finally the stuff began to get harvested. She didn't know about other regions but suspected that locally grown produce when in season was unrivaled. It was even tempting not to eat vegetables during the winter because most everything from the chain stores was so disappointing. That night she wanted corn from the nasty sonofabitch off Highway 14. Once she asked if he had any bicolor corn and was nearly tossed from the property. "Why the hell would I grow that shit!" he blazed. Charlie didn't know whether to run or pee or cry or stand her ground. How can a mean man like that do what he does so well she wondered. She knew if he didn't love anything else he loved his corn. There was the reason not to run. Like other days he wasn't even outside, just bushels of corn, paper sacks and a bucket under a big tree. There was a brown cardboard placard affixed to one of the bushels, *bag your own, $2.50 per dozen* it read. On the small white pail in black, *please put money here.* The pail was atop a cut log among the bushels the height of a short stool. Charlie didn't open many of the ears as she felt she had to in the grocery store because it was a time she could count on it being good. The most she could go home with was twelve, any more and it dried out in the refrigerator before they could eat it all. She scrounged for the broad ears, more length and heft but still tender, then put them all in one of the sacks at her feet. Wrinkled dollar bills were already poking out of her pocketbook so she straightened out three and put them in the bucket with the smooth gray rock already there. There were a couple coins around the rock but she thought it was silly to have to reach into the container. It was still a good price and the fifty cents earned not having to get caught looking dishonest during an honest act. She reversed out of the drive onto 14. Behind a gully a little off the entrance to the property: *open sun up till sun down* read a sign staked in the ground. "Never saw that before," Charlie said out loud. "And here I been waitin." She felt like she wanted drive more places. Ross would be ready to go to church though.

181

"C'mon Durry, you gotta be home by now," Gwen said picking up the phone. She was going to call later but decided to call right away before Durry was off again.

"You're there, I can't believe it!"

"You found me. I been around anyway. Just forgot my phone yesterday," said Durry.

"I don't blame you. The best is not knowing you don't have it. If you remember you don't have it then you panic. If you don't know, you don't know. You get back and see it and think that was *great*. I *can* live without it." Gwen started to laugh.

"Yeah, that's pretty close," Durry answered chuckling. "Sometimes I just leave it behind and I'm too far out to go back and get it. Like you say, I can always check when I get back. Most stuff isn't so dire."

"Well, I'm glad you're there, been wondering... what did you do yesterday?"

"Had to go to Madison. Was nice to see the water. It always changes size on me. I try to remember how big it is then when I'm there it seems not as big. But goin over the bridge it looks huge. Kind of a strange view just seein all those campers on the other side too. There has to be a better way to do that."

"Really, I mean, how are they, or what are they doing?"

"Just a million campers, looks like a shore littered with giant white pillows. When your eyes focus all the pillows have wheels and black tires and you know what they are. I remember I felt funny when I realized it, just so gaudy." Durry paused to see if Gwen was still with him. "Kinda funny, things like that everywhere, I see."

"Huh. You went by yourself?"

"Yeah, just took off. Didn't really plan on it, just woke up and felt like it. The wife and kids didn't mind."

"That's right. I forget about that sometimes. The Madison Kid there to preserve the shores from all the heathen, camping, motor homin assholes. Clear the beach in the name of good taste, I know. Too bad you can't arrest em and get em outta there. I imagine that's what you want."

"Yep. But I don't think I'm in the right area to bust people for ugly."

Gwen erupted with laughter. "No, I don't think so! I don't know if anybody here has *any* taste. Not a lot one way or another... But *you* can teach em..."

"Did you call only to make me look crazy or is there somethin else?"

"Oh, yeah, been tryin to reach you but you're down South, I guess, drivin all over."

"Well, its summer, wanna just have some fun before its gone again. Can't stand the thought a *that*... Would really like to go somewhere farther away, like on a plane but can't, gotta keep on the gas."

"I know. You have to, but you'll figure out a way. One of those guys can watch things. Well, I could watch everything. Somehow, we could come up with something. Give you some time off, if you want."

"Yeah, there's a way, thank you."

A pause.

"Well, guess what I've done?" said Gwen.

"Hmm, I..."

"I invited everyone you know and a thousand people you don't know over to your house for a party."

Durry suspected it wasn't a joke. "What for?"

"Well, your birthday is comin and since its not that easy for you to get away we wanted to give you something else. Something at least that would be fun—I don't know about unforgettable... we'll see." Gwen spoke cautiously, waiting for Durry.

"You mean at my house?" Durry began to think it might be a joke.

183

"Yeah, over at *your* house. I thought it would be the best place. You have the pole barn, lots of room in your yard, big trees for shade. Make the place lively. Don't you think so?"

Durry was still deciding if she was serious. "My birthday's this week so what day...?"

"Saturday. We'll have it Saturday. Yeah, no one'll come if we have it during the week. *We* would but everybody else wouldn't. Not people who don't know you so well. Just people who love you." She paused. "I was thinking about one o'clock. That's a good time. We'll have lotsa food, people can play games. We'll light fires. You know, fire a pit or something."

"I think I'm gonna hang up and you can call me back in about an hour."

"No, no... you don't like it?"

"I do like it, I just have so many questions. Like who's going to do everything, the food, who's all coming? I don't know. But, yeah, it sounds like it could be great. I mean, how many people did you invite—who are they?"

"I told everybody to invite who they wanted. They just have to bring something, especially drinks. I think its going to be very hot. I don't think we need a tent thing, though, you have a porch and people can go inside the pole barn if they want, we can open the big door."

"So there is a plan. You're gonna run the whole thing? I mean, are we talkin weirdoes too, just everybody?"

"You and Perry and Dale can handle any weirdoes. Beat em up and bury em if you want to, but I think its gonna be fine. There'll be a lotta people who just wanna have a good time, probly some drinking, yes, but you're okay with that, I know. The whole thing should be just a big picnic."

"Adults only, or kids too?"

"Kids too. Lotsa kids."

"Who's Dale?"

184

"Well, Sandy has a new friend, and that's the girl's dad. I don't know im but I've been gettin to know his wife. You'll like everybody; if you don't you can run away. I'll clean up everything so when you come back there won't even be foot prints. Oh, I remember now, you can't forget to clean your house. That's all you have to do."

"Where're people going to pee? You don't think everybody needs to come inside to pee do you? I don't think I wanna picture that."

"Well, they'll have to go somewhere. Maybe I'll get a couple portable toilets. Yeah, that might be a good idea. I didn't think of that. That's a lotta people peeing. I mean, they can go in the woods when it gets dark. Why can't people go in the weeds?"

"Is Sandy and her new friend going to pee in the woods?"

"They'll be the first ones."

"Well, what about her mother, and Dale?"

"I don't think we have to worry about it. Let's not worry about it. I'll clean your bathroom, okay. Forget about any inconvenience. That's not the point. Somehow it will get clean, okay?"

"If you get portable toilets they'll never leave, it'll look like some official event."

"People go home from official events all the time."

"Okay, you promise to clean the bathroom, or figure something else out and I'll be ready. Do I need to do anything?"

"Just what I said. Somehow the whole damn thing should be a blast. I don't know what's going to happen. I thought you would like that too. I mean if they destroy the place you'll just build another house. You can stay with us and you can see Sandy swim one morning. It was a big decision to do that this year, by the way. Its been better for she and I too. I can't really explain it. We're both more relaxed. I like it much better. It feels natural. Does that sound stupid?"

185

"You can say natural. I'm sure its good for her. That's probly what it is."

"You need to see her. You need to know her friend's name. Its Tera. I had no idea Sandy could get along so well with someone her own age. Her mother told me Tera was kind of a problem, but Sandy can handle it. It makes me feel that sometimes I do something right."

"Not ashamed to take credit, are you?"

"No way."

"Even if you have to lie to yourself."

"I think that's all I do, so don't ruin it for me, dammit!"

"I've been thinkin lately there's no other way. If it got broken down into statistics every night, not many would make it. It feels okay to lie and be happy."

"So you're okay? Not gonna change your mind or be upset with me?"

"No."

"I don't know how I came up with this. It seemed like having a lot of people at your house, especially people none of us knew, would be exciting. I'm a little curious who might come. I thought you could handle it."

"You're right. Its only the anticipation but I don't feel like I have a lot to worry about... Seriously, I don't wanna have to worry about food, you're gonna do all that?"

"Everything, yes."

"There's other things I'll do that'll be easy, but I don't wanna worry about a menu and how much to buy and..."

"I told you..."

"Alright."

They both took a breath.

"You call me this week," said Gwen. "Also, I might be over a few times. I wanna see a few things. If I need to get inside leave a key for me or let me in if you can. Just leave a key. Don't be afraid to let me in."

"I'm not afraid. I won't be after I clean."

"I'll hide a key. I don't wanna come home in the day if I don't have to, you know?"

"I'd like a key. I can do things then that I don't want you to know about. I really would prefer to be there by myself."

"No problem. I'll tell you where the key is when I think of a place. I think I'm starting to like the idea. I shouldn't tell *you* though. Can't believe you had the whole thing going without me knowing. What were you gonna do if I was doing somethin else or workin or I don't know?"

"There was no other plan, this was it. Get you a stripper on your actual birthday."

Durry thought about what Gwen had done off and on during the day. She once again reminded him he wasn't alone. That was the message he received, anyway, the biggest part. His mind went to work on what he'd need to do at the house. It was clear, really, and he thought he'd spend time during the week getting ready. He wanted to do things Gwen hadn't thought of, maybe an awning off the shed for tables and food. A few conveniences may cost a little money but the items could probably be reused or returned. He still shook his head at Gwen's initiative, to assume he'd be okay with such a large gathering of people he didn't know. She was right, since it was such an absurd and dangerous thing to do it became appealing. For an instant he wished he could drink again, be twenty years old taking drugs again, something to bring the high closer, make it last longer. There was a desire to preserve certain states in amber, instead of letting them pass through.

Durry looked out a window at the sky. The grass in the yard was ready to be mowed again. He read the last section of the paper then changed into shorts and a t-shirt. He knew beach sandals weren't safe for using the mower but he only knew of one instance someone's toes had been cut off by the blade and that was when he was nine. A kid on the other side

187

of the neighborhood slid on some wet grass and got the top of his foot chopped off still in the shoe. That was the legend anyway. It was nicer to have cool feet Durry thought. Sneakers weren't going to stop rotating steel.

Durry stopped many times for water, though the moisture in the air should have been enough on its own to drink. When the sun came from behind a cloud the heat's intensity rose and with the humidity was like a tropical land. But there had been little rain, lots of leaves from his tallest trees had been falling in the wind because it was so dry. The soil's reserve depleted and some of the deciduous species fooled into autumn months ahead. As the chore stretched out the wind blew stronger, it seemed to him he was emptying the collection bag and filling trash cans with clippings all day. He stood in the kitchen after he was done drinking a glass of water. He saw water droplets on the windows and searched for his cigarettes. He couldn't tell the difference in taste from a recently purchased pack or his six month old one, maybe longer. There were periods he smoked sometimes. Certain weeks he'd realize he smoked five or six sticks. Then sometimes for whole seasons, nothing. The pack would come out again at some opportunity, a recent tangle of events. The storm began outside, the wind pulling hundreds of leaves away from their branches, rain almost a white sheet that moved in from the west. Durry watched from the back of the house, the door in front of the patio. So many leaves were coming down, they blew almost clear of his property toward the field. At least I don't have to clean up so many he thought. But the yard was filled with enough. The wind worked on the trees turning the tops silver while the overdue rain apologized to the crisp grass. He watched to get an idea how long it might last, he knew not long at its intensity, the heat was too much and the climate too changed to keep the water on for the needed amount of time. When the storm slowed in about an hour he went out to the patio which was

188

now covered again in brown and yellow leaves. He stood smoking in the light rain toeing at the sticky leaf bunches.

Gwen found the extra key and opened Durry's front door. She was going to leave the key in the lock to keep track of it but instead pulled it out of the deadbolt, held it in a tight fist. She could feel the metal teeth digging into her palm, along with how hot it was in there. She didn't know where to put the key, set it down somewhere in an unfamiliar place and it would be lost. If she put it in her purse it would be lost. If she put it in the pocket of her jeans, hard to remove. If she carried it anymore she would continue to wonder where to put it. She put it in her jeans pocket. Relief at the decision and she relaxed. Sandy followed her mother who was just creeping along rather than walking. She was looking extendedly at everything, as if she'd won a contest in a store to let her shop for free. Gwen wasn't exactly sure why she was there. She realized she brought Sandy mostly for protection. Protection from what she could not fathom. But she knew she was *using* her daughter on this occasion. Its alright, she thought. I brought the kid into the world anyway. Helping me along is part of the job. They went farther into the house. For all my lurking this seems like a pretty happy place, Gwen thought. There's custom woodwork every-where, naturally. The kitchen is bright and inviting. Gwen didn't think Durry had done the curtains himself because they were too perfect. If he did them he couldn't be the man she thought. That would make him too precise with luscious fabric. And though she would still love him very much the new twist would suppress her primitive side. That's why I brought my kid, she realized. I was worried I might do something *illegal* if she weren't here. What, like sniff his underwear? Or maybe hold his shampoo bottle and razor a very long time. Gwen smiled and shook her head. Sandy was opening drawers in the kitchen. "Knives and forks just like

189

us, mom." How did Sandy know? Well, I'm behaving like a cat burglar! The kid sensed how apprehensive I am. What am I even doing in here! Well, I'm getting a feel for the place, the layout, for Saturday. Did I really need to get a *layout* in my mind? Couldn't I have just come on Saturday or Friday night with most of what I planned to bring over? No, I needed a layout, some idea of where everything is going to go. And I want to see everything, the bedrooms too. I wanna see everything, even what I don't need to. The kid's here, she can explore with me. I *need* to see everything. He's a great man so I need to see the whole house. If Sandy is paying attention she'll get to see how weird her own mother can be. But this is more than I can resist so I'm willing to endure her reaction. A little kid's reaction. I won't be able to explore the house the day of the party because it would be so strange. Too many others. The adventure of a first sighting would have to happen now. Gwen was thrilled at having the place to herself on the first visit. She'd just been in the drive before. Well, invited in for the quick tour. She was married. Strange though. Sandy was never close behind, usually stopped for a unusually long period examining something Gwen hardly found interesting. Gwen realized the difference between her daughter's visit and her own, reverence. Gwen was selfishly stealing images for a thrill while Sandy's only impulse was to invade as little as possible. She found simple objects plainly in the open, enough to remind her of her fondness for their owner. Gwen wanted to loot everything, the word lust came into her mind. I don't mean anything, Gwen thought. He's just such a mystery, and so private. I've always wanted to see more inside of him.

"What are we gonna do, mom?"

"I just wanna look around. See where we're going to put everything." Gwen was still panning the room. Her eyes ate everything they saw. She loved the man after all. She just admitted it to herself. She believed she would never act on

190

the emotion but she loved him. If Perry got run over by a cement truck she'd run to Durry the moment after. I love the sonofabitch, she thought. I love the hell out of him. I can't believe I love the hell out of him. It feels good to know, she thought. She smiled at Sandy who was looking out a window, concentrating.

"Mom, there's a barn. That's where we need to be hunting. Have the whole thing outside. You can put the food inside the barn. It will be perfect for that. People can get their food inside there then walk around outside, play badminton or toss bean bags or something." Sandy didn't look at her mother as she spoke. She concentrated on those big doors on the pole barn. There wasn't ever anything that interesting inside people's homes, it was their garages. "Goin outside, mom."

Gwen nodded as she approached a window in the back of the house. It looked out toward big trees and sunlight. Gwen didn't resent her situation in any way. This new information actually made her appreciate it more. She was grateful for everything she had, both men, both daughters. Realizing her feelings uplifted her instead of depressed her. Women were made to love, right? God, I'm going to make myself sick, she thought. Okay, maybe I would jump him if I were drunk enough and Perry was in a coma but its nothing I have to do or want to do. Thank God I have him as a friend though, I'd be missing a whole side of myself I really like. She turned away from the window and examined the living room, her view again refreshed. With Sandy outside there was no feeling of having to get away with something. She honestly wanted to know the man and fantasize about him, just like looking longingly at some lovely page in a magazine. He has excellent taste, she thought. Some things would have to change, like the obsession with edged weapons. He's got knives all around this place. *Any girl that came in here would think she's never going to make it out. Oh, he's got a*

191

freakish side, doesn't he? Gwen was in full enjoyment, a tour bus in her mind. *Men only need to see a woman naked and they feel they know her, but a woman can tell more about a man by what he surrounds himself with. But I still don't know him. His collection here is complicated. There's too much from all over to figure it out. I like that even better. If I were married to him there'd be no more mystery. I'd hate him for things like I hate Perry for things. And he'd hate me for my things, clogging the drain with hair or ruining the food or something. Friends can last but a marriage is unstable right after intercourse. I like it like this. I'll still think of him when I'm not supposed to but that's because I can't have him.* She went upstairs.

It was hotter at the top of the cramped stairs. Neither bedroom looked like where Durry slept. Each was small and had an steep angled ceiling. Good as a kids' area but tight for grown-ups. And the bath area was all clean, no signs of regular or even recent use, which to Gwen meant no sleep-overs of any kind. *He wouldn't put her up here anyway, right, unless it was me or Sandy or someone else who would have no business in his bed? Oh, I wouldn't stay up here long, he'd be in for it!* She found no incriminating sundry items in the bathroom, disheartened, she withdrew to the stairs. *Someone's doin these damn drapes, though.*

Gwen found the master. *He's got a first floor master. Always wondered how that would be.* She remembered dating a man briefly before Perry who had a king size water bed in the living room in front of the television. Bachelors, no restraint. She found herself disapproving of first floor bedrooms suddenly. Or maybe just king size waterbeds with irritating men in them. *Oh, this is good, come back now, remember your daughter is out there somewhere probably playing with paint thinner or dirty mouse traps.* Gwen stood in the threshold of the master bath just staring. Her eyes bounced from one object to the next. *Just so damn curious,*

192

no will power. Well, he's family, I have to know im. She found his razor and shampoo. She didn't hold either to her bosom, shaving cream residue and hard water deposits deflected all longing. She wanted to lie in the bed but decided that was an awful thing to do. *Its inimical and exhilarating to be so whipped again.* Instead, she sat on the bed and thought about where to run the food out of. *Sandy was right, I could prepare the food at home and in the kitchen over here but we can serve it to all the reprobates in the barn. It's the perfect place. One day soon I'll have to get out there and check on my daughter. I know she's probably cut her arm off in a fan belt by now but damn, I haven't enjoyed myself like this... forever!* She had the feeling of being high. She remembered quickly that everything around the besotted tended to go to hell. She glanced at the kitchen for reassurance of her plan wanting to return in a little bit to look more closely.

Gwen opened the white service door on the side of the pole barn and went in. Durry said he'd leave it unlocked. It was perfectly quiet like she feared. But instead of calling out loudly she rounded the knee wall allowing her to see most of the enclosed space. Sandy was squatting beside a motorcycle holding a dirty towel.

"Gettin ready to go for a ride?" asked Gwen.

"I was gonna check the oil but the engine has to be hot," she replied. Sandy was reveling in the discovery of the machine. "I can't ride it anyway. Look how big it is. Way too heavy, I think."

"Yeah, probly too much for you, huh?" Gwen was mystified along with apprehensive about what she looking at. Its beautiful, she thought. *Now that Sandy knows, how do I keep her off it. Dammit Durry!* Gwen would now have to decide if she needed to keep Sandy away from the motorcycle, *another* job. She knew Durry wouldn't take her out if Gwen was against it. *I'd* like to go out on it, Gwen realized. *So this is where he goes... This is why I can't reach him sometimes...*

193

Sandy would never stop asking if she could go. I'm going to lose my daughter, I know. Is it time? Lord, screw all this panic, I just wanna feel healthy like before. If the motorcycle doesn't kill her she's just going to leave! I was happy only losing her a little at a time, now I might never see her again! Durry would never let her leave, she'd listen.

"Sandy, whutta you think about that?"

"I don't know, mom. It's too big for me. I don't know if Durry would ever give me a ride. It was just sitting here in the dark. I like it a lot, though. I'd like to hear it. I don't think Uncle Durry ever told me about it. I like it more of a surprise, anyway."

Gwen could tell her daughter didn't know exactly what to think either. They all loved Durry and didn't want anything to happen to him. It wasn't cool to be like that, though. Tough motorcycle guys can't be questioned about safety. Gwen started feeling high again. Her body remembered some of her earlier years. It was like chemicals were being unleashed taking her right to the past. The same woozy faith, wrongly knowing things, medication was an okay refuge, it suddenly made her somber but alert. It was the same blinking warning light helped her all along. She never thought about it once it had gone out, didn't need to. Everything was on the right track now. The stress and excitement had drug some things up. Happiness had been winning over death defying feats. She thought about how cold it had been not knowing herself. The years she spent not nearly as whole as she was now.

"Would you be afraid to ride this?"

"I don't think so, mom, not with Uncle Durry."

"I might wanna ride it too, okay?"

"Mom, you can ride, if Durry lets us. If he asks me." Sandy smiled twisting the dirty towel. She felt like she wanted to unscrew every bolt on the motorcycle then put the whole thing back together again. She wanted to find out what every part did. She never looked at the workbench for a tool but her mind saw the machine before her in a neat pile. A pile of smaller machines, smaller and smaller. Some parts would be unnecessary and not used again. Sandy dreamt of one wrench only to do the whole job. She looked up at her mother.

"I'll bet he has a lot of fun on that," Gwen said. "I was trying to call him the other day but he was out on this I guess."

"Maybe. She's almost like a girl for him. Sleeping quietly here in the dark until he comes home. She does whatever he says. I'd do whatever he says if I were her," Sandy finished.

Sandy's words were thoughtful and strange to Gwen. "Do you think that's what he'd want, do anything he says?"

"She doesn't care though, if you're going to be loved that much you don't ever care. Its like perfect, so you don't have to fight." Sandy kept twisting the towel moderately. It was filthy in big spots, black, oil mixed with dirt.

Sandy moved her mother. It was one of those moments where accuracy wasn't as important as depth of feeling. When this came from her little girl it awed Gwen. She contemplated for a moment what it would be like to have the love Sandy pictured, her heart expanded and almost blew up. She touched Sandy's head, felt bolts of hair between her fingers. She loved that, feeling her hair, was almost going to have to eat the girl all up. "Nice kinda love isn't it?"

"Well, you have to be ready, and listen..."

Gwen kept stroking Sandy's hair. "What else did you find in here?"

"He isn't here so I couldn't look at everything. Just yard stuff in here." Sandy pivoted to look around. "The motorcycle. A wheelbarrow..."

"Yeah, I see."

"It looks like he has an office over there," Sandy pointed. It was a corner where Durry had placed an old wooden writ-

195

ing desk. There were some papers, some with black finger-prints that looked like receipts, pink, yellow, white.

Gwen suddenly got the idea to look around for any furniture. She was certain he would have incredible furniture stashed away somewhere. In the garage was the perfect place! She jerked her head in every direction seeing nothing. It was fairly dark but light enough to see sticks of furniture. Nothing. What about up there, she thought. There was a partial loft above the end stall where tarp covered merchandise dwelt. Gwen's mouth now contained more saliva. *I am a treacherous woman, she thought, thinking all these things about my brother in law. My judgment has been run over. I've been so hungry all morning.* Gwen didn't do a search of the loft, next time, without Sandy.

Sandy stood over a box by the desk.

"What's in there," asked Gwen.

Sandy lifted the box flaps. "Bottles," she said. "Nine bottles."

"What's he got, wine? A big dusty case a wine." Gwen shook her head. "I wonder why he has that?"

"Well, are you gonna start cookin today or why did we come out here when he's not here?"

"Yeah, I just wanna see where everything is gonna go. We'll use your idea and put the food right here on long tables. Everybody can serve themselves and I'll keep bringing out more from the kitchen inside. Maybe you and Tera can watch these tables, stand behind em or something, in case somebody needs something or something runs out, like at a restaurant."

"I don't care but Tera will. She won't stand there very long, she'll probly get upset."

"She doesn't have to, maybe I'll ask your sister. I think she'd be better. Anyway, just some ideas right now. But that's how its gonna go, Sandy. I'll need your help a lot. This party is for Durry but we also have a lotta people to think

196

about. You'll still have fun; once everybody has eaten the real work'll be over.

Sandy gazed at her mother.

"And your birthday is comin up soon, your uncle won't forget that. You're gonna have a lotta fun. Your uncle will wanna git you in trouble. Your father too. God, your father, I think I have to worry about him more."

Sandy smiled faintly.

"I think Durry's gonna get toilets and I'm gonna talk your father into getting us a grill big enough. Or maybe more than one, whatever he thinks."

"Durry's getting toilets. What does that mean?"

"Well, we need toilets, isn't that funny? Everybody can't go inside or Durry's bathroom will be a mess. And they can't go *outside* so there has to be a place. Extra toilets, like at construction sites."

Sandy looked confused but nodded that she understood anyway, her eyes large. She didn't expect to need a toilet at all.

"I see the guys cookin on the grill. You and I and your sister organizing the cold food, salads and desserts, there's gonna be a few that wanna help, always are, that's good! Some stuff might have to be cooked or heated up. I can do that in Durry's kitchen, but I think everything should really be done before and just brought over here. We'll use the refrigerator and buckets of ice to keep things cold. The kitchen will just be a place for extra stuff and dirty dishes, maybe. I think it should be fine. I'll jist have to figure out where to put everything. Its supposed to be hot, hot this weekend. Hotter than it is now, if you can imagine."

Sandy appeared bored listening to her mother. She sat on Durry's desk while her mother thought out loud with her arms crossed. Sandy peeked at the case of wine again, deciding if she should steal a bottle. If she did she didn't want to drink it alone though. It would have to be with Tera. Maybe

197

at the party. I wonder if its good, she thought. *Durry can have some with us.*

Gwen was positioned next to the far stall, looking toward the opposite wall, imagining the space needed for the spread. "We'll be fine," she said confidently.

I can't handle many more assholes, Perry thought. People from other areas were building large homes in the hills, many as their own general contractors. He assumed they brought along money but it seemed like every work estimate he and Allen gave lately was being ignored. Commercial customers too were screaming about prices, quoting with numerous other shops, shrinking a lot of the incentive. Allen said great work wasn't important anymore, just speed and price. God help you if something went wrong but if the work simply held up through the warranty that was good enough. You could have built the aqueducts and for a hundred dollars less they'll pick someone else to plumb the space shuttle. What he and Allen didn't talk about was being ashamed. So much concern and strain in a job only to have a lot of people think you're just ripping them off. There were a lot of missed chances at that time, a lot of bids curling around the edges with follow up emails and phone calls wasting only more. A lot of work they were quoting still hadn't been rejected but during the wait it was the minor jobs that bought gas and food. I don't care, Perry thought. He guessed he didn't mind much that is was slow. It was tiring trying to dig up jobs though. He still liked to do it instead of Allen but was almost ready to admit he needed help. Whenever he thought he couldn't pitch another the phone would ring and they'd make a couple hundred bucks putting in a new faucet and garbage disposal. It was bullshit inconsistent wife hired service work but always profitable.

Being between significant jobs gave Perry a moment to think. For some time being around his brother never seemed

198

that pleasant. But the party Gwen had going sounded like a great idea to him. He truly wanted to help. He looked forward to seeing his brother, even felt a little pride. Gwen asked if he'd figure out what to do about a big enough grill. Perry wasn't going to eat meat cooked with gas fire so decided to build a charcoal grill for what they needed. After dropping off a quote to another tightwad housecat turned construction boss he decided he'd need to see a customer he used to know from High View Electric. He and the owner of the welding shop worked on some special orders together after hours. But Perry first had to stop at a food processing plant past Dillsboro. He went quickly to the loading docks in back where he knew he'd get the reception he needed. The employees in the front office would have told him to get lost, some with big smiles. His temper would rise and he'd dream of carving them up as he walked out, always so predictable were the worm people he thought. He wanted to find a couple food grade steel drums, maybe unpainted. He was still told he couldn't have anything inside but there was a row of four white drums near the dock outside that were damaged with small creases. Perry examined the barrels which were sticky with vegetable oil residue. He was suddenly struck by the heat of the asphalt and sunlight reflecting off the white-painted steel he was squatting to look at. Really hot these days, he thought. He felt that draft of heat enter his nose and swirl around inside his head. He looked at all four containers but any two were fine. No one felt comfortable accepting money but a guy did come around with a forklift to load the drums. Perry dropped the gate on the truck and moved some of the mess around so the load would fit up close to the cab. He strapped the drums in tight after again trying to offer a few dollars to the lift man.

He drove away thinking about overweight people and the suffering they said the heat caused them. Perry tried not to let the heat bother him. He loved summer, hated winter, no sense being upset with both. He didn't even know if the air conditioner in the truck worked because he never turned it on. He was driving with a friend a couple years ago who requested it be turned on so as a courtesy Perry did. Dried leaves, dead bugs and dust flew out one of the passenger side vents hitting his friend in the face, making him laugh. It was just cultural differences, thought Perry, between those not as strong and those who faced certain things without trying to make them softer or more comfortable. So much was already *pussified*, stuff needed to be endured.

At a stoplight outside Engadine Perry had the whole design worked out in his head. The most important aspect was cutting the can exactly in half. He realized he probably wouldn't need both of the barrels. He wasn't going to put a lid on either of them so he was one hundred percent over on material. It took Vic only seconds to slice the barrel in half at the welding shop. Rather than smell burning paint the outside of the container was first sandblasted. Since the interior originally held food oil it was left alone. The oil residue would quickly be charred away, odorless. The sizzling paint aroma would have been difficult to bear and the appearance of the invention even worse. It was like him to leave on the enamel to watch how it faired, breathe it in a little, and also the time it took for the finish to bubble up and peel off in hanging strips. Perry was glad he was wise enough to avoid his own juvenile curiosity this time, and probably make a lot of people sick. He still had to picture that it was wrong and a criminal's delight that the impulse was there at all. Would the finish simply cook away without affecting anyone or hang heavy in the air, burrow into the lungs, changing the structure of the cells there? It might be the fumes only trigger the gag reflex even if they smell no different than the inside of a paint and body shop. If food was cooking on the grill at the time would the paint in a gaseous state be absorbed to poison it, enter my blood that way? Perry still wondered.

Vic welded three-quarter inch trim pieces over the sharp edges where the cut had been made and decided to remove the manufacturer's pour spout and install a solid plate. He and Perry decided on iron pipe for the frames, they made two. Perry wanted two single frames so they could be easily moved. Vic splayed the legs out somewhat on each one for more stability. He welded brackets slightly inside the opening near the top to catch the actual grill. Perry didn't know where to find pieces that were going to fit. Vic said he could make them but Perry would have to come back. Still no charge as long as Perry helped him out some time. The two were really just friends who had always done each other favors but after Perry was fired from High View amid rumors of theft their relationship was shelved. Only one frame fit into the back of the truck. The half barrel nested perfectly and Perry said he'd come back again to pick up the other frame with the new pieces of grill.

At every stop the heat rose in the truck cab, it was strange then that Perry should shiver. He thought it might be his body reacting as the air temperature came close to his own. He drove away from the intersection while the radio announcer told him it was eighty-nine. Perry wondered as he accelerated if dogs could commit suicide, especially if they were unwanted, and what was it about the hot sun that the elderly and overweight couldn't manage. He needed to know at what age it became too dangerous. But you can't avoid the sun he reasoned. *I know a lot of old people who garden when its hot.* He remembered thinking if they die its better than staying inside and being afraid. Perry reached over to find the half container of warm water laying sideways on the passenger seat. He took a small sip but couldn't drink anymore. He was trying to figure out the best way to Durry's house from where he was.

It was irritating to have to put some thought into his route but Perry now formulated his best version of the way. "I'm gonna get there and if I can get in I'm gonna find somethin to eat." Payment is always good in food, he thought. If everyone paid in food, well, we'd figure the rest out. His phone rang. It was Allen wondering what he was doing. Perry told him he just delivered that bid. Allen said he had another one to take out, also a residence.

"Just drive back and git it, wouldja," Allen said. "Sometimes its like this, I really have to try to get business. Then it always comes from some place it was impossible to guess."

"Don't worry. I'll be back soon to take it out."

"Where are you?"

Bosses were forever wondering about your location when you have the privilege to drive, Perry reflected. "On my way back now."

Allen was immediately more at ease. "Alright, see you when I see you."

Perry folded the phone and confirmed his route, glancing at a street name through an intersection. He was going the right way. Talking on the phone sometimes he'd miss turns, even subconsciously take a heading as if he were to go home or some other familiar place. He was afraid he'd look too fancy in one of those ear pieces but heard it was easier to drive with one and keep your hands free. He really hated to talk to people unless he was right in front of them. Writing something down was second best, all the electronic stuff was too maddening. It was then he realized he drove right past Durry's shop while on the phone. See! Screamed his mind. I didn't wanna stop but I would like to have said, "There's Durry's place, I'll bet he's workin hard in there, or somethin like that." It just woulda been nice to enjoy that. Instead I'm scarin people, runnin over wild dogs and kids like some old country bitch shoppin in the city dressed in a white Cadillac! My head turnin everywhere but the road, the whole world goin under the tires! Perry braked hard as a squirrel ran out. "Which way you gonna run now, my friend?" A few years ago that squirrel would have been paste. Even now an observer might have thought it uncharacteristic. Helping his brother and wife and in the absence of stress from work he had become a life giver. All he knew was for the moment he didn't feel the urge to destroy. The squirrel chose a direction then disappeared in the scrub. Perry pushed the accelerator to get out of there. The next living thing probably won't be so lucky, he thought, there must be balance. This thought uncomfortable above his neck, altering the peace. He tried to hold on to the feeling of good will he had found. I don't wanna be shitty today, he thought. I just want it to be all right. There will be no destruction only creation and some spirit is gonna help me to do it! He drove through a short wooded area where a couple people had cut room for their modular homes. The green forest with an empty spot filled with a white structure. He thought it didn't look too bad, you gotta live somewhere. At the next "T" he turned right. Hard to forget about Mule Barn Road, my brother loves it for some reason, like he picked the name himself. Of all the damn names it does stick with you. Perry chuckled. My brother knows nothin about mules or any other kinda livestock, friggin mule head *himself.* The hills around the road rolled like a green sea, only fully mature trees here and there by the road or an oasis some-where out on the green water. Perry found Durry's place and pulled up the drive. Like his own, it was a nice little piece of track right to the shed barn then cut around a little toward the house. People will have a good time here he thought, place'll handle a lotta bodies. He got out of the truck for a look around. It was such an awful beautiful hot day. The wind coming up off the field made him feel that the Spirit could take him anytime. Every time one more good thing happens, Perry thought, he can have me. The Old Man can have me. I wanna fall over when

203

the sun's shinin. Don't wanna go when I'm down. "Take me Old Man when I'm on top, you sourpuss. Take me now that I'm on top." "Love this place," again aloud. Perry looked around for a place to stow the grill. He thought he already had a place so took more time poking about. It had been a couple months since he stopped over. Durry let him ride the motorcycle when the snow melted. To Perry it was never warmer than that first day when the snow is all gone and warm wind comes up from the south. He still wore a jacket but if he could, loved to ride on one of the first couple warm days of the year. Durry said he could show up anytime and take the bike out as long as he replaced the fuel. Sometimes Perry left it empty just to cause conflict. But Perry came over less anyway as the warm months progressed, winter boredom was gone.

The house was locked but Perry wanted to see if the back door was too. It was. Dammit! How am I supposed to get a sandwich, he fumed. He shook the door handle one more time anyway. Alright, let's unload the grill. He stepped to the front again, stood with his hands on hips. He decided to place his cargo behind the pole barn. He got the truck in position then got in the bed and lowered everything.

He got out his phone and dialed. "Hey asshole, I just dropped off a grill behind your shed."

"You gotta grill?" responded Durry.

"Yeah, I built it, my wife made me do it." There was no way Perry was going to let him know that he actually wanted to do it *himself*. Too much squishy pink crap in the world already.

"Well, that's great, thanks. Just put it against the back wall."

"Its already there, picking up one more too. The grates are being made. I'm also afraid I'm gonna have to do all the cookin, sorry. Most people can't be trusted. Rather go without than eat somethin nasty by somebody I don't know!"

"That's fine, you can cook. I have no problem with it. Gwen will probly be happy. You're gonna be busy, though, in case..."

"I don't wanna talk to people anyway, they can say *thank you* when I put the meat on their plate, that's it. All I wanna hear is *thank you* and *can I have more*."

"Well, you're the one then. No one'll have to worry who will do it then."

"Hey, I want somethin to eat. How do I get in the house?"

"The key's in the barn, in my desk drawer. If the side door isn't open that's it, I got the key with me. It might be open. But don't jimmy it, bastard. And don't smoke in the house."

"Right, I'll see if I can get in. You got anything good inside? Whadaya have?"

"I don't know what you want, look around, man! Probly not a lot, maybe."

"All done here, but I'm comin back, I don't know, tomorrow. Have fun."

"See you."

Perry slammed the gate shut on the truck bed and looked out. He lit a cigarette trying to judge the distance between where he was and the next house. He thought about trying to locate the cricket making noise somewhere behind him and give him a taste of the lighter. Perry rolled up his short sleeves like a dude and smoked against the truck. Allen is probly thinking I should have been back by now. No work, anyway. I'll just tell im I stopped for somethin to eat. He smoked the rest of the cigarette but put it out in an empty pop can because the ground was so dry. It probably wouldn't have caught but Perry was in tune with goodness that day. He didn't want any trouble. Maybe he was hoping he would be taken that day and he felt on top. If something swooped in and grabbed him for the final ride he wanted to go straight, not having to answer for doing anything that day at least. Ah fuck it, he decided. *Probly did a hundred things today already I don't even know about. I don't think I can ever be redeemed because I don't know how, like a dog who goes out to roll in the mud right after a bath. Also, if I can't git in this damn garage for a key I'm gonna be breakin into the house to get somethin to eat.*

At home Perry told Gwen about his project. She was pleased with what he had done. She knew Perry didn't show it but he was human. He was one of those men who worried that kindness and weakness were the same thing. Gwen thought women married them because they were easy to tell apart from the gay ones, and also their secrets would be safe because they had a hard time seeing inside. Gwen knew many sharp women who had married or were planning to marry closed minded men. It was many times easier to have only one in the union who was a well of emotion. It seemed smart to Gwen to wed a man who knew what he had to do. But there were hazards, stubbornness, alcoholism, a colder heart. So when miracles happened like enthusiasm for a brother's birthday party it was enough for her to go on. Enough to subscribe to a sturdy arrangement, herself, Sandy and Perry.

"I'm also cookin, so don't hire somebody else. Okay?" Perry said.

"You think I was goin to hire somebody? No way. So you're it! You volunteered! Thank you! We have so much to do Perry, that's one key position I didn't know who was goin to fill. I never thought about it but you're the perfect one... Ahhh, so they're wood burnin, aren't they?"

"You know it. This way I can eat, know what everything's gonna taste like. People anymore don't even know how to cook over coals. 'Oh, no, its not gas, its gonna take too long to cook!', Perry imitated in an effeminate voice. "Think they're gonna get cancer or somethin."

206

"Well, you're it. Thank you, that helps a lot. I was over there yesterday with Sandy and we think we have a good idea how to set everything up. You can also be in charge of games if you want. I was thinking volleyball and something else, not as strenuous." Gwen knew now how much she was asking.

"I'll think about it. Might be a job tomorrow. Have to pick up the other grill and git it delivered too."

Gwen gave her husband a kiss on the cheek. He just looked at her.

Sandy came in from the porch and asked, "What kinda games?"

"I thought volleyball. How'd you hear out there?"

"I can hear you both yellin when I'm outside." Everyone paused and looked at each other. "It'll be fun watchin the drunk people try and hit the ball!" Sandy proclaimed.

"There won't be any drunk people, will there Perry?"

"There might be." Perry began laughing.

"Ok, well, I just can't believe you would think that's funny," said Gwen.

"You will too when you see it. I think that's why you want volleyball in the first place," added Perry.

Gwen looked at Sandy and cracked a smile. "People will always drink too much, I wish they wouldn't. You don't have to get wasted to have fun." Gwen finished the sentence looking at Sandy.

"I don't care, mom. That's what some people are gonna do. I thought about having some myself. But I won't get drunk like everyone else till I'm older."

Gwen was horrified. Even Perry leaned back in his chair. "What! I don't want you *having some* at all. You stay close to me. Who gives you a little, anybody?"

Sandy anticipated her mother's reaction and thought it might be a good time to get her used to shock. There would be many shocks ahead, Sandy knew. Not many from alcohol

207

or drugs but other shocks, however, though unknown at the time. Sandy looked at her father who wasn't saying anything. She suddenly felt as if she might have hurt him, betrayed him. Strangely, she had less hope for him accepting what lie ahead than her mother. She sensed she would have the effect of making her father increasingly sad, not because of her actions but because he wouldn't understand her. That's okay, Sandy thought, I've already been sad about that and a hundred other things.

"No one has given me anything to drink, mom." She looked at her father. Perry had a slightly concerned but more neutral look. "I was just joking. I don't wanna make you nervous."

"Have you ever tried any?" asked Gwen.

"Dad gives me some beer sometimes, in a little glass. I had beer and apples with him once, outside. You were here, picking weeds or something."

Perry's expression didn't change. He made sure Gwen saw. He would never feel he did anything wrong. Kids get a little beer, that's the way it is. Half a juice glass and they love it. I expected it when I was little, he thought. Gwen glanced his way once in a while, never long in that moment.

Gwen looked at Sandy, more calm. "Do you think we're yelling in here when you're outside?"

"No, but I can always hear you. It helps me because I know where you are and what you're talkin about, I can see if its me."

Gwen smiled. Her daughter was amazing to her. "Well, just so you know where we are." She gazed some more at Sandy. My other daughter wasn't like this, she thought. Someone must have cast a spell or I musta had Sandy at a strange place on the earth, where there's no gravity and everything has the ability to move in any direction. When they took her out she was drenched in my blood and I knew she was different. *How I love her and her soul.* Gwen turned back to the sink.

"Durry likes bean bag toss, mom," said Sandy.

"How do you know?"

"We've played it before. He loves it. We played for a couple hours before. He was playing pretty serious. Call im and ask him. Its his birthday, you should get what he likes."

"We'll find something," said Gwen.

"I know that game," said Perry. "It is fun. Seems like a pussy game but once you get a few beers in you its fun as hell." Perry looked at his daughter bearing his teeth. "I've seen guys get into fights…"

Gwen put both hands on the edge of the sink and shook her head. Today she was losing. They are at home wherever they are she realized.

"It is fun, mom. But you won't get to laugh watching the drunk people like with volleyball." She smiled at her mother, enjoying making her uneasy.

"Where do you find one?"

"Durry has one. He plays at the shop to help him think," Sandy said.

"Well, you two are way ahead of me, I guess it'll be alright."

Sandy left the house again after dinner. She said she was going on the porch but instead went down to the river. Her head was clearer than usual and she felt happy. Saturday was raising everyone's spirits. She squatted at the shore floating sticks in the shallow. Light flickered perfectly in the water, brown water. Her sticks turned in circles and collided with one another, most eventually getting caught on shore. One made it out and she went to collect it, group it with the rest. A tiny deer came to the water on the other side. It was so small, looked at her, caution in its eyes. More thirsty than afraid, though, and began to drink. Sandy waited. She knew the adult deer would be close. First she saw the mother. It came to drink with the fawn. The adult male appeared upstream about twenty-five yards. He watched Sandy carefully. He would tilt his neck in a way that was humorous, Sandy almost called out for him to stop trying to make her laugh. He was always trying to get a better view, moving his head around the brush. Only he didn't move his body and he pivoted his head as if it were attached by soft rubber. It reminded her of the way she saw some of the kids at school dance. She thought of the word *staccato* from music class. She felt engaged by the male deer and they stared at each other. Sandy's sticks were beginning to travel, she sensed them below her separating, more water between each. With no threat the male came to the shore but didn't drink. The fawn and adult female glanced again at Sandy. Sandy could tell they weren't afraid but there wasn't any way the deer would come to her either. She resented the hell out of that. How can I get them to do *that*! The little one and the female climbed the bank, lingered, then the scrub closed around them, they were gone. The male was kicking up the bank already and was away too.

10

Durry sat on the front porch to watch the people come. His family, Gwen, Charlie, Perry and Sandy were in his kitchen pretending to be organized. Sandy mostly observed or was given small tasks. Durry didn't want to spend any more time in there with them under the circumstances. It was his birthday, unofficially, and a bit of narcissism overtook him, and he chose peace. A chair on the porch gave him some. He looked away from the road to the bushels of corn beside the barn near the grills Perry had assembled earlier. Five bushels Charlie was able to fit in her car, one in the front seat, three in the back and one in the trunk. I wonder if we'll eat all that Durry wondered. The night before he had gone to his brother's house to be near them all, especially his favorite, Sandy. She warmed his heart like no other while sweet Gwen and loud Perry decorated the background. That night, his true birthday, seemed better because it was exactly what he wanted. Today the taste was gone and it would seem more like work. He'd be surprised if anyone came. *And who's going to show em where to park?*

The first cars arrived and since no one else was outside he went to meet them. He didn't know what to expect with each person, didn't know any of them. He thought it was highly probable he would know some people just because, well it was inevitable he believed, but many he wouldn't. In a way it was nice because they didn't know him either so wouldn't jump out of the car to scream *HAPPY BIRTHDAY* at him. It was much less personal than it could have been and Durry was good with that. If too many people around knew him he'd have a difficult time enjoying himself. Being too self-conscious would have made impeded his stamina. Now instead he was directing strangers where to park or where to put the dish they brought. So far people were bringing too much food. If each car brings as much food as he'd already seen Gwen would not have had to pick up anything at all.

Parking turned out to be easy behind the barn, in the yard or along the road. Perry helped for a while until going back inside. Durry still didn't recognize anyone. He didn't do any of the inviting and had left it up to Gwen. He sure liked that it was all strangers. There wouldn't be a lot of unnecessary talk so he could relax among the crowd and enjoy himself. He already planned on eating too much then working it off playing volleyball. He hardly ever got to play so would put some time in. Sandy already approached him about the motorcycle. He'd not considered what Gwen might see if she were to come to the house without him like she did, especially bringing Sandy. They'd try to go for a ride at the right time. He wasn't sure anymore if there would be a right time, just planned on having fun at home without the burden of operating a vehicle. If one went out with him, they'd all wanna go out he knew. He didn't want that to happen. He laughed to himself while he guided a car in for a landing behind the barn. *Am I just not used to people around? Is this why I'm alone, because I don't care for intrusions? Am I not willing to inconvenience myself. Yes, just for those who have an impact on my life. The rest won't ever be as important.* In his head the matter was resolved. He took a baking dish from a woman who gave off a matronly air. He reflexively wanted to call her *mom.* But his mother wouldn't be at the party. He took the dish and helped the woman out of the car. She was a bit overweight, but in the same merry way as a baker or a cook in the kitchen of an elementary school. Durry took the dish to the table in the garage after directing his new mother to a seat in the shade. He had Sandy make sure she had something to drink. The serving table was filling up. Each dish separately might have had some appeal, not every one,

212

but all of them close together made a weird band of color. There were a couple times in the barn when he was all alone, a banana cream pie almost disappeared into his little refrigerator by the desk. The one who created it would ask questions he thought, and decided not to do it. He looked over at the motorcycle as if for support.

He had been watching the beer arrive too. Durry expected people to drink alcohol. It wasn't hard on him to be around it. He had gotten himself to where he felt pity for those who had to drink. He wasn't now rigid and pious either, just felt a little contempt for anyone who used it. If he was going to be full strength he wanted everyone else to be too. I don't want to go away from myself anymore he thought. It didn't really matter; people he loved did it all the time.

By three-thirty Gwen figured everyone who was going to come was already there. A new car would pull up sometimes. They'd keep coming, some going, most of the night. Perry had one grill fired, decided two was unnecessary. The flow of food was steady, never too much waiting. Perry sweated in the smothering heat but worked his station in earnest, as if his life depended on it. Guests were starting to relax into a rhythm. After being fed people played volleyball or sat in chairs they brought to laugh and talk. Kids were everywhere, boys running from imaginary enemies while the girls ordered each other around. Durry became an enduring volleyball player, after each game he kept going. Many others stayed on too, on both sides. He hadn't had this much fun at his own house before. Sandy was busy with Tera but she noticed her uncle once in a while. He looked over to see her standing off to the side of play, pretty sure he was having a better time than she was. He'd wave or smile at her, grab her shoulder. But Sandy wanted to be included. "You're too short, girl."

213

"Don't tell her that," one of the female players said. But Sandy knew he was only kidding. She did it to Durry a lot too.

"You'll get killed," he warned. The woman player tried not to look at him this time. Tera came up beside Sandy and they went off together. Durry was amazed someone in the world smiled at him like she did. It was only the last few years he and kids were able to relate at all.

Gwen and Darling kept each other company in the kitchen dipping potato chips in blue cheese salad dressing and drinking beer. Gwen didn't really feel she should stop running but did anyway, laughing incredibly loud sometimes as they told each other stories.

Perry was on a seat, smoking a cigarette, having a beer. There were a few servings of various kinds of meat away at the back of the grill. Perry looked out or talked to men who approached once in a while.

Durry wanted to get out of the game, eat a little more. He finished the last match then went over to watch the guys at bean bag toss. All of them were intensely focused and extremely drunk. Liquor seems to change the way a person perspires Durry decided, thicker. In the incredible heat he watched as clear jelly stuck to the faces of each wasted man. They'd argue ambitiously then voices rose up to a yell or a cheer when the beans flew true. Durry wasn't able to even locate the empty banana cream pie dish. He just wanted to have dessert while he watched the lunatics play. He ended up with a pile of something luscious looking, couldn't say what it was called, crust and chocolate custard, fresh berries. He ate watching the nuts continue their bag toss game. Perry knew a couple of them and sometimes would call out to antagonize. They'd answer back with a blend of light humor and submission. Perry realized they probably all thought he was a thief. It was his brother's house which made Perry kind of the king; he wasn't going to shrink no matter what.

214

His status as the cook also helped he thought. It was only his imagination because he heard nothing from those who came. I am either accepted or they don't care or they don't know Perry thought. Anyone else should have kept away if it bothered them.

Durry stood in the shade under the canopy he'd put up eating raspberries and blackberries and chocolate custard, watching the tossers. Perry growled at him once from where he was sitting after making more taunting remarks at the contest participants. Most everyone had eaten so Perry got to direct his interest toward innocent civilians. But mostly he drank quietly never too far from the grill. Gwen passed by a couple times on her route to the barn from the kitchen while Durry ate in the orange and yellow shade created by the fabric of the canopy.

"Happy birthday old brother," said Gwen as she walked under the canopy.

Durry smiled and nodded, ate a berry with his fork.

"Did you like it?"

"It was great. It's not over, lotta people still here. How many do you think came?"

"What, maybe a hundred?" Gwen paused. "Maybe we should've started later so it could go into the night."

"What is it, about six? People are still here, its starting to cool off." Durry looked around. "Yeah, its cooling off, just a little."

"I'm glad you like it. There's some people here I never would have dreamed would come!"

"Yeah."

"But that was supposed to be the fun of it. People could invite anybody."

"I had no idea what was comin, either." Durry laughed.

"Look at that guy with all those tattoos." Durry turned his head. "He seems very serious."

"Who is he?"

"The girl looks nice, though." Gwen examined her. "I don't know, part of what we were goin for."

"Is it *your* birthday?" the girl asked.

"Its mine," Durry replied. Gwen had that look women get when an unknown female has a perceived interest. She made this quick hopeful face that embarrassed Durry.

"Well, happy birthday."

"Thanks." Durry wondered why Gwen would react that way when the girl was with someone else. The girl looked back to the dark featured young man she was with. The guy must have been about thirty Durry supposed. The girl about the same. Durry inspected her profile and her butt.

"I'm goin now to clean *your* kitchen," said Gwen. Durry looked at her. "Perry seems happy, relaxing at your place." Gwen shook her head.

"Where's Sandy right now?" asked Durry.

"In the barn, giggling and running around sharp tools. If anything happens to her or Tera you're takin em. I'm lettin you know, you're takin em."

Durry snorted and smiled. "There's a first aid kit in the desk out there. We'll just tie it off and turn her loose again. Anything worse she won't tell you about."

Durry could also be annoying sometimes, Gwen thought. "Well if you hear a scream, I need to know."

"There won't be any screams." Durry was annoyed too at how much Gwen usually worried. He went toward the girl with the profile.

"Clever man," she said as Durry came up. She pointed, "This is Burt, and I'm Tamara."

Durry liked the name, Tamara, it shot a warm hole through him. Burt was maybe five feet eight inches tall. He was built solidly, handsome kid with close cropped dark hair. He was hard though, Durry could see, seen a lot no doubt. These days Burt was someone vicious who had been reclaimed. His eyes and the gray skin on his face under the

216

stubble told secrets. The cutoff sleeves of his mechanic's shirt revealed detailed tattoos of figures with horns and other devilish menagerie. He had a relaxed air about him though, almost in balance with the terrible side anyone could see. Durry thought he understood a bit more about the girl.

"How did you hear about this?" asked Durry. It was going to feel strange talking to Tamara near Burt.

"I don't know!" Tamara said then laughed. "We heard about it somehow." She was a little embarrassed by her witless answer. "I know, but somebody told somebody, you know?" She seemed to want to come across as authentic.

"Well, good." Durry smiled.

"We like it here," she said. Burt widened his eyes slightly to confirm. Durry didn't think Burt was going to be too vocal. His chick was alright though. She had on black shorts and a white tank top, brown leather sandals on her feet. She was a couple inches shorter than Burt and shaped much differently. Durry tried to enjoy her shape without Burt getting wind but then Durry figured that a guy like Burt knows all that shit already. Even more interesting to Durry was Tamara's shoulder length straight black hair. He noticed it wasn't dyed. If she were slightly more beautiful she would have resembled a dark heroine in some comic book. "You wanna talk about something interesting?" she asked.

Burt's expression didn't change. He acted like he was looking at something else. "Go ahead," said Durry.

"Well, is this your place? It seems like it would be someone else's." Burt turned to sit down in one of the many chairs under the canopy. Some of the bastards at bean toss yelled again before Durry could answer. Tamara made a surprised expression with her eyes.

"Yeah, this is my place. My family wanted to have a party for me and we decided here."

△

217

"They don't have to clean up that way!" After crossing a boundary Tamara turned more flirtatious. "Maybe...," she followed. Durry caught her eyes this time.

"You're probly right."

"Who are they?"

"Well, the woman who was standing with me before is my sister-in-law." Durry turned and pointed. "Her husband is the guy on the grill." After a second: "And my niece I'm told is in the barn possibly hurting herself."

"What if we go see er?"

"We can go."

"Can you leave for a minute?"

"Its my party."

Tamara smiled warmly. "We'll talk about more interesting things out here later."

"Okay."

"We're goin over there," Tamara said. She was speaking to Burt and pointing at the barn. He nodded gently back.

About three inches of spine in Durry's neck felt like it froze. "So Burt's on his own?"

"We're just friends. He's a good guy. We just do things together." She realized how that might have sounded. "Go out, see people, have fun." She looked ahead as she spoke. Durry saw she was contemplating the truth of her relationship with the man. He thought they may have been discovering it at the same time.

He opened the service door of the barn near the desk he kept inside. The two of them went in. Tamara had that extremely curious look as she turned everywhere to see. Durry watched her as she walked ahead of him. She touched certain things with her hands also being careful where she stepped. "What do you use this place for, just storage?"

"Not much more. The business has enough room. I park the truck in here, store the lawnmower, that's about it."

Tamara saw the motorcycle and walked right up to it. She leaned over and put a hand on each of the grips. Just then Durry imagined pushing her against the wall and tearing away her clothes with one rip. I'm almost there, he thought, and I'm gonna try and get you there... He folded his arms.

"Nice...." She looked at him with a big smile. "I like to ride." She looked around now. "Where's your niece?"

"I think I hear them upstairs." Durry motioned with his head. They started up the stairs to the loft, Tamara leading. The murmur of children's voices hit their ears about half way up, whispers reeling secrets back in. Durry watched Sandy's face as Tamara emerged in the room. She was a little startled and confused until she saw her uncle. By then her eyes widened and she couldn't wait to talk. "What're you doin up here?" she asked. She and Tera had been drawing on stored boxes with various markers and pens. Durry saw the two had been there a while.

"We came to see you, and Tera." Tera looked up then continued drawing. The pictures were humorous to Durry, he caught himself before a laugh. Little girls, he thought, everything so special. Now he had funny looking pictograms on boxes that contained his extra pots and plates. Free art. He realized too he was very comfortable beside Tamara. He really wanted to pull her next to him, rub his hand over her back, move his fingers onto her neck, into her hair.

"We're just drawing," Sandy responded. Tamara smiled.

"Sandy and Tera, this is Tamara," said Durry.

Sandy looked up at Tamara with eyes that had no mistrust. "Are you staying?" she asked and then returned to her drawing.

"We wanna stay," answered Tamara, beating Durry.

"Well, you can't draw," said Tera. "There are no more things to color with."

"We'll stay for a minute," said Durry.

"You don't wanna draw, Uncle Durry?"

219

"Its okay. We just thought we'd say hello, haven't seen you much today."

Sandy thought a moment. "Mom took your wine inside."

"She did?"

"She thought people would get into it."

"Okay."

"Tera and I wanted to try some, too."

"We just didn't know what you'd think."

"I think it would be alright if you try some. Just another day." Durry looked at Tamara who was smiling.

"You have wine in here?" she asked.

"Just one old case. I don't know why I have it."

"Sure you do," replied Tamara.

Durry shrugged.

"You've got women stashed all over this barn, might be good."

"Its just some dusty old case. I can't believe anyone even knew it was there."

"The world goes right to somethin like that, huh?"

"Hmm."

"I'll have to take a look," she said. There was no mistaking her interest in cocktails.

"Are you goin for a ride?" asked Sandy.

"I don't know, probly stay here for now," said Durry.

"I didn't know."

"Know what?"

"About the motorcycle. You never said anything. Is it new?"

"Kind of, about three years."

Sandy kept drawing. "We'll have to go on it." She smiled looking up from the floor.

"I don't know how yet but I think I'll be able to getcha on it."

"Today?"

"Probly not today. We'll need some time, so we can go for a ways."

"I'll bring a jacket, I think. Gonna be windy. You can let me borrow some sunglasses?"

"Yes, got plenty a gear... it'll be a fun time. How bout we see you both downstairs?" Sandy nodded slowly but never looked up. And to Durry, Tera seemed a very intense girl, unbalanced, probably capable of great ruin. It was not difficult liking her.

Durry went first down the stairs. Tamara followed behind without saying anything until the bottom.

"Give em some wine Uncle Durry."

Durry turned around and Tamara had a great big sarcastic grin. "You can get em lit then go on the bike."

"Yeah, *me*," Durry replied. "The little papers down here would love that." Durry thought a moment. "Probly though, if *I* wasn't drinking I'd only have the mother against me."

"Do you reckon?" Tamara said.

Durry looked at her pretty face, her slight frame, thought once again about ravaging it keeping her standing.

She kept laughing or making noises that sounded like laughing as she wandered toward the daylight outside. Passing the motorcycle stimulated Durry to take off. The feeling of being trapped had surfaced. It was a feeling that had been gone for a long time. Durry saw it as a survival tool against making a poor choice. It was reflexive, Tamara didn't seem like a bad choice, his stomach relaxed.

"Come on, I need to see what Burt's doing."

Durry slowly caught up, didn't want to leave the barn he discovered.

Burt was talking to Perry. They both had their legs stretched out on chairs, smoking. Perry had somehow been able to keep the grill hot all day. There were a couple wrin-

221

kled hot dogs and dry pieces of chicken still at the back but the temperature could handle anything new.

Tamara and Durry stood beside the reclining men. Burt was making his point about a guy he once knew who liked to cut himself. He said he was at work one day, looked up from a phone call and the guy was standing in front of his desk making shallow slits in his own forearms with a carpet knife. Burt was one of those people who never talked about how an experience made him feel, just what he saw. Durry was eager to know much more but didn't think Tamara would understand his curiosity.

"Guy just wants attention," said Perry.

"I don't know," Burt said quietly.

Durry knew getting attention was only part of it. What motivated the man was deeper. There are less disturbing ways of getting noticed. What made the man behave that way?

"I think that was his drug," said Tamara.

"He might have been on drugs," said Burt. "I'll bet he had to be!" Burt and Perry laughed together.

"Drugs are kind of the same thing," Tamara continued. "Doing drugs is a way of saying something. Its not like, 'Hey, look at me, I'm doing drugs.' Its like, 'Hey look at me, just *look* at me.'" Everyone was quiet. "I know its complicated. Most people who do that just want to let somebody in. Or somebody *back* in. Someone who has hurt them that they care about but who isn't helping them. Their feelings of loss are so great they start out numbing themselves and the chemicals released in the body from self-mutilation might be another kind of anesthetic."

Perry and Durry looked at Burt who was smiling inwardly. He knew the girl, she rubbed his head saying, "Well, I thought you'd wanna know!" She was clearly embarrassed about speaking her analysis, turning bright red.

222

Durry thought that his sexual desire had dissipated. The conversation had been just as fun. He wanted to know more about Burt. What else had he seen? But the painted skin was a big deterrent. If only Burt would volunteer. Durry decided he didn't want to trek inside on his own.

Tamara went flirting with Burt now. Perry just looked ahead to the yard and field beyond. The bag toss game players looked like they were deciding on more beer and a few kids tried playing volleyball. Durry watched as they tried serving like the adults but the ball would travel only a couple feet never approaching the net. For some reason he felt sorry for them. Maybe it was their weakness, no chance of a good game.

Tamara reached for him as he was sorting out the upside of childhood. "Durry has a nice bike," she said to Burt. Burt nodded slowly.

"What kind is it?" asked Tamara.

"Springer."

Perry looked over.

"You ride it a lot?" asked Burt.

"I try," replied Durry. Durry wanted an answer that'd for sure satisfy Burt.

"Work gets in the way, huh?"

"All the time, I think." Burt's life seemed miniaturized to Durry now. He wanted to tell Burt that sometimes work was another kind of high. He wanted to mention that he didn't have to hide in his work because he loved it. After a few good days at work it was unreal to consider endangering himself on two wheels when life lately had been alright. It was also difficult for him to remain under the speed limit. The road was only one more thing to be overtaken but the statewide increase in police took much of the sexiness out of any run. Durry was baffled by how often he was pulled over. It used to be every three years now sometimes it was twice a month. He fought every ticket, though, and used a lawyer to

223

help. Some violations he completely escaped with the tactic. But there was always another pending that he worried was going to stick. If he forgot to feed the parking meter they caught him. If he wasn't wearing his seat belt they caught him. If he ran his motorcycle without a permit they caught him. Durry held onto the teenage idea of only needing a standard license to ride and that the police were too hated and far between to be a problem. He innately didn't recognize their authority, no more lowly profession in the world. It was unimaginable to him to want to impede peoples' actions for a living. The difficulty for Durry was in knowing that it could be *you*. It was one thing saying something then doing the exact opposite in everyday life but constantly correcting people and charging them for it while knowing your own fallibility was to mock human nature. To Durry that's what most people found ridiculous about cops, the stupid little rules they enforce which they probably break all the time themselves, taxing others' mistakes. And there was always more debate about going even *further* with law enforcement by politicians. If it was a matter of helping someone being hurt most people would do it automatically, especially Durry. But it was the shrinking freedom by paperwork that nobody saw, leaders spreading blankets over deep holes.

Durry wondered if Burt would care to know that when he rode he usually did it alone. He went out by himself because he didn't like clubs or adhering to a schedule. He even hated planning trips with most friends because his day's routine and more importantly his mood changed often. Something too far ahead pushed the air from his chest.

Perry rose to throw a couple bean bags. The guys who had been playing were still gathered under the canopy talking too loudly to each other. One of them had renewed interest after seeing Perry.

Most of the people still there looked in no hurry. Durry was happy to have everyone and felt they could stay as late as they wanted. His home had never been so alive. He wanted to go riding with Burt. Bring the girl, don't bring the girl, they only needed another bike. The girl was cool but he seldom found anyone he was interested in riding with so this was an opportunity being missed. There was no way he would leave, even if Burt had ridden over but with almost four hours till sundown, the nicest part of the day, it would have been a great time. He then thought he would probably like to go on a short ride, it was his birthday, just for an hour. He didn't know why but he'd rather Burt take the girl. Durry reflected how strange that seemed in view of their connection. Just hated the feel of the weight added in back. So many things I've gotten comfortable with doing by myself Durry thought. He couldn't tell if that was bad or making progress.

"Let's go out for a while," said Durry.

"Where?" asked Tamara.

"Just a little drive, we'll throw on some ribs when we get back."

"All this food and I haven't really had anything," she said.

"Maybe there's nothing here that you want."

"There's something here I want."

It had been a long time since a compliment like that came his direction. "Anywhere, a breather, what do you think?"

"Sure, we can go for a little bit," said Tamara.

Tamara smiled at Durry while Burt slowly rose. "Jeep's over here," he said. Durry was glad their route took them in front of the barn rather than behind where Perry would see them. He wanted only to slip away because he was afraid people would start to leave if they realized he wasn't there.

"I'm drivin?" Burt asked. He was pulling keys from his pants pocket.

225

Tamara nodded. "Its my Jeep but when he drives I can just look around."

The Jeep was along the road so nobody else had to move their vehicle to let them out. Burt and Tamara swung into their front seat positions while Durry stood for a moment deciding what to do.

"Well, climb in," said Tamara.

Durry used the rear tire as a step to get into the back seat under the roll bar. The brown Jeep was wide open with no canvas or top. To Durry it felt like riding in the snug stern of a power boat.

With the motor running Burt said, "Which way?" Durry indicated for him to swing around and go east on Mule Barn.

Durry put his arms out sitting in the middle of the seat. Tamara turned around to look at him and saw he was enjoying himself. He watched her black hair flying forward over her face.

"Anywhere special?" she asked. She became preoccupied keeping the hair out of her face.

"Just keep goin. We'll drive a little bit then grab somethin if you want at the end. That alright?"

She nodded, snuck a hand behind her to squeeze his shin.

Sometimes Durry needed to feel he was leaving the planet momentarily. These two allowed that rare feeling. He hadn't met anyone as unique as them since his move down and he drank in their presence. He thought they probably didn't know the effect they were having which made him feel a little guilty but it wouldn't be for long then they could be without him if they wanted.

At fifty miles an hour the stagnant heat turned into hot wind. Being in the back Durry was in his own world and there were times when everybody felt comfortable not saying anything. It was great just driving ahead looking at scenery with people who also had no plans. Durry had an order of sights though, and would point a certain direction when he wanted them to see something or if he wanted to see something he thought they all would appreciate. Wind deflected off his sunglasses while he turned his head to look at the two in front of him he'd discovered or the bucolic view. He liked the woman in the front seat but couldn't really think of anything to talk about, especially over the wind. She didn't say a lot either. He thought the words might come pouring out of him if they were ever alone.

They stopped for a few minutes on a patch of gravel near an elevated part of the road. Durry often admired the way the land fell away from that point, rolling and rolling off to the horizon. He thought certain country roads were the ocean beaches of their realm. He missed big water a lot so his mind helped him experience it another way. Burt stood at the edge of the gravel looking out with his cigarette. Tamara went with Durry as he walked into the field. He looked back at Burt, his plentiful tattoos, wondering if there was anyplace other than a bar or machine shop that he might seem like he belonged.

Durry stared off, wondering how long the view was, next to Tamara. They didn't hold each other, his hands weren't ready, Burt also back there. It was just a warming experience. She didn't probe his history like women usually did.

There was relief back in town after the time afield. Durry just needed to be in motion for a while, like he said. There had been a lot of anticipation over the party and now all the unknown had factored out.

"What kinda meat you want, lady?" Durry asked inside the grocery.

"Are we hungry enough for that?" she said pointing to the package of ribs Durry was holding.

"Hopefully still plenty a people around. If we can't eat everything..."

"Who's cookin, you?"

227

"My brother, probly. I think he can get these goin right away. Sandy loves ribs too. Maybe she'll want some. And her buddy." Durry laughed.

"All right, get em." Tamara waved her arms. "Should we get anything else?"

"The thing is, don't know what's left. What about a bag a potatoes?"

"Yeah, get something to go with just in case. And there's gonna be some people left if we have too much."

Durry held some barbeque sauce then handed it to Tamara to carry. "I don't know what I have at home. It'll be extra, maybe, because I don't wanna come back."

"Where do you live?" he asked in the checkout lane.

"About an hour from here," she replied.

"How come I've never heard about you before?"

Tamara just looked at him.

"You a teacher or something?"

"I'm a counselor and manager for a non-profit."

The information didn't register with Durry. He heard it but didn't know what it meant. The name just made him think of Christmas time.

"You're a contractor or somethin somebody said?"

"I have a wood shop, do refinishing, things like that."

"Production, I like that."

Burt had stayed in the Jeep and his eyes were closed when they approached. "Wake up, man," Tamara said.

Burt did that quiet smile then stretched out his arms before turning the key. "Whuhjuh git?"

"We got ribs, you want some?" said Tamara.

"I'll eat some," Burt replied.

He didn't know the way back so Durry had to point out where to turn. There was still plenty of daylight left and that sweet smell in the air again that was a surprise every single evening. No human deserved to take a breath that seasoned, couldn't ever believe it was happening, and from something Durry couldn't see.

"You're back. We been waitin for you, Uncle Durry." "We didn't know if you were comin back. Mom thought you fell asleep somewhere."

Durry put the grocery bag down next to the grill. Perry not to be seen. Still a lot of light left at eight o'clock. "Just went out for a few more things. What're you guys doin? Where's Tera?"

"Mom, I think, has a cake for you. She wanted to wait till later because so many people singing. She thought it would better *later*. I told her it doesn't matter and you would like *everybody* to sing."

"Where is your mother?"

"In the kitchen with Tera and Tera's mom. They were thinking about making something to eat then remembered the cake." She paused. "Tera might have to go home."

"I'll go see your mom." Durry nodded. "We gotta lotta ribs, you want some?"

"I think dad's gonna cook em. Yeah, I'll eat em."

Burt found a seat again near the edge of the canopy with Tamara. Durry looked at her and she knew he had to go inside. "See you soon," he said. She waved gently. He wanted her to come with him but that would leave old Burt alone.

Sandy looked between Durry and Tamara. She decided to walk with Durry. All the faces he was seeking stood in his lit kitchen. Tera was sitting across from her dad at the table. Durry had met Dale and Darling earlier in the day and intended on visiting with each of them but didn't get around to it. Darling and Gwen had spent the day mostly as co-workers and were standing against the counter still in aprons not ready to give up the role. Perry stood closest to the threshold drinking a beer. Gwen had been talking but broke off.

"You're back! We thought you ditched us!"

"I don't know how you do it. I snuck outta here without anybody seeing... so how...?"

"We *saw* you... and we don't blame you!" She continued after some laughter from the others. "We thought that was it for you though. He's not comin back! We were just gettin ready to eat your cake and the piece of banana cream pie I saved for ya, leave the dishes in the sink and the door unlocked!"

Durry couldn't tell if Gwen had been drinking because he didn't remember her being so funny. He looked down at Sandy who had a perplexed smile. Durry put his hand on her shoulder then rubbed her head. "Let's eat some cake Uncle Durry." He looked down at her.

"I almost got away," Durry said to the crowd. He smiled warmly though just in case.

"But you're back, we're glad," Gwen said.

"Put some ribs out by the grill, wanted to eat some dinner then might have some cake. And you know, if the kids are ready they can eat some now. You can do whatever it is you need to then give em some."

So the song got sung and the kids had their cake while Durry worried what an isolated man he'd become or was becoming. All alone in his house every night after work. He didn't care to go out on his own for the evening anymore, only saw his family or people in some way related to his work day. Durry stopped worrying but that cold feeling of loneliness during the song scared him. He leaned against the door jamb working very hard on a smile they'd believe.

Charlie and her husband were outside sitting under the canopy together with a plate of three eaten ears of corn on the ground between them.

"Hi Durry." Ross stood up and walked to him. "Nice to see you, thanks for inviting us."

"Of course, Ross, always." He shook Ross' hand looking at him affirmatively. "Hi Charlie. I know you brought the corn. You're the only one who knows I'd rather have corn than birthday cake." Ross turned to see his wife. Durry had always liked quiet Charlie. Everyone else including himself was so much louder. Charlie smiled as she chewed, bringing her hand up to her mouth.

"Happy birthday," she said. "You're not tellin anyone how old you are, are you?"

"I don't care. You can tell people."

Charlie just looked at him. "We're gonna make some ribs, you want some?" Durry was mostly looking at Ross.

"Maybe, if you have extra," he said. Charlie rubbed her abdomen slowly like she might be full.

"I'll find you," Durry said. He began walking away.

When he saw Tamara she was seated apart from Burt on top of a table with her hands under her. The two voices calm. He couldn't tell by looking if the feeling had passed, if soon was going to be an exit line.

"Heard you inside," said Tamara. "Did you blush?"

"I wanted to fall through the floor, yeah."

Tamara didn't say anything.

"Still want some food?" Durry asked.

"Cook it," Tamara said. Burt nodded.

Durry hauled the grocery bags into the house to boil the meat. Perry watched but not too closely. Durry was back and forth outside to be with Tamara.

Perry finally did come out to see how Durry was doing on the grill. With Sandy usually under Durry's arm food preparation made highly attentive moments only sporadic. Perry sat with his beer among them. Sandy went over to Tamara, placed her hands gently on Tamara's knees and looked up at her. Tamara held Sandy's face for some reason.

Sandy ran to say good bye to Tera and Darling and Dale came over.

231

"Understand you're in the wood business," started Dale.

"Refinishing mostly. We're starting some cabinetry," replied Durry.

"I've been working in mills most of my life. That's why we came down here, another mill they want me to do somethin with."

"Thanks for comin, we're gettin ready to fill up again." Durry twisted toward the grill with his hands on his hips. He looked at Darling, she was sexy but in a bland way.

"Wish we had more time to talk," said Dale.

"Well, come by and sell me some wood sometime. We don't buy a lot but we may start. Got some bookshelves to build."

"We think we're going to start to mill more exotic stuff. Bring it in for cabinet guys and furniture makers. We think we're going to do it." Dale was ready to talk work for hours.

"Well, come by, I'd like to see whutcha have."

"Gotta go home, put her to bed or its child abuse." Dale smiled pointing with his thumb over his shoulder toward Tera.

"We'll pick it up next time."

"Happy birthday, Durry," said Darling.

"Thank you."

Dale and Darling turned going for Tera. Dale called her and all three set out for their car. Sandy came over and now stood near Tamara. "Where's the ribs, Uncle Durry? You've been sayin we're gonna get some. First you boil em, then you put em on the fire...I don't know why you ever wanna put em in water..."

"I smeared yours with extra dirt and grass."

After the food Sandy couldn't calm down. The new calories and Tamara's presence kept her excited. She later followed Perry inside, however, when he went to check on his wife, doing the clean-up Durry selfishly expected, prayed for. Gwen showed Perry the spot of burned hair on her arm, laughing. Sandy thought they both seemed stupid. She just kept asking if she could stay over at her uncle's house. But Gwen told her another time.

Burt had gone completely quiet for about two hours. Durry still wondered what a man like that thought about. He wondered what he was like when he thought he spotted an opportunity, the certain things which brought him out. Durry just knew that despite his temperament today Burt would travel obscenely past where Durry would disembark, especially around men who raised him, his need to advance in their eyes. Durry knew the emotion was there and could become disconnected. There was a way for people to go under, not realize they were without restraint, some kind of clear justification replaces any hold or forbearance. Others might sue each other at that point, might even forget the whole thing, find something else to do. But there are those who will cross and don't stop. There were all kinds of reasons why and Durry didn't care. It has to be a choice he reasoned. He used to think he would be the most perfect criminal, his makeup would have fully allowed it, even tried on a small scale when he was young. He didn't want to be a rotten man. The pretty face of a young man with only tragedy behind it. So he sat there judging Burt who was silent.

Durry did not know why he started hating the man. He thought he knew him, knew everything about him. He probably did. He also knew after a deeper conversation they would both want to kill each other. Poised exteriors had nothing to do with wanting to be liked. He was suspicious of anyone not reaching, without the will to go longer, faster. He needed to calm down, forget about being boss.

There were still a few people hanging around in the dark Durry didn't know. It pleased him though that they should be so happy at his place. They could stay all night.

233

Sandy, Perry and Gwen all came out. "We're going," said Gwen. Sandy was near her father. "Anything else you can think of?"

"I'm embarrassed at the help you already gave. You don't need to do another thing. I'll tear all this down and clean up on my own. You guys did great, thanks."

"Well, its all cleaned up inside. That's your birthday present. Just out here maybe tomorrow."

"Nope, I'll do it, okay?"

"Okay." Gwen looked around. "Still a few up and alive, look."

"Yeah, one on one drunken volleyball," said Tamara.

Perry laughed.

"Everything was great, the food was great. And Charlie brought my corn," said Durry.

"Charlie still here, mom?"

"Nope, got rid of em after the meal," said Durry.

"They stayed a long time, didn't they? I couldn't believe Ross wanted to stay that long. I was glad, though. Good for them to be out all night," Gwen said.

"Yeah, he marched to the car about a half hour ago with the food I gave em still in his hand. Charlie was tellin him he better wipe his hands or the steering wheel will get too slippery, come unscrewed or something. Over here we just looked at each other after hearin that." Durry paused. "It was good to see er tonight."

Gwen nodded.

"Sandy, you wanna sleep in the barn?"

"I can't. Mom says another time." She looked at Durry pouting.

"Durry, I just got her over the idea," said Gwen quietly. "You don't know..."

Durry began to laugh.

"I can leave er if you want," whispered Gwen.

"That's alright," said Durry laughing more.

234

"Huh, happy birthday, again," said Gwen. "We'll call you tomorrow."

"Thanks for cookin tonight, Per. It gave me the night to relax."

"I like grillin, you know that."

Durry nodded.

"Happy birthday, Uncle Durry."

"Thank you, sweetheart. Thanks for comin. I'll see you soon."

Tamara offered the Jeep to Burt, said she'd call him when she needed a ride. He rose, waking up. Durry knew well the feeling of being the odd man out. He sympathized with Burt who seemed like he was trying to make his way back after quite a while away. Lack of excitement is a great way to do that Durry knew. When you face all the quiet you can stand the mind gets eaten into making a person nuts or its best friend, some of both. Burt shook Durry's hand and gave Tamara a light hug. She handed him her keys. Durry feared any moment Tamara might fly away.

She miraculously stayed. Now Durry and Tamara went slow, taking all night. Durry thought it was the most exciting time he'd ever had with a woman. He wanted to control his feelings, though, because he didn't know her. But he knew himself. He got attached too easily. He hoped the experience wouldn't somehow instill emotion right off. He just wanted to enjoy having a woman in the house. It had been a long time. Her lightness was all he could feel or see.

He didn't sleep, didn't know if she did either. So hard resting nude, didn't know whether to keep on screwing. But he was hungry for breakfast. He decided to find food, hoping for something left over. He lifted the sheet to slide out, view Tamara's body. He was already in the bathroom when she said something. He looked in at her, she wasn't moving, so he trotted away undressed for grub. Being in the kitchen and

235

eating naked was regular for Durry, especially in summer. He told Gwen once the food just adds to the sensual feeling. She laughed, feeling much the same without admitting it.

Durry prolonged being in the kitchen but Tamara still didn't show. He was so used to waking up early it was difficult to lie flat while his mind began to run. He was sure he'd crash after she left. He almost wished she was already gone then return to him after he had a couple hour nap. Durry opened the front door for a look outside, wanted to feel the warm air on parts of his body that were usually covered. He had a nice stretch there in the already oven-like atmosphere. He loved the weather, grinning and massaging his sack before stepping back in.

Much later in the day after a nap and some work outside Durry sat on the front porch watching a black cat creeping around near the mailbox. Tamara had called for a ride about eleven that morning. Durry couldn't understand why she didn't want him to take her home. She replied that it might be unwise being seen with a strange man while her husband was away. It had happened to Durry before but never with someone he liked so much. Someone who seemed so free. He kept watching the black cat, envying it because it knew what it was hunting. Durry knew that he'd only want Tamara a couple more times then leave it.

11

Durry got more work done in the first two days of the week than he usually accomplished in five. The experience with Tamara was incredible and so overdue but now typical how it stood. Durry was never a cynic. It took years of interaction with the opposite sex to make him one. He even hated that aspect of him that kept expectations low, wouldn't let him act stupidly. That self-governing part of him decided he should be alone instead of combining with another in chaos. Trouble was everywhere and if they weren't in trouble they were too young, more trouble. It wasn't that Durry was jumping to conclusions or generalizing, he had early given himself the task of mining each kind of possibility. After the best kind of possibility slipped away from him and being unable to find it again the experiment started. He tried situations with married women, women with kids, ethnic women, lesbians, girls much younger, or some combination. After maybe a hundred results were that few exceeded an average football game. He sincerely wanted to do more research in the ethnic area though. That was the one difficult thing about his choice to leave Chicago. Dark skinned beauties hardly showed themselves in the countryside. They were in the city, generations of Americanized Italians, Spanish, island heritage, Eastern European, on and on, had produced to Durry some astonishing women who seemed to work better with family, had much less drug and alcohol use, not twisting themselves into tattooed beasts with surgical smiles and oddly hanging breasts.

Nevertheless, Durry went around energized at work like it was all new. While he was with Tamara it had seemed positive, so he got a glimpse, helping to keep him hopeful. It was time to expand the business into cabinet making. He had been bothered by the idea for years, preferring just restoration but the market was changing and it might be that he could make a name for himself ahead of others as a shop that could produce meticulously made goods with corresponding high margins. He never wanted to be purely production, usually choosing jobs and customers that were challenging, desiring him more than being anxious over cost. You can starve either way, Durry reckoned, why not do what you like?

Gwen came by Tuesday to do a little talking. Sandy was with her hair still wet from swimming. They were in Durry's office standing while he was sitting, giving him the feeling of being cornered.

"Uncle Durry, can I talk to Mike?"

"Yeah. You see im?"

"Yeah, over there," Sandy pointed. She went into the shop.

"Mike's here?" noted Gwen. Quality should be up around here at least for a couple weeks."

"The uncertainly gives me a thrill for some reason," Durry responded.

Gwen thought for a moment. "Did you like the party?"

"It was a great time. I can't believe you did it. It was a big thing to pull off. I'm still kind of amazed."

"Good. I hoped for something like that." Gwen was moved that he apparently liked it so much. "How bout the food? I couldn't believe what some people brought! Things I never thought of! That there are recipes out there like that! Yuck!"

"I guess I only saw what I wanted. Most of the stuff on the table looked good. I just didn't move fast enough to give it a try."

"I know, but one or two of those dishes I couldn't figure out. Anyway, it made me wonder."

Durry nodded.

"So what's goin on around here?" Durry was sure she would want to know about Tamara. "Mike's back, that's good...what are you doin for the Fourth of July?"

"I don't know, something without a lotta planning, sound good?"

"Yes. You come over. It'll just be us. I'll make something to eat and then you and Perry can do fireworks with Sandy."

"That'll be nice. It seems like there's something else going on that we were all supposed to do but I can't think of it."

"We already did it," said Gwen.

Durry could see Sandy standing near Mike who was looking at a drawing. It was a basic rendering for bookcases they had been asked to make. Durry smiled as the two talked, amused Sandy might find it interesting. He moved his eyes back to Gwen. *What a good woman* went through Durry's mind. "Yeah... we got along great but she seems to be with someone."

"That *guy*?"

"Nope, somebody else. I can't figure it out—don't know what she's doin." He leaned back, destabilized. "We didn't talk too long about it. Progress was really encouraging then it all reversed and I think I just blocked it out. At this second I'm one of those mice who can clean a trap without setting it off. But I always set the trigger lighter after that. If I see her again I'll be caught in all of it. She'll do the best she can to describe the reality of the situation and I'll just wanna be dead."

"Well, you're too nice for all that and I would just stay away. Its too bad but that's what you need to do."

"I knew you were gonna say that but when something's so nice and then cut off... it just woulda been nice, you know?"

239

Gwen could see his disappointment. "I know, sweetie, but you don't know what's goin on with her. She's pretty, I know, but she's got the one guy she's goes around with and now she has some other guy and then she's also with you. I mean, c'mon." Gwen straightened. Durry was just staring at her glassy eyed. "She's married, right? It sounds like she's married."

"Yep, says she's married. It was a bonus she told me right at the end."

"So you slept with her?"

"I had to," Durry said.

Gwen made a mildly disapproving face.

"It was incredible." He breathed a laugh though feeling a bit of a fiend.

"Yeah, adulterer.

"Not sure about my title here."

"Do you know anything about her husband?"

"I'm not sure, maybe an army guy." Durry shrugged.

"He's fightin for are country and you're with his wife."

"Like I said, I didn't know, especially since she was with the other guy too. I'd do it all over again because she was so open, reminded me when we were in school and the girls were all available and had no past or any *situation*. She really seemed like that. I knew it was too good to be true but I didn't feel anything negative at all coming from her. If she's in love with someone else I never would have been able to tell. There seemed to be nothin holdin er."

"What're you gonna do?"

"I don't know. Be nice to see her again but too complicated."

"I would just remember it as a great experience and leave it. If you run into her at the store sometime you two can reminisce about the best sex you ever had."

"It was too. How did you know?"

"A dog as thirsty as you…"

240

"Thanks."

"What's my daughter doin out there? I forgot all about her." Gwen raised herself using the arms of the chair but stayed seated.

"I don't know, she's out there with Mike. I'm sure they're enjoying having her out there. I haven't heard any talking."

"Well, gonna drop her off and go into work again."

"Nah, leave her. I'll bring er back. Be nice for me to have her nearby, help take my mind of this other crap."

"I'm gonna leave before you take back the offer."

"Let me say good bye," said Gwen. "I'm going to leave her... well, she doesn't have anything with her, only her pool stuff in her backpack. She'll be fine."

"She doesn't need anything. Lotsa stuff to do here."

"I was thinking a book or something—she's fine."

Sandy came into the office occasionally to see Durry. Because he was usually on the phone or concentrating on the computer she would just sit in the chair across looking at him, waiting for an opportunity when she might get a thought over. He tried to give as much attention as possible. Her presence did what alcohol did for him once and much more. His heart rate slowed, he could breathe.

"You gonna eat with us tonight?"

"You cookin?"

"No, less you wanna be sick. I'm sure what I make will make everybody sick." Sandy felt embarrassed.

"Nah, make somethin easy. You can just put cookies and candy on my plate if that's better."

"Okay, you get cookies and candy."

"How bout fish, can you cook fish?"

"What did I say? That's one I'd make you sick!"

Durry only smiled.

"Okay, I'll learn how to cook fish for you."

"We'll make it together sometime, alright?"

"Catch it and cook it and eat it?"

"I'll show you how. Do you like fish?"

"Some."

"You'll like the way I cook it." Durry suddenly thought of several things he needed to do.

"Thanks for havin me today Uncle Durry. I didn't wanna go home, nobody there, too lonely." She made her body quiver in the seat.

"Where's Tera?"

"Don't know, home I guess."

Durry glanced over his desk.

Sandy went back to the shop to build a model house out of wood scraps.

He ate dinner at his brother's house. Nice visit because he didn't care to be alone quite yet for the evening. When he got home he went into the back yard to fire off a few mortar shells from his fireworks haul. This year they were more powerful than anything he'd gotten in the past. The obese, video-game addicted man with the chin bolt had not been wrong. But selling fire to those with a love for it isn't hard, nice just once to have all the talk from somebody turn out to be true. He sat one of the tubes in the yard far back from the house and patio, lit the long water-proof fuse with the miniature butane torch. Durry went outside himself then to see the man alone in the dark except for a tiny hissing blue flame lighting fuses like a reproved fire bug. The hanging fuse was now burning in the tube. Just a few more seconds! It had to be one of life's strangest feelings Durry imagined to know someone intimately and then no possibility of future contact... Boom! There was hardly a trail to follow the projectile, faint orange sparks only for a short way up. He lost sight of it, couldn't tell how far up it had gone. Boom! A multi-colored kaleidoscope of light bounded across the sky in a spectacular circle above Durry and the house.

12

Family in rural Kentucky, any that were left, were spread out. Perry would have gone to visit his great uncle sooner but birthday parties, swimming and work forced it to the end of the month. He selfishly saw himself hiring a van and taking a trip alone to Appalachia. The mountains and disappearing sounded good to any man he was sure. It didn't resemble any kind of trip home because that had been so long ago to have all attachment or feeling cancelled. He thought it would only be a brief vacation with cherry-picking at a junk giveaway, not even justifying the cost of the van. He thought if he could come back with some tires or car parts, something to turn into money, he'd be lucky. Ahh, but the family would be coming he was afraid. There would be no bad behavior including flirting or drunkenness around firearms. Durry wouldn't be too much trouble but the wife and kid? he just didn't know what to expect. He didn't know if his uncle had any room, what condition the house was in or who else was around. That was the tired question, who else might be around? If there was going to be conflict it would arise because of people who were an irritation. It could be anyone, been a long damn time Perry reflected. But he wasn't afraid of home, of the mountains, like Durry who didn't ever care to have a thought about it. There were only trees rolling off toward Heaven from a deep crease in the surface of the earth, rock and people folded in, the base of the slant hard to escape. Perry watched the river as he drove. He had begun the dangerous habit of paying more attention to what interested him while he was driving instead of looking ahead. Each day he found himself swaying past the centerline or running over the noisy man-made cuts in the shoulder. Driving usually bored him. He urged himself to keep alert in between thoughts about what souls still dwelt in those long gone hills.

Allen had him installing sink and shower fixtures in some rich lady's house who was completing a remodel about thirty minutes north of home. It was easy work and since she had relocated down from the city with her husband the guy she normally had fix the plumbing refused to come because of the distance. Perry could tell she tried, might have even pleaded a little, having been used to the old bastard who was only probably cheap as hell. Wealthy people fell in love with kind, cheap contractors, might even offer a pop or bottle a water as a way to continue their generosity. Huge muskmelon sized tears if they had to change to somebody else who charged more or was supposedly not as nice. And Perry never stopped hearing about how *reasonable* they were or what they did *extra* that was included. When the bill came it was time for the final reminder. Perry wondered if people thought about how the man they hired lived. If they knew his own plumbing needed more repair than most of the customers he worked for.

Perry could not have cared less about another party or get together but it was the Fourth of July then soon Sandy's birthday. He only wanted to camp by the river till he had to go to Lied so his patience was all saved up. Go to work, home by the river, a big fire, meat from his favorite store cooking. He didn't think he wanted any fish, not from Smoke River. Pretty to look at but as much spilled in as out and over, the quality always had to be ignored by a person. He sat there by the water having affixed his fixtures, waiting for the right time to depart. Allen wouldn't be chasing so hard today because of the holiday. Susie would hit him on the two-way just to check up. He hoped no one was having an emergency ahead of a million guests who would be using the toilet. Holidays created deadlines and panic. He lit a

244

cigarette to symbolize, watched the low river, not nearly as wet now from the high heat, rain's refusal. He went back to the truck, thought of eating the extra burger from the two for two dollar deal, saw Susie had hit him on the radio.

"What?"

"What're you doing?" she asked.

"Floatin down the Ohio playin cards."

"Only because you didn't bring me am I gonna have to say somethin."

"I'll tell you the whole story which'll be jist as good."

"Allen just wanted to know how you're doin out there. He wants to bill it."

"Already gotta check."

"Oh, you did? He didn't know, I'll tell im." Silence. "You comin back in?"

Perry knew the only reason he'd be needed back was to drop off the money. "Thought I would deposit it but no banks are open. Ask him if I can bring it tomorrow."

"Yeah, jist go ahead, bring it tomorrow."

"No emergency calls today?" Perry wished he hadn't asked.

"Allen went on one, water heater. Said they could wait but he went out anyway. He said he had the guy's son help him carry it down."

"He doesn't need me to go out?"

"I think he's okay."

"I'll keep on the river then."

"You do that. Have a good Fourth and I'll talk to you tomorrow."

Perry had a bite of the burger, threw it back in the bag with the bite he spat out. He thought it was strange how the weather could not keep his food hot. He'd have another cigarette to hold his appetite. It was only three so he was deciding whether to show up early at home or go somewhere and have a beer. He assumed the mood he was in would lead

245

to more than one if he started drinking. He smoked against the truck in the semi-secluded spot he was parked. No hurry. I'll stop by the store and get some food, make Gwen happy. He knew she didn't really feel like a big deal either. Tonight I'll just make something everybody can eat. Gwen won't have to feel like she has to go back to work. He looked up, now thinking about his wife without clothes. After that came a realization his parents weren't dead. Nobody ever talked about their graves or which direction they might have traveled. As much gossip as people are capable of and no one has said anything. *I know they're not dead. I'm going to realize that down there, aren't I? Who even said they were? Durry. He made it up so he could handle it. He thought they were bastards who deserved death. If you leave people when they really need you then you're pretty much dead to them in time. It was just stupid memories as a reminder of what happened. Then no one even wants to remember and it gets shoved away to a place and closed off. That's where this thing is. I'm only gonna go to the mountains to pick up some trash. Oh, fuck.*

Perry walked up to the river, knelt down and put his palms in the water, moved them back and forth slowly. Stirring the quiet river, quiet as all he thought. His knees started to hurt so he rose, moved his wet hands together, flicked his fingers off his thumbs. He looked at the footprints in the soil on the path back to the truck.

They were about sold out of his favorite cuts of meat. Perry was maddened people bought all the meat. Why couldn't the store have bought more? He flipped through the packages that were draining red liquid looking for a piece that impressed him. He thought about asking the guy at the counter if he had anything. The man in the dirty white apron said there was nothing else, no unfrozen cuts of the kind Perry wanted. The hamburger meat looked stale and fatty. He didn't want ribs. All the good sirloin was sold out, only puny or ugly cuts. It was going to be pork tenderloin. He hadn't made that for some time on the grill. If he made it right his family would ask him why they didn't have it more often. He bought two packages, about four pounds each. They were almost giving it away at one dollar forty-nine per pound. He bought some seasonings he liked, beer, a carton of cigarettes, a huge can of peaches and three chocolate bars.

Durry was already on the porch when Perry got home at about a quarter till five. He had his sales book next to him on the small table by the chair. He was leaning back, might have been dozing but not after Perry pulled up. Sandy ran out of the house to meet her father, disappeared around the side to go by the garage. Durry reached under him into the brown sack for a pack of firecrackers. When he was kid he'd light one at a time, they were scarce. He lit whole packs now still unconvinced some wouldn't fly at him to explode.

Sandy soon came back around to see about all the noise. "Are you lighting firecrackers Uncle Durry?"

Durry just snickered. He had left work early and been on his brother's porch figuring out how much money was going to be left after paying the shop's expenses, resisting Sandy's desire for him to come and play. When she finally accepted he wasn't going to move, she left him alone. The math revealed enough money after all bills to pay expenses at the house for two and half months. He was hoping for consistency in that outcome, be easier to finance some kind of retirement that way, and each month so far had been about that except in the very beginning. He considered himself lucky in an area where people were always complaining about their meager livelihoods or lack of opportunity altogether. So after the rigorous counting he leaned back in Gwen's wicker chair, in the wonderful heat, listening to the leaves rattling and himself snore. He was only awake now because someone came up the drive. It was in him to take cat naps of only twenty or thirty minutes and be refreshed right after. Many

247

he knew said they couldn't rest for short periods, becoming tackled by sleep lasting for hours.

Durry reached under his seat for another pack of fire-crackers. Sandy was standing at the bottom of the stairs in front of him. She hadn't *run* over to him after hearing the noise but come after some time, unhurriedly, when her father had gone inside through the door opposite the garage. Kids came running immediately at such explosions that were presumably caused by the their misguided uncles. But Sandy was suddenly poised. Damn, Durry thought. He was almost heartbroken at the change. He didn't want her to be a young woman yet. He wanted that little kid to hang around, maybe indefinitely, so he wouldn't be the only one.

"Come up here," he said.

Sandy slowly came up the stairs. Durry peeled back the red paper around the firecrackers, flicked a lighter at the fuse then spasmodically chucked the lit bunch off the porch. Sandy covered her ears, blinking and they both turned their heads away. Duds or chunks of exploded firecrackers rico-cheted around them and they'd duck, yelling, almost wishing it was over. They both laughed and Sandy was that little kid again cheering the destruction and raucous.

"Do it again," Uncle Durry. That was the child he knew, encore after encore.

"What's your dad doin?"

"I don't know. Probly sleepin."

Durry smiled. That meant he would enjoy making noise even more. He peeled the paper off another pack and this time let Sandy light it. He found himself having to throw it side arm now and was afraid a couple might come unattach-ed from the bunch. He thought he heard some come loose and land on the steps before the explosion. Enough were still bouncing off the ceiling and the wall behind them satisfying the worry of a depleted show. Sandy just wanted to do it again.

Perry came out the front door holding a beer. He stood for a second spreading his rib cage in a stretch. Durry tossed another lit pack of firecrackers off the porch as a demonstration for his brother. Durry saw Perry had a wrinkled brown sack in his right hand. Perry continued down the porch steps, across the drive settling under the saw tooth leaves of the lone basswood tree. He sat down against the trunk to drink his beer and soon opened the worn paper sack. He laid a few bundles of bottle rockets on the ground to his left then lit a cigarette. Sandy went over to him. She examined the little rockets closely before Perry decided to take some of them from her hand. He lit a single rocket with his cigarette and not even standing up tossed it by the stick away to his right but the inertia of his throw didn't allow enough time for the propellant to ignite and the rocket came to the ground quietly fuse still burning. He screamed, "Look out!", and tackled Sandy in mock emergency. They heard the rocket make a strong hiss then the sharp *bang* in the grass a second later. Sandy scrambled to her feet to locate the fired rocket.

"It was close to us!" she said excitedly. She held up a purple stick one end splintered, showing the natural color of the wood. She rolled the stick between her fingers slowly, inspecting it.

Perry, now standing, held out another rocket lighting the green fuse again with his cigarette. He let the fuse burn down about half way or better then whipped the rocket upward by its tail. This time the propellant ignited at the height of the toss with the rocket still pointing up. The rocket shot up almost perfectly straight with a much fainter *pop* now that it was so far away. Durry sat on the porch steps watching, delighting in someone else doing the entertaining. He thought living alone did have the effect of making human interaction richer. He wondered how others kept their lives rich if they were *constantly* interacting but then quickly knew most could never get enough and couldn't take being by themselves. Relationships between parents and kids were fascinating because there was nowhere to go for anyone but back to each other. Durry's head swam while his niece and brother came to life in front of him as the only people on earth. Perry threw a pack of firecrackers into the brushy field behind the basswood tree. Sandy held, waiting for the *popping*, but her father covered her with his arms, twisting their bodies away, wanted to tease the girl by not letting her see; couldn't imagine something happening to her eyes.

With it being daylight each man was just firing off the cheap stuff, just went *pop*, bigger stuff waiting for closer to dark. Perry made a launcher from a long piece of flat wood. He leaned it on a log he got from the stack by the garage. He knew Sandy could safely execute a barrage from there without him worrying. She lit one after another in rhythm, like she was picking up twenty dollar bills spaced exactly the same distance apart on the sidewalk. Perry stood near the tree finishing a beer then used the empty bottle as another launcher. So now each of them were firing while Durry relaxed from the porch. He had nothing at all in his mind other than what he was watching. Sandy would urge him to come over and light one with her and he did but it was really the thrill she got that he wanted to see.

"I thought you were going to save those." Gwen stood on the porch watching them all, hair not all the way dry. Durry craned his neck to see his sister-in-law who was wearing shorts and an old t-shirt with no bra. Durry wondered if she knew he sitting below her.

"They're just doin some small stuff. Firecrackers and rockets," said Durry.

"What about for later? It won't be dark for a while."

"We got lots for later. We actually needed to get ridda summa the other stuff."

"Well, says he's cookin tonight so I'm off. Its been really nice." Gwen smiled out to the world.

250

"Whenever. You work today?"

"Yeah, for a minute. I just can't get it to come together in there. The more I try to make some things easier the more fighting I get. You know, from other people who work there. There's usually a clear way to do something but it seems like I'm the only one to see it. If I push it on em I'm accused of tryin to be the boss and *who do I think I am*? So, I don't know. I think I'm gonna have to talk with Bret. If he wants me to do all the things he says then I need less obstacles. God I sound like most of the people I hate. Maybe I should just stay home and make gift baskets with dried flowers and figs." She laughed at herself. Durry turned to see her sometimes up above.

"I could offer you a few things but I'm not workin anymore today."

"Yeah, I don't wanna talk about it either. I just don't want to be someone I don't like or I'll look for something else."

"I don't think you need to look for something else. The problems there seem fixable. Your thinking is right, just have to get the authority and trust."

"Mmm. I think you were workin there."

"Yep."

"Mom, look!" shouted Sandy.

"I see..." It was clear she didn't want her daughter too near the fireworks. "If she hurts herself out there... you two aren't comin inside again."

Durry didn't bother looking back. He smiled from there on the step. He knew there was some truth to her words. Girls, in some ways, are greater than women he thought. They love everything around them and aren't afraid to be ridiculous. They have less lust and usually receive none, except the desire to squeeze them till their backs crack.

"Are you still bouncin around back there? Why don't you go over and watch your daughter as she learns to be a pyro."

"You think I'm kidding... she better not..."

251

"*We're* watchin her. Nothing will happen. Perry can pour his beer on a wildfire if he has to."

"Yeah, can somebody get me another, too?" Perry called from across the drive.

"You want anything?" asked Gwen.

"I'll go in a little while. Got ice water right now, thanks."

"Listen, get him a beer wouldja, and I'm gonna finish upstairs. Try to feel him out about dinner. Is he gonna start soon or what? I'm tryin not to care. But I feel like somethin good just without all the stress. It was fun but I really don't wanna do it again right now."

"Alright. I'll see you later."

"Maybe. This is really nice for me. I might take another bath, actually open a magazine or take another nap."

"We'll wake you up in a couple hours one way or another."

"I'll be *comin* back down."

Durry followed her inside but made the left into the kitchen. He opened the fridge to find Perry another beer. The shelves had lots of tempting items including that slimy nacho cheese dip he could easily eat with only his hands. He removed a beer from the bottom shelf above the drawer where it looked like raw vegetables were stored. He could never bear opening that compartment because it was full of shame. A career of not eating vegetables, they just didn't taste good to him. He placed his water glass by the sink in favor of bottled water he found in the laundry room. He was going to open Perry's beer but saw it was a twist off cap. Perry could open it himself. Durry really just wanted to sit down at the breakfast table in the nicely semi-dark kitchen and ruminate next to his fresh water. Only when he took some extra time off did he relax enough to only want to sit and think. It was amazing to fall into a place sometimes where nothing bothered him and none expected anything. Instead he put his

252

bottle on the table and stood leaning on his arms just for some idea of what it might be like to have the privilege.

Durry returned to the porch and before delivering the beer set off another pack of firecrackers. He walked over to his brother and Sandy who was trying to figure out a way for the rockets to go farther and higher. Perry told her she could build whatever launch pad she thought would do that. He leaned back watching her with amusement from near the base of the tree. Getting the beer now took away most of his original interest. Durry lit one of the rockets and tossed it up by the stick. It ignited and hissed away traveling horizontally into a tree, many leaves falling. Sandy's excitement grew toward uncontrollable. To have her father and uncle with her supervising a derelict activity was a dream.

"Your wife wants to know when you're gonna start cookin."

"Yeah, soon. You see those tenderloins? Oughta be good. Been sittin here thinkin how I'm gonna do em."

"I can help."

"You are, just stay with her," Perry said as he was standing up. He was cleaning away grass he thought might be stuck to his backside. "Where is she?"

"Upstairs, probly. Had a nap but still bein lazy."

Perry nodded and started toward the house.

"There's more to launch Uncle Durry."

"Just keep em away from the house."

"We can put one in the ground. I found some ants we can blow up." Sandy stuck the tip of the rocket in an ant mound she'd seen. She didn't try to work it too far into the loose dirt. Durry laughed to himself seeing the girl act so purposefully to get it in place then with the long stick still pointing upward, the rocket upside down, their afternoon had degenerated into the pure love of ruin. Sandy lit the fuse of the inverted rocket, running away clumsily. The fuel burned trying to move the projectile forward, still a surprise when it

253

tilted. The report left a small crater and the ants had been blown away. Durry saw some stumbling around many feet from their old village.

Perry had astounded Gwen not by how well he cooked the meat but because other dishes got made to go along and were presented at the same time. The food ate as Perry wanted with the other three agreeing the meat was light as whipped butter. He decided to just cook one of the slabs he'd bought and freeze the other. He hated it when there was a lot leftover because he got bored eating it. He hated that he hated something he not long before relished. He preferred the friendship to last. It was at least difficult finding more new friends. The meal then had been eaten outside. Durry asked Gwen if he could save his plate for later so he could give them a show while they had theirs. With one statement from her he was chewing with all of them. Sandy was last to the porch because she began to take too seriously the trajectory of the rockets and was walking the property scouting new launch paths. Since her location had been difficult to keep track of she was able to get her mother to believe she had already washed her hands before sitting down. The lie was because she wanted to preserve the aroma of the black powder.

Durry and Perry began the show after the dishes were done, much too late Sandy was quick to let them know. Gwen watched the natural competition between the two from the porch steps with Sandy sometimes when she wasn't official fuse lighter. The fireworks were the biggest and loudest Gwen had ever witnessed except for commercial displays off high buildings or something. She couldn't believe what she was seeing in her own yard. Her early terror gave way to awe. Where had these men found what she was sure must be incredibly illegal? They assured here everything was legal and she should just stop worrying and look up. She did.

She finished almost three beers watching the brilliant colors flash after huge booms. It was the bass sounding explosions that jarred her. She felt as if she were in a war. But when she looked out, the people she loved were yelling laughter and having fun. It was loony to her. What happened to sparklers and smoke bombs? She decided she wasn't as advanced as she thought. She was the same person who had reservations about a lot of things that were dangerous. She knew she was somebody she could rely on. A huge boom and a crack and an expanding halo of glittering red light shown above her. She smiled and thought about asking Perry for a cigarette.

If there was a competition, Durry had won. Not only were his explosions bigger but his show lasted longer. Perry was sitting with Gwen for almost half of it. It gave Sandy the occasion she needed to become totally involved. Sometimes Gwen could have killed Durry for a close call or letting Sandy do something she seemed unsure of. Perry was so relaxed, though, and leaning back on the steps that she found her reassurance.

Perry told her he wanted to go to Kentucky on the 27th. He couldn't wait anymore and he'd go by himself if he had to. He thought it might be more of an adventure with everybody along but schedules made it hard to organize. He'd take Durry for an extra back if necessary. He apologized but said that was what he was going to do. Gwen was sure she'd be able to make it and Sandy's swimming would be over. They didn't think they'd need more than two days but decided to set aside three.

Sandy hadn't entered the house almost all day. She stood by her bedroom window at midnight listening to the distant pops coming from unseen back yards somewhere out there. She wasn't pleased that others were still celebrating after she'd run out of stock. It had been a really great night anyway, the noise and smoke; she brought her hand up to sniff her fingers. Under one thin sheet she looked at the ceiling,

255

heard the faint pops, wondering why her uncle never stayed the night. *He always went home. Mom offered but every time he went. Said he liked to sleep in his own bed. But most relatives stay over. Everyone stays over. Uncle Durry never does. He likes to drive home in the dark listening to music. There's no one at his house so why doesn't he just stay here?* She was glad the air conditioning was on because she wouldn't be able to sleep. *Dad would leave the windows open if mom didn't make him turn on the air.* She told him not to get cheap on her or make her suffer and he said he wanted to smell the outside air and hear the sounds outside at night. *I don't believe I can sleep while others have so much goin on out there.*

13

Durry had written on a piece of grocery sack:

Stray dogs in the middle of the road. Mist halfway up every vine covered hill. Coal visible in the sliced hillsides as you drive. Lied is tucked into the clutch of the mountains like an armpit. The slope makes all the buildings group together in the crease. Everywhere people are huddled in doorways, looking, quiet. A place more like a box trap placed in the path of an animal. A huge gate across the one road into town from the north. Flood gate they say.

More on the back, written faster, difficult to read:

Nothing in the streets of Lied any day. Usually no people. Sometimes a person looking out from under an awning, still.

The hills prison walls for those who stay.

"Burning House Path"

A country covered in broad leaf vines and rope bridges. Coal oozing from hilltops. Hardcore hillbilly. Always mist at higher elevations.

Mad the war didn't go their way. 4WD climbing machines covered with mud at every gas station. Plane rides $22 per person. Min. 2 people. The land sliced open and people living in the cut.

Discount stores every mile and a half. Heavy, uneducated accents. Still something holding you against your will in that cut, a magnetism, to make everything the same as it. Like being digested.

Rusted red brick buildings at the center of a shack village.

Orange clay blood where there are no trees.

Unwanted dogs, almost hit a little one.

Police chopping down everything out of place, especially Yankees.

A lot of grandfathered exhaust systems.

10,000 churches.

Gwen liked her job but began to think she just hated working. After a lot of the learning was done the routine felt too predictable. The level of tension that went along with her assumed responsibilities bothered her to where she had images of trying to kick open the door of a cage she was inside. By ten o'clock in the morning adrenaline filled in the disgust. That was the part she liked, really, keeping up the high level of energy. But to cross from who she wanted to be to what work needed was getting harder. She decided to talk with Bret about her role. If she was to continue to have so much responsibility she wanted them both to be clear on her specific duties. Right now she was serving as an unrecognized supervisor. She either wanted the full role with everyone knowing or a plain job that was much less demanding. She wasn't going to ask for the time off she wanted at the same time but decided she could afford to be bold. She had an idea that Dale's lumber company might hire her if there wasn't a way to be happy where she was.

Gwen shopped through the big lie that was lunch. No one ate *lunch* anymore but did errands instead. After buying birthday presents for Sandy she phoned Darling to be sure everything was okay. It was Sandy's tenth and the idea to have a party at Tera's house seemed fine. The girls could be together for a while since swimming was about over. Gwen actually remembered the coming Saturday was it. She loved the program but her schedule would calm down when it was through.

It was a girls' afternoon. Everybody else was a at work. It was only going to be a couple hours the women imagined. Sandy of course wanted everything chocolate. Her cake was as rich as Gwen could find. She didn't feel as bad as she thought she would buying one instead of making it herself. Gwen only wished her hands had a part in the creation.

She watched her daughter across table eat cake next to Tera. The two girls didn't need their mothers in the room. They might have even forgotten they were there. Two half grown girls exchanging ideas, easily relenting to each other's worlds. Gwen's pride swelled and she believed she didn't have to worry so much anymore. She ate her cake and talked to Darling about life at work. She never mentioned anything about a job at the company Dale worked for.

When Sandy and Tera appeared again after being absent from the room for a while Gwen told Darling how nice it was to see her. The women liked their time together, Gwen felt much better. She rose from her chair as Sandy talked to Tera about seeing her Saturday. Its so much easier getting her ready to leave since she's older Gwen thought. She's as agreeable as anybody. In the car Sandy asked when she was going to see her uncle and Gwen said he's probably at the house already.

Gwen could choose for herself what position she wanted at work. Bret also said she could have whatever days she needed for her trip. He's great at that, letting me decide everything, she thought. That's what I do every day. How does he do it, get me to do everything? He must need me and trust me. It was worth the meeting with him just to realize that. But I can't let him arbitrarily put it all on me. I told him we wouldn't make any changes till I got back and made up my mind. What she really wanted was something else. She already knew the offer she'd make. He would probably go along and she could let herself out of the box she unknowingly let him keep her in. She couldn't leave the job so decided to accept it, maybe make it better. *I used to have so much more patience.*

The dark colored van Perry rented made it seem like they were all off to the robbery. He said he still didn't understand why everybody wanted to go but he wasn't going to fight it as long as they stayed with the schedule. Gwen didn't care, really, about junk that needed to be cleared out. She wanted to be away with her family and Perry did too which is why he didn't get really stubborn and go ahead by himself. Also, with Durry along, it seemed like a real vacation.

"And down there we're pickin up furniture, mom?"

"I guess, Sandy, we'll find out."

"Jesus, shit! That's my stuff, and Durry's. I don't want anybody bein greedy an tearin into everything. Let's see who's down there and what we can do. I'm sure there's gonna be some work to do before anybody lets anything go. They haven't seen us for years but its not gonna be free. There's gonna be somethin we have to do. And that's okay. I don't mind some sorta payment. If its all garbage we'll wind it up quick and take off."

Durry looked at his brother with a laugh.

260

After going over the river from Madison they spoke in shorter sentences. The heat and sun sharpened the scenery, making it sparkle, too defined to behold. Gwen had to remind herself certain things were real. It was a whole culture that existed in hilly communities between the larger cities. Around some green and gold bend would be a large open air produce market. It seemed to those in the van that the region itself had turned out. It was where they met to talk with other human beings before going away again around some other steep turn toward the sky or down into the earth. Space would suddenly open up again to fields with prickly, crooked trees hurt by the wind.

Perry finally got on the highway in Frankfort to get to the southern part of the state. By noon they were going east on the Daniel Boone Parkway.

"What's the name of it?" asked Durry.

"Lied," answered Perry.

"Lied...not yet, we'll take the exit in about sixty miles. Let's eat, anyway."

"Yeah, let's eat," agreed Sandy.

"Lied, Kentucky," mumbled Gwen.

"Can we eat, mom?"

"Well, its very beautiful down here," said Gwen, nodding to her daughter.

"Yeah, I had no idea," said Durry.

"So are we stopping?" Perry asked.

"Anytime, Perry. I need a bathroom and let's get a snack or somethin," Gwen said.

"Be somethin comin up here soon," offered Durry.

"Well, keep a look out where you wanna pull in," said Perry.

Sandy drank a cold Coke through a straw sitting at a picnic table outside a fast food restaurant. She picked at a chicken sandwich claimed to be made in the same tradition as *your momma.*

261

"Can't forget the color of the water up north," Gwen said. "It was mint green."

"A lot different than our mud, huh?" said Durry.

Perry was thinking about something else.

"How far down now?" asked Gwen looking at him.

"Ask Durry, he's handlin that."

"South on this road into the mountains," Durry pointed.

"That sounds amazing to me," said Sandy smiling as she reached for her cup.

"Probly bout two hours."

The road they followed offered other worldly sights that Sandy couldn't believe. The mist or clouds in the mountains, she couldn't figure out which, made it into a dream. The pavement seemed to slope down so much sometimes she thought they were just going to slide away. Durry said to watch the turns because the moisture on the surface. At what seemed like the top they drove through a low hanging cloud and drizzle.

Lied was a blanket stain village backed against the Jefferson National Forest of West Virginia. The most outstanding structure they had seen was a franchise gas station. Its shiny plastic signs letting everyone know money was still around.

Durry told Perry to take the road south from the gas station along the mountain slope, where to the right was a wide rushing stream. Durry watched the water as they drove. It was clear and not the color of dragon skin Sandy saw earlier. But the water's sure moving fast Durry observed. He had to pay close attention to figure out which direction it was flowing, which maddened him. Reminded him of wheels spinning, after a certain speed they appear to turn the opposite way. He still couldn't be sure so turned his head feeling stupid.

The property wasn't as Perry remembered. He wasn't sure now if he had any memory of it at all. They crossed a small wood bridge over the water. It was the first time Sandy

262

had a view of it from her window. "What's this man's name, mom?"

"He is your father's great uncle. Uncle Bless." Gwen warmed after she spoke it. What a man he must be to live back here. His name, the land, she had no idea what to expect.

They followed the clay drive two or three hundred yards till they saw a large white box house. Getting closer, also two large outbuildings, mostly gray wood, some slats flaking white. Gwen stood taking in the house. Perry parked as close as he could in front. He thought that one outbuilding could be used as a deep garage if the sagging frame got some attention.

Uncle Bless' hair was the same color as the high mist that day. He stood on the stoop to give a wave. There was no portico which Durry always thought looked unfinished.

"C'min side now woan chuh?"

Perry started walking ahead. He'd determined he had no recollection of the property or the people. Time made him believe he was obliged to uphold a connection with everyone. Usually turned out actual events were different than how they were remembered. Twenty five years was enough time for his mind to be subjugated by nostalgia.

"Perry?" said the old man.

"Yes, that's me. How are you?" Perry went up and shook the man's hand, put a hand on his shoulder. "My brother, Durry. And my wife Gwen... and Sandy."

Durry shook Uncle Bless' hand. Gwen and Sandy came after with their niceties.

"We'll walk around out here later. Show you everything." He was motioning with his arms for them to come in. "That your van?"

"Yeah, for the weekend," replied Perry.

"Looks comfortable," said Bless. He held the door for everyone, they made their way into the darkened rooms.

263

The house was just a big box with choppy flowing rooms. Gwen would have called it lived in. It wasn't as unkempt as she feared. But an older man living alone wasn't expected to make them all envy his housekeeping. Gwen and Durry did as much exploring as good manners allowed, mostly just what came into view. Pill bottles in a group to the left of the kitchen sink. Gwen watched for the fold up table, seeing it. He had it set up in the aisle before the dining table in the back of the kitchen. There was a set of clear glass shakers keeping an ashtray company, also papers in uneven stacks, burn holes in the vinyl top in front of the most popular seat. Across from the chair sat a tiny television on the counter. There was a radio built in. He sat with his friend during meals Gwen thought. The large dining table was hardly enjoyable alone. How old is he she wondered?

"Come inside, Perry. Come inside. You've made it all this way. Its nice everyone came." Bless' words weren't as thick with the sound of the hills as imagined. It was still there, comfortable speaking, but not uneducated gibberish. It was clear he didn't quite know what to do with everybody. "You wanna sit?"

"Sure," said Gwen. They found themselves in a living room in back of the house. Sandy was looking about intently but thought she shouldn't touch anything. Gwen watched her behave very well without having to be told a thing. Gwen looked at Durry as they were sitting. The upholstery was so vulgar and dated Gwen was afraid it was going to hurt against her. The furnishings so far were mostly shabby but the house was wearable like one of Perry's holy undershirts that Gwen had to sneak to throw away. Poor taste is a malady nothing to do with income she thought.

Durry studied the old man. Plain looking but walked erect. Durry believed he was still active, working the place, enjoyed labor. His eyes awfully wrinkled but he still had all of his hair though it was a crew cut. When he stood he was

264

about as tall as Durry at five foot ten, a little less from shrinkage. At eighty, his slim frame was more than just a rack for hanging clothes on.

"Its nice to see yawl. Not many left down here. If you didn't come I'd be afraid a dyin without anybody havin benefit a things I saved. Not very interestin maybe, and I guess the stuff is mostly mine, your father didn't have a lot. Your grandfather rescued most of it when him and your mother left. So there's your father and mother's leave behinds, I got some and your grandfather wanted you to have summa what he had. I don't know how you feel today but its all out there when you wanna go look. And you don't have to take it all, or any of it I guess, wanted you to have first pick anyway. Your grandfather thought the same way. He's been gone about ten years now, wife long before. Seems men in this family live longer than the women. I always thought it was supposed to go the other way. No matter what somebody goes on alone."

Sandy could have listened to him talk the rest of the day. He was so steady and sure. She loved him after just meeting him.

"You wanna apple? I have lotsa nice apples," Bless said to Sandy.

"I'll have an apple." Sandy looked at everyone.

While Bless was absent the adults had nothing important to say. He already spoke of the reason for their trip, so they were at ease. He returned with a green apple in slices on a plate. He handed the plate to Sandy and sat down.

"I got beer for you, Perry, but I forgot to ask. I'll go git it in a minute."

Perry gently shook his head. "How long have you had the place to yourself?"

"Three years. Lotta house to run, lots to do. Work sends me some help sometimes on big things and I can get your cousin Sim out."

"You workin?" asked Perry.

"I remember Sim," Durry interrupted.

Bless looked at Durry and nodded. "Not workin anymore, but they don't forget about me. I like to go over when I'm feelin up to it. See how they're doin it without me."

"Where did you work?" Gwen asked.

"Mine supply in Pikeville, was manager for thirty years. They finally made me quit but then gave me an office where I could do all the orderin." He smiled. "Suppliers wouldn't work with anybody else, were used to me for so long. I don't think anybody really wanted to get ridda me anyway. I was always a steady parta the place." The lines around his eyes more raised and deeper.

"Who comes out, Uncle Bless?"

Bless looked at the young girl. "Not a lotta traffic anymore, darlin."

"You got animals anywhere?"

"Everything is wild around here, now. Had chickens, dogs, cats and one cow. Since muh wife died, she loved animals more than me, I got ridda the animals for eatin and the dogs died." He thought for a second. "Those dogs both died inside a week. Found em each in different ditches. Couldn't tell how they were killed. Thought they musta been killed by *somethin* strange cuz they wouldn't wanna ditch to die in I don't think. Funny. Guess I did like those dogs more than I thought." He winced as he looked at Sandy.

Sandy was disappointed the animals were gone. After three apple slices she quit.

"Hard to keep animals out here sweetheart. Too many bigger ones wanna take em. We got too many fox and wild dogs. We even got bears sometimes come on the property. You'll like it, though. I'll show you everything, you'll finda lotta animals, bet on it." He winked.

Sandy suddenly thought about eating another slice of apple.

266

"Why don't you see your rooms? Had only one ready but there's another we can make ready. I don't know how you wanna do it. Will two rooms be enough?"

"We'll be fine in two rooms," said Gwen.

"All got twin beds. Never wanted anybody to get elbowed in their sleep."

The rooms were four white walls with two beds each. Sandy almost feinted from joy when her request to bunk with Durry was approved. Gwen looked at Durry with a *good luck* expression.

Bless had them in the living room some more, pointed out other things he thought would make them comfortable. He apologized if the condition of the house wasn't what they were used to. Everyone shrugged, took a sip of beer or whatever, eventually got a trip to the sagging building

Gwen cooked dinner in the old man's kitchen. She went for the stove because she didn't like using a strange oven. Perry and Durry found a grocery somewhere. She told them just potatoes and hamburger meat and something for morning. Perry got eggs and bacon and more apples for breakfast.

When they were out the men discussed the size of the van. "Its not close to big enough. Unless we only haul a few things. And I feel kinda like a thief taken this stuff at all. We don't know im. He's a nice old guy," Perry finished.

"I feel kinda the same. Try not to look too greedy. We coulda shown up in a box truck." Durry laughed. "He does seem like a nice man. Bein down here by himself, though… you gotta learn to like it or go crazy. Crazy can help when its against your will."

"He seems alright. Bet he's got some stories."

"Sim, you remember him?"

"He was Aunt Trissa's kid. You played with him more than I did. Whenever I said somthin he could always catch me. I never thought he'd be able to because I was older."

267

"It never seemed like he was mad but he'd come after you!" Durry laughed even harder now. He knew Perry had worked long to transform himself from a jackass. "There was the other boy too, but he was older. I remember you tried bein friends with im but he didn't want to."

"God, I forgot about all this! Guess they're all comin to life, fillin with air. They all been sleepin in my head."

The hills towered above to a white sky. Perry got to see the stream on his side of van.

Sandy shuffled through the wet leaves with Bless as they saw some of the property.

"How much is there?"

"Bout sixty acres. Used to have four hundred."

"Why didn't you keep it?"

"Don't know why."

"Did you have kids?"

"My wife couldn't have kids."

"Oh."

"We thought about adopting but I don't think I woulda felt the same when it was somebody else's."

"I could."

Bless just smiled.

"I'm not used to goin up and down so many hills. I don't mind. Its just unusual. And there's so many huge rocks in the woods. We don't have that either."

"Mm-hmm. Cave up here too. Can only get in on your belly."

"A cave?" Sandy wanted to go in but when she saw the small entrance imagined something else already occupied it.

"That's just one entrance, very small. There's more round back here."

"You ever been inside?"

"One time. Its not a big cave but its spread out all around. Not much good in tight places."

268

"You mean you're claustrophobic?"

"That and small places…"

Sandy shook her head. She had never seen so many slender gray trees. With the overcast sky and dark floor they appeared as skinny omens. She wanted to live among them. "If we keep going?"

"Mountains. You'll go into the western mountains."

"You bin?"

"I walked as far as I could in a day when muh wife died. That was in the snow. Other times we were huntin.

Sandy tried to notice if Bless was getting tired. "Can we keep going?"

They came upon a slat shack before a clearing. For the first time Sandy could see the how close the mountains were. They went inside and sat down on log stumps in front of a stone fireplace. The musty smell, sight of scorched rock around the firebox penetrated her senses. *This is far away.* She had finally gone someplace. It was a feeling of harmony, loose from the earth. The fireplace almost spoke it had witnessed so many scenes. And the upturned logs were polished slippery by people she wished she could see.

"We used to cool our drinks in the stream behind. Stay down here all day shootin, have our lunch inside." He made an expression like *right here.*

Sandy couldn't get over the fireplace. Huge roundish rocks streaked black so violently. The fire had to be in the *room.*

Girl saw the hole in the skinny trees. She doan know I like to lie there by it sometimes and looks at the sky jist for the feel.

Bless suggested that in the morning they should start going through all the things in storage. He'd also held a few items that he wanted to keep in the house. Two Fordney

269

Pennsylvania rifles he brought out that night were part of it. He handed them over like he was passing the salt. Perry and Durry could hardly speak, eyes stayed wide. "Now these are yours. I wancha to take em." For another hour he brought out more guns and semi-valuable things he said he didn't want. *Take with him.* Once he began he couldn't stop. He was liquidating. He wanted everything out of his possession. It struck them how lonely he must be and that he just wanted to move on, start again much farther away. It wouldn't have been smart to put the things in the van so the stuff stayed in the open all night downstairs.

Sandy wanted to slide into bed with her uncle in the morning but he wouldn't let her. So that's what Gwen meant. He'd already woken not knowing where he was or who else was in the room. Sandy was now nestled between him and the wall. He didn't have enough fight that early. He thought the bed on wheels might role away. He lay on his back with her forehead by his right shoulder. Gwen looked in at almost eight. The creaking door stirred Durry. "That's what she does," she whispered. Durry waved.

Gwen had moved the card table to the stationary panel of the sliding door. Her first customer was Bless who'd risen by six. He wore deep gray trousers with a standard white under-shirt. She wondered what he'd been doing. She saw the paper was unfolded on the dining table. He ate his eggs there as well. "Already been out. Went to where Sandy and I were yesterday. Took the lock off the door for those boys. Perry's been out there an hour."

"You know you seem alright to me." Gwen saw his bushy white eyebrows raise.

"Been okay. I jist wanna be thinkin clear when I'm doin this. And be sure its how I want it." He held his fork. "Other people more greedy than him, spoil it, doan wanna leave that

270

behind. Seen that, not the peoples' fault either. Shouldn't a been left so there'd be fussin."

His wife must have not wanted him to possibly ruin a shirt ahead of the day thought Gwen, seeing the scar on his neck. In the light from the window he was a humble man, the point of his crew cut aimed at his plate. They smiled together kidding about the greedy one in the garage already.

The sun was trying to come out, steamy by then anyway. When Durry got to the shed Perry was in front leaning against some oak drawers smoking a cigarette.

"Too much out here." Perry shook his head. "Some stuff is nice, other stuff I think is just old, smelly."

The two were quiet. "What have you found?" Durry didn't want to rummage through junk.

"Well, there's some good things. I found a couple work benches, there's tools. He's got some nice wood furniture out here, Gwen might like it." He hit his cigarette. "How do *you* think we oughta do this?"

"Well, if we can get the guns back, summa the tools, the wedding gifts he was bringin out, come back down for the bigger stuff." Perry looked around the space. "I have a truck we can use, he's already made it worthwhile, we're not set up for anything but small stuff."

Perry nodded, crushed his cigarette on the floor. "Weird gettin it handed to you, huh?"

"How bad you want the guns?" asked Durry.

"Don't care, just lemme see em sometimes."

"And the tools?"

"*Like* the tools," Perry replied grinning. "You got everything at the shop you need." He wanted to toy with Durry.

"I don't care, either, maybe we can decide about the work benches?"

"I don't have any room, we'll see, maybe." Perry looked around again. "So come back, huh?"

271

"Yeah, how else we gonna do it? We gotta take summa this, don't you think?"

Perry nodded. "We'll be sellin some of it."

Durry was already thinking about fixing up some of the more desirable furniture for sale at his shop. He'd ask if they would want to split the money.

"You and me come down, soon, spend the weekend, load the truck. That's less for him to worry about. Have a few beers together," said Perry.

"So let's tag what we want. Get the girls out here, git what they want, come back again and load it."

Bless watched as they went through the contents of the shed. He never put on a regular shirt. He didn't do much directing, pointed something out, gave an explanation or a history. It made him happy they were interested. He talked to Sandy mostly, about items she brought out. They told him their plan, about coming back. He said he really wanted to be done and they should rent a truck locally, he'd pay. He told them they were welcome to return anytime but he was soon going to donate whatever they didn't want. He'd put himself on a schedule, didn't mean to be difficult. Once it was taken care of he'd feel better. The brothers went to Pikeville, hired a bigger truck, came back. It was a sunny day so driving in the mountains was an unexpected benefit. The family hauled out and loaded the things they decided on. Gwen had the same vision as Durry with regard to some of the furniture. No one cared who got what only that each got what made them happy. They laughed about where to put it all anyway.

They locked the truck and thought about what to do before dinner. Bless was elated because they made the effort. He wasn't disappointed they didn't want everything.

Gwen took the van to find the grocery store. She wanted to go alone, wanted Sandy to spend time with *him*. It was an opportunity for her to know someone like a grandfather. Gwen's father was gone before Sandy was born and her

272

mother who was another state south didn't drive. *If I could I'd leave the girl with him for a week or two...*

"Let's take the guns out," he said. Bless, Durry, Perry, Sandy marched in a line to the back shed. "Clays already out there, gotta use em up."

The group ambled around by the shack until confidence set an order. Durry would be the first up and Bless was going to throw. The bird was little more than a dust cloud as it was hit. The crowd took a step back, Sandy was inspired. "Are you gonna let me do that?" she asked.

"Course we are," answered Bless. The other men glanced at each other.

Bless threw another and on this shot the bird merely split in half.

"Go ten," said Bless and threw another. Sandy watched with her arms folded. She didn't think there was any way she could hit one of those targets in the air.

After his turn Durry handed the gun to Perry who looked at it slowly before reaching into his pocket for shells. Both shotguns were modern Remington auto-loaders, standard skeet weapons. Durry knew, he snuck away for a round whenever he could, used a twelve gauge Beretta. Perry looked like someone handed him an oboe. Bless stepped over to show him the how to operate the gun and to point at the target not aim. Loading the shells pinched Perry's thumb but he finally got three onboard.

"Ready?"

"Goin ten?" asked Perry.

"Goin ten," answered Bless. He drew his arm back then threw one about as high as he could so the shooter would have a good chance of a hit. Bless' throws didn't go very far and were an advantage but Perry still missed the first five. He didn't want to give up so Bless offered more instruction.

273

Perry missed the last five targets as well. He went to look at the other gun.

"You don't want that, son." Perry looked up. "Smaller bore, less shot, use a other one, you'll hit somethin." Perry, puzzled, replaced the gun against the shed.

Still the manager, Durry liked him more and more.

Perry wasn't sure if it was the gun's recoil that was making him miss. He felt like a kid again, awkward at something new.

"I'll throw to you now," Durry said. Durry was used to at least a hand thrower but quickly adapted to pitching them up without.

Bless brought the Remington up to his shoulder. Durry tossed the bird, the old man made it disappear.

After a few shots, Bless had to stop. "Breaks too many my blood vessels," he said with a cocky grin. Durry looked at him. "I got a few in."

Sandy stood with one leg wrapped around the other, arms still folded. Bless went to the shed, took the other gun, set down the twelve gauge. "Come on, Sandy."

Sandy looked at her father who just smiled broadly, nodding. She stood next to Bless while he gave her the basics. She couldn't believe what she was about to do. She just didn't want to hurt anyone.

"This is a smaller gun than the other one, okay? Better for someone your size." Sandy just went along. It seemed a bazooka to her.

"I'm gonna load only one shot." Bless breached the shell, slammed the action. Sandy's jaw clenched at the sound.

"Keep it pointed that way. You say ready."

Sandy held out wood and steel that seemed a mile long. "Ready."

The bird went up and came down, she fired off toward the mountains when the target had already landed. *Some* of the men chuckled but Sandy was thrilled. It was the loudest sound she ever heard. Her shoulder ached and her ears rung.

"Wanna do it again?" Bless asked.

Sandy nodded. She pointed the gun while he loaded another shell.

Her next shot and the couple thereafter never connected but she got to live through it. "These men here are prouda you, see? Jist for tryin."

Gwen could hear the distant shots when she got out of the van. *Havin fun without me.* She placed the brown sacks on the counter, still not comfortable with the kitchen. She found the note by the sink, *In back with Bless. Love, Us.* She put the note down deciding whether to walk to where they were. She stayed instead, made time for dinner. She examined the stack of papers at the far end of the counter, picked up the laminated, wallet-size picture of St. Jude, read the words on the reverse. *Wasn't he the one...?* She quickly looked at some of the other papers, medical receipts, receipts for about everything else, banking, coupons. *Dealing with all these people...* Cooking began on the avocado stove.

They were all out of shells. Sandy helped pick up the empties. Like to leave it as I found it," Bless said. He looked west, horizon was silver and purple, for an idea of the time. They wanted to go into the shack. Durry noticed a hand thrower in the back corner of the room. Sandy seated herself on one of the stumps then the others followed. "What kinda gun is that?" she asked.

"Twenty-eight gauge," said Bless. Both guns had been brought inside. "You keep that one for her." He raised his chin at Perry. "I wanna hold on to that other'n for a while." Perry didn't reply.

"Found a man here cuttin down trees once. Said he didn't know he was on my property. Had the permission of the property owner next to me. That's all government land I told him." Bless paused. "I watched him a while, he didn't know

275

it, took his time with leavin. I walked toward the house then fired a shot in the air. When I went back he was gone." He laughed, his eyes slipping behind the wrinkles.

"We haven't been down in a long time," said Perry.

"Well, you needed to see it again. Your aunt raised you, then you left, probly a good thang. Butcha always wonder, now you come back." He waved his hand. Durry felt nauseous.

"How is Sim's mom?" asked Perry.

"She's old, not like me but looks it. Everybody like that aroun here."

"What about our parents, anybody ever hear from em?" Durry suddenly saw himself at the edge of a dark pit.

Bless shifted his eyes between the two men. "I think people know em, might know em well." A moment passed. "They're out there somewhere, growin that good smoke like they always done. Each uv ums been in trouble. Some a that may be the reason they weren't aroun."

"Thought they were long gone, moved to who knows where," said Perry. "Arizona or somethin."

"I know they looked for somethin else. Kept endin up here. They like growin." He nodded his head but looked away.

Durry's stomach relaxed. His heart stopped beating so fast. He was glad they weren't dead. He also knew if he pressed, he'd find out their location. Bless wouldn't have held back, not with that, might only leave us to do some hunting. But he and Perry didn't ask, Sandy didn't know to, thank God.

Bless crunched the empty ammo boxes into the fireplace, checked the flue with a lighter. Perry lit a cigarette tossing in the empty box. He and Durry didn't really look at each other. It was good to have the flame as a diversion. Sandy wanted to burn more trash, inside getting smoky. The paperboard

276

quickly went up and the diversion quit. Bless tapped his wrist and they got up to go.

That night Sandy had concerns for Bless. "He has no one here with him. We need to stay longer, I think." Durry looked at her. "I wonder if anyone ever comes over?" It wasn't a conversation, really, she didn't exactly look back at him, she kept turning to different tasks in the room as she got ready for bed. Durry was standing next to his suitcase which was on the floor, getting ready to pull back his all white bed cover too.

Attempting to explain changing circumstances and why the hell people find themselves living their lives alone would have disgusted him, Durry didn't know anyway. The logic and reasons would have come out sounding like a sales pitch. Words memorized for excuses when people had objections.

"He walks through the lighting bugs when they first come out to some road that scares him. If we're not here we can picture him doin it. What did he say... where houses were on fire?"

"Burning House Path. We saw it," Durry said.

"He just walks to the street and back but the street's a scary one. Sometimes he doesn't even go there, just to the end of the driveway." Durry always enjoyed her meanderings, which he sometimes couldn't interpret.

"I don't know why the road is named that," he said.

"He's given us a lot of things. Its important that we see him. It's a big house, so dark outside at night."

Durry, of course, didn't see it through her eyes. Bless wasn't asking for anything in return.

"We're taking all his things." She lay on her side looking at him.

Breakfast was hard. It wasn't easy. Basic tasks usually make it better. There was enough wood around to make

277

needed repairs Durry saw. Perry's impulse was to give everything back, no way to leave a man. Leaving it behind was worse, hurt him even more, made everyone wonder what plans he'd made. Hot morning to the sound of an idling diesel. The girls had become attached, spent the rest of the time being sure he didn't need anything, two sworn servants. The engine sounds irritated the family, no one was ready, hugs and promises. Gwen had cleaned the refrigerator and tried to highlight nutritious food items. She looked inside one more time. I should have filled the shelves for him she thought. Some kind of guilt. He wouldn't want us to feel that way. It gave her enough peace. There was nothing else to do, it was all packed. The men were waiting in their vehicles, Sandy of course went with Durry in the box truck. She was again disappointed she couldn't see the moving creek from her side. Durry was prepared for her resolve about how much still had to be done.

From the window Bless caught a final view of both vehicles as they were turning down his drive, a dark van followed by a medium sized box truck covered in loud advertising. When the vehicles were no longer visible he kept his eyes where he imagined they'd probably be. Soon, though, it became cumbersome to estimate their location given the minutes gone by so he turned, faced the rest of the house, fixed on the card table that had been moved.

It was a nice size hole dug at the edge of the beech grove about two years ago. The pile was high beside. He'd clean it out after weather threw too much back in shallowing it or giving it the appearance that the idea was past. He'd lay near the lip on dark days staring upward just to get a feel. His heart was failing which he knew. He died instead seated in the fire shack about three weeks after the girl started school in the fall. The gun was next to him with two shells loaded

278

and the safety was off. He felt it coming and didn't have to be saved.

The river was low enough for Sandy to wade across. It seemed hotter at home. The water so clear, unstirred by days without rain, strange to see all the long stripes of algae writhing in the current, fixed to the bottom. In the middle she was able to step on dry rock the rest of the way, stopping to put her shoes and socks back on below the slope before the bank. She carried images of Bless, the shack, stray dogs, constant mist, rusty red brick buildings, waking in the same house as her uncle, and the mountains where certain places looked laid open, cleared for mining, dripping orange mud. The old man kept walking in her mind through fireflies to the end of the drive or in the woods among the skinny American Beech trees. They did it together many times. Durry assured her he wouldn't be forgotten. It would be good to visit before very long. He said something about having to look at it in a new way, laughed then about so many churches. His parents were also down there, she knew that, and that he'd want to talk to them. She started downstream on the other side this time before dinner as she liked.

To receive additional copies of this book or to send a gift please visit www.cadanhenry.com or use the form below:

Burden Books, PO Box 501938, Indianapolis, IN 46250

Please send me _____ copy(s) of Cadan Henry's *Country Folk*. I am enclosing $14.95 plus $3.50 to cover postage and handling each.

Mr/Mrs/Ms_____

Address_____

City_____

State_____ Zip_____

Gift to:

Mr/Mrs/Ms_____

Address_____

City_____

State_____Zip_____

*Please allow 1-2 weeks for delivery.